NOW

JOHN NEWBOULD

Copyright © 2024 John Newbould

All rights reserved.

ISBN: 9798326077370

Front cover created with Adobe Firefly. Back cover image by Daniel Olah, Unsplash

As a woman I have no country. As a woman I want no country.

As a woman, my country is the whole world.

Virginia Woolf

The only possibilities are now world government or death.

Bertrand Russell

Zach's Journal – Part One

Chapter 1

I

13 January 2018

Unbeknown to many, the untimely demise of Angelina Fontana in the white-washed mountainous village of Cómpeta in southern Spain was a grave loss to humanity.

The crude, radio-controlled IED went off at 10.07am, tearing through the flat, Monday morning serenity of Casa Antonio's café in Plaza Almijara, the village square.

Splintering dark mahogany and the oak banquette from where it emanated, uncompromising and changing everything, the explosion took out all in its wake: furniture; half of the old brick and marble-topped bar and the glassware, bottles and cutlery that sat atop it; framed photos charting the village and bar's history; the blue and white tiling delineating Andalusian pastoral scenes; the newly-installed and incongruous Art Deco lighting; the obligatory flat-screen TV; a considerable section of the lacquered floorboards; the café's front window; the left arm of proprietor Antonio Romero; and, quite comprehensively, Angelina herself.

Then silence. Momentary but absolute. An eerie, evanescent stillness. Just air levitating, sunlit flecked beams of dust slicing the ordinarily musty interior, piercing now un-shuttered windows, illuminating previously dark corners, angling off glass, broken and intact. All this, suddenly punctured by screaming, groaning, a hissing of mephitic pipes, the strident shriek of car alarms and immediately followed by dogs barking, shouts, wailing and movement.

Pablo, the village Guardia Civil, was fortuitously at hand, himself having been fleetingly ossified by, in turn, the blast that shattered the hitherto tranquil morning, the contiguous, fleeting silence and ensuing cacophony. Stood where he was meant, by default, he was one of the first on the scene, having been disclaiming Senora Garrido-Zambrano's daily tirade against teenage moped riders. Thrust into action by the screams of onlookers, he bustled, already perspiring in the early January sunshine, selflessly towards the acridity of the still smoking café; his pronounced girth bouncing as he shouted at people to get back. He was met by three apocalyptic figures, stumbling and bloodied, who emerged from the tangled debris that had once constituted the front of the cafe. Young Miguel, son of owner Antonio; Francisco, the long-serving chef; and part-time local mechanic Federico, the only other guest besides Angelina. All fell out, dazed and dishevelled. Having guardedly entered the premises, Pablo stood stock still, his stomach turned by what was left of the body of Angelina as his gaze took in various parts of her strewn in unlikely corners. Her midriff had clearly taken the full force of the blast, offering a futile shield against the makeshift but effective home-made device. Without warning he wretched, after which his mind cleared quickly and he noticed for the first time the slightest of movements from behind the crumpled bar. It was a semi-conscious Antonio who had been knocked witless, the blast having propelled him rearwards into the back wall and the shelves of spirit and wine bottles.

The first two ambulances took just over an hour to snake their way up from Vélez-Málaga, slowed by the winding road through the foothills of the Sierra Almijara. Pablo, leaning on his imperfect and half-forgotten medical training, had created a tourniquet from a towel, which seemed to partially stem the blood seeping from Antonio's shoulder and, along with two holidaying paramedics, had tended to the superficial wounds of the other café dwellers and a couple of passers-by with minor abrasions. Guardia reinforcements from nearby villages and coastal resorts helped Pablo marshal the sizeable crowd that had gathered, cordoning off the village square prior to the arrival of medical assistance. By the time the firefighters, *los bomberos*, had arrived from Nerja, locals had already dampened the pockets of low-level conflagrations.

The identification of Angelina took several hours. It transpired that she was relatively new to the village and had been indefinitely renting a small flat on Calle Picasso. A semi-concussed and half-deafened Antonio recalled her as a polite, quiet *extranjero*, Dutch he thought, who had slid into his café most mornings for the past few weeks, shortly after it opened. Almost always alone, she sat in the same corner and ordered a *descafeinado* and *tostada* before taking her laptop out and locking horns with the scratchy wi-fi signal. Both her wallet and her phone, which may have offered up clues to her identity, were decimated in the blast. There was no sign of a laptop. When questioned, Antonio recounted that it had been busy the previous day and that many customers had sat at 'Angelina's table', none of which had struck him as suspicious.

It was not until mid-afternoon that a young German couple presented themselves to Pablo, who was still overseeing matters at the taped off crime scene. They wondered if the woman who had died was one that was staying a couple of doors away from them. They explained how they had developed a passing acquaintance with her and had gone out for drinks a few nights earlier. She was called Angelina, and yes, they confirmed, she was indeed Dutch; they told how she had spoken obliquely of taking some time out from the daily grind. She had said she was married and was a feature writer who split her time between Amsterdam and Stockholm, but nothing much more than that. She had seemed a little edgy to them, troubled even.

Having forced the door at Calle Picasso, 27, Pablo and his colleague Manolo conducted an exacting search of the thinly furnished premises, finding nothing that might shed light on why a thirty-something tourist enjoying some *r and r* might be blown to smithereens. The only possible hope of explication was her laptop, which, clearly, she had not taken to the café that morning but, despite Pablo's clumsy thumbs, remained resolutely locked. That she had been a news reporter set off alarm bells in Pablo's head – he knew it could be a dangerous profession and that, around the world, dozens of journalists died every year with hundreds more languishing in prison. The chances of this incident remaining local, he surmised, were vanishingly small. It may well be down to the computer forensic specialists in Malaga.

II

26 February 2018

Why begin my account here? In many ways Angelina's premature passing comes mid- to late-story. And, of course, I forget my manners. Really, to make sense of all this, I must begin by introducing myself and explaining how I became acquainted with Angelina and why I am compelled to write about it. But wait, first I need to deal with the here and now.

'Sir, are you okay? Can I fix you some breakfast?'

'Yes, I'll have a double rum with a splash of soda water.'

So, who is telling me all this, you may well be wondering? As my journal unfolds, you will naturally form your own conclusion but, at a superficial glance, I am a single, 37-year-old male named Zach Boocock from Hebden Bridge, a small town nestling in the Pennine valleys between Manchester and Leeds in northern England, working, up until recently at least, as a photographer on a local newspaper, *The Bolton News*.

I need to take you back in time.

Chapter 2

22 April 2017

My story – sorry, the story - really begins a year ago when I was contacted somewhat unexpectedly by an old friend from my university days. Geir, an affable Norwegian, and I had formed an instant bond when we first met while studying photography at the Gerrit Rietveld Academie in Amsterdam at the turn of the millennium. Beyond photography, we found we had common interests in the other things that matter in life: football, humour, indie music, alcohol and partying. In our first year of study, we shared the same hall of residence and after that, along with several classmates, we went on to rent a number of crumbling student fleapits across the city. From the outset, I was openly in awe of Geir's mastery of nature photography and I wasn't in the least bit surprised to learn that he had, since graduating, picked up a number of gigs with the environmental campaign group Greenpeace.

His telephone call didn't come as a total shock; we had kept in touch intermittently through social media and the odd lengthy email and had met up on a few occasions for dissolute, bibulous weekends in European cities, loosely revolving around photography. I knew he was making good – if somewhat erratic – money as a self-employed shutterbug, undertaking assignments for glossy nature magazines and websites. As I said, I was also aware that he had already enjoyed several extended projects with Greenpeace, travelling with them to Indonesia and South America. I knew too that he had been all set to join them as assistant to their permanent photographer and videographer on a two-month expedition, sailing out of Amsterdam on the *Esperanza* to the clement waters of the Caribbean.

When I took the call from a hospitalised Geir – a broken leg and concussion in a car accident – saying he needed a stand-in, I'd decided, before I put the phone down, that I was, if you will forgive the pun, on board. I briefly wondered, why me? Why not National Geographic's Nature Photographer of the Year or some such luminary? I suppose the answer was that I was relatively cheap, came recommended and, most importantly, was available. I had to move quickly. I sacked my job with the newspaper that day; they were increasingly paring back their pool of photographers and I knew I wasn't their favourite so I saw it as jumping before I was pushed. There was even a vague arrangement that I might be able to undertake some contract work for them after my trip. I had no accommodation to worry about as I was living with my parents at the time. It meant they got the freedom of their house back and I am sure they were more than happy to see the back of me for a couple of months.

My role aboard the *Esperanza* was as an assistant photographer, essentially a helper and a gopher, and I was more than comfortable with this. I saw myself as a half-decent nature photographer, even having picked up a few awards over the years but I did not pretend to be in the same league as Geir. I was a strong swimmer and had a PADI diving certificate, which I thought might stand in my favour. However, I soon learned these attributes were extraneous, the ship being equipped with state-of-the-art underwater monitoring equipment, including a drop camera that could plummet depths of up to a kilometre and a remotely operated device, which could comfortably shoot video at 300 metres below sea level. Geir's call had come just three days prior to embarkation, which meant I had little time to put arrangements in place. On the other hand, it gave me an 'in' to a once-in-a-lifetime opportunity.

Chapter 3

22 April 2017

Founded out of Vancouver in 1971 by a handful of environmental campaigners, Buddhists and hippies, Greenpeace now operates on a budget of tens of millions of pounds, employs 2,000 people in offices in over 50 countries across all continents and is headquartered in Amsterdam, the homeport of *Esperanza*. For its funding, it relies on small donations from over 3 million supporters and foundation grants and on some 36,000 volunteers who help with regular campaigns and actions. Wary of being enslaved to a paymaster of any kind, it does not accept donations from governments, businesses or political parties. Personal accountability and non-violent confrontation are its watchwords. In theory, I'd signed up for a world of imaginative peaceful protests, blockades, unfurling banners, painting colourful slogans, creating provocative artwork, pioneering research and jaw-dropping stunts. We set off, in finest Greenpeace tradition, to bear witness and denounce. Whilst Gandhi-type pacifism was our lodestar, this would not stop others hurling abuse, intimidation and death threats at us.

I knew the job would not be without jeopardy. I was conscious that a photographer had died when the *Rainbow Warrior*, one of Greenpeace's early campaign boats, was bombed and sunk in Auckland harbour by the French secret service in 1987 – nothing more than an act of state-sponsored terrorism. Remarkably no government in the world, apart from that of New Zealand, condemned the action. A pretty clear signal of the esteem Greenpeace was held in at the time. The flagship had been on its way to the Moruroa atoll in the Southern Pacific to protest against planned French nuclear testing. There was, of course, initially much denial but, some twenty years later, Francois Mitterrand, the French President at the time of the bombing, admitted to authorising the mission. Now, I might be missing something here, but in any other walk of life this would surely make him, and the French state, a murderer and other countries accomplices? Politics, it seems, offers immunity from such crimes.

The Greenpeace project I'd enlisted for was to photograph and document the state of the Caribbean Sea and all that lives in it or by it, in order to help promote a wider campaign called 'Save our Seas'. The big picture was to continue to lobby world governments to sign up to a Global Ocean Treaty, whereby 30% of the high seas would become protected through a number of inter-linked ocean sanctuaries. There was once a time when fishermen would organically work their near coastal waters but, as I was to learn, those days are long gone. Huge fleets now trawl the open seas, which account for two-thirds of the ocean or half the planet and lie beyond national boundaries. It's like the Wild West out there and the Greenpeace endgame was to have these waters protected by international law. I was amazed that they weren't already. The aim was to create a kind of national park at sea, enabling pollution to clear, human interference to abate and for marine stocks, coral, phytoplankton and plant-life to replenish themselves. A rewilding of the seas.

Our expedition would shine a spotlight onto humankind's despoiling and exploitation of the sea by oil drilling, deep sea mining, nuclear testing, plastic dumping, sewage disposal, poisoning by industrial run-off and contaminants as well as stressing by overfishing and shrimp farming; all of which contribute towards spiralling species extinction and acidification.

Our mission was pretty much summed up by the quote from the renowned marine biologist Dr Sylvia Earle, which was painted on the wall of the *Esperanza's* campaign room and said: 'We need to protect the ocean as if our lives depend on it, because they do.'

Chapter 4

27 April 2017

The first 24 hours on board the *Espy*, as it was affectionately known to its crew, were pretty manic as each of us focused on settling ourselves into our confined berths, unpacking and checking our equipment and familiarising ourselves with new workmates. Most already knew each other to some degree, but there was a handful of neophytes like myself. For the sailors and engineers on board, their time was spent navigating the busy North Sea Canal that took us out from the Hook of Holland, underneath smothering, leaden skies and into a gusty and dirty grey North Sea. We had a multi-national crew of 32, comprising the captain and his mates, engineers, scientists, researchers, a journalist, the ship's medic, two cooks and half a dozen campaigners and comms specialists that doubled up as volunteer deckhands – plus, of course, the ship's photographer and his assistant, yours truly. Everyone seemed purposeful but friendly, cheery even, smiling and nodding acknowledgements, swapping pleasantries where time permitted.

I was to share a work station with my boss for the next two months, Philippe, a thirty-something Brazilian photojournalist who had been with Greenpeace for four years and with the UN prior to that. A handsome man, in good shape, he was a little reserved but oozed calmness, methodical efficacy and professionalism. I came to learn that he was a perfectionist, quite happy to spend hours preparing and waiting to get the photo he had half-imagined in his mind. He was more than content to spend an entire day in pursuit of a single image. While he had all the technical know-how, his real skill was in having an aesthetic eye - an ability to see things from a new angle as he framed his picture in order to capture a moment that cut to the very heart of an issue. If he did not get what he wanted then, no drama, he would come back the following day or, if needs be, the day after that. If patience and creativity are the two greatest traits of a photographer, then he had them in spades. His existence, it seemed, was given over to his passion. He was very comfortable with spending long periods of time on his own. Throughout our time away together, he let little slip about a life beyond the confines of his calling; he talked sparingly of family, and while he hinted at there having been women in his past, it seemed there had never been anyone long-term or special.

We were initially headed for the French Caribbean islands of Guadeloupe, set between Dominica and Montserrat. The *MV Esperanza*, my home for the next eight weeks, was named by Greenpeace members and means 'hope' in Spanish. Built in the 1980s for the Soviet Navy as an expedition, search and fire-fighting ship, there was little on offer in the way of creature comforts. It was recommissioned in the year 2000 by Greenpeace – made more eco-friendly, boat cranes were added and a heli-deck installed - and launched in 2002. These days it's instantly recognisable, emblazoned with the environmental campaigner's eponymous white capitalised logo and rainbow livery, on a backdrop of emerald green. It is the largest and fastest vessel in the Greenpeace fleet. Predominantly powered by a highly efficient combined diesel and electric engine, it has two back-up diesel engines which can kick in when required – perhaps to chase down illegal whalers or ships dumping nuclear waste at sea. Its career highs included delivering aid and humanitarian relief after the 2010 Haiti earthquake and after Typhoon Botha, which struck large parts of the Philippines a couple of years later. A rather clever reverse osmosis machine allowed sea-water to be turned into fresh drinking water.

Once we were out into the English Channel, we assembled for our first whole group meeting. Collegiality and friendliness were parked as team members adopted implacable business demeanours, reminding me of the stoic gazes of Moai statues. Most were content to sit back and ruminate attentively on the Captain's sailing assessment for the next few days and to absorb the allocation of duties and expectations for daily life as delivered by Dr Francesca Ballotelli, our Chef de Mission. Slowly studying each impenetrable face, one by one, I was suddenly brought up sharp when I settled my gaze on a pretty thirty-something Dutch woman. I could not actually believe my eyes; how could it be that I was only just seeing her? As I said, the first day or two were fairly frenetic and I guess our paths had just not crossed or perhaps it was down to the hard hats we all wore on deck. However, unforgivably, we had been in the same meeting for five minutes or so and still I had overlooked her. It was Angelina Fontana and we had a past. There was one or two lines, a fleck or two of grey in her dark shoulder length hair, a slightly more elegant disposition perhaps, grown up and mature I suppose, but unmistakably her. I could tell she was conscious of my intense glare but she did not throw me a look and I suspected she had seen me before I had seen her. She was the reason I had studied in Amsterdam. We had first met in England, when she attended the same college as me in Manchester. Things had not ended well.

Chapter 5

1 May 2017

On-board life saw our working day begin at 7.30am. Apart from individual specialists, everyone was also a volunteer and this meant contributing several hours a day to domestic duties, which might include laundry, cleaning communal spaces and basic food prep. After lunch, each of us absorbed ourselves in our own personal work. Later in the day, there might be a fitness or yoga class on the poop deck for an hour or so or a little time in which I could read or try, with scant success, to unpick the thoughts and backstory of taciturn Philippe.

As we arced south-west into the Atlantic, the skies gradually brightened, the wind subsided, temperatures steadily rose and I began regular postprandial perambulations of the deck. Partly an attempt to keep fit, partly to relieve the *longueurs* of early afternoon. On one such occasion, after a protracted session in the video editing room, I'd paused and was clearing my mind by staring vacantly into the mesmeric, timeless ocean while leaning into the ship's rail, when Angelina was suddenly alongside me.

'So, were you going to ignore me for the whole trip?' she asked, teasingly.

'No, no……not at all,' I stuttered, momentarily thrown. 'I thought you were ignoring me. It's been a while, hasn't it? How are you ….. I mean how have you been? What are you up to now?'

'Good, I guess, all things considered,' Angelina measured out each word carefully before pausing briefly, looking out to sea to consider what she might say next and then continuing: 'I am a freelance journalist; a features writer for the most part. I split my time between Stockholm and Amsterdam. I went on....' and I noticed another moment of hesitancy '...after we separated, to graduate and then stuck around and did a Masters before moving to Prague to complete a PhD in Journalism. I met Jochen there, who is now my husband, and when he got a job in Stockholm, we moved to Sweden. I've since bought a flat in De Pijp in Amsterdam too, as I still have family in the city. I often spend time there as it is such a good jumping off point to cover stories across Europe – one of the advantages of being multilingual is that my stories can be placed in more than one market. I earn my living by predominantly writing about politics and the environment – gifts that keep on giving, as you can imagine. But what about *you*? What have you been doing? How have you been keeping?'

'Fair to middling, I suppose. I went back to England after uni, lived way beyond my means in London for a few years and gradually drifted back north. I had a number of part-time jobs; I suppose I was part of the gig-economy for photographers. I even did weddings for a while but that turned out to be harder and more stressful than it looked. It took some time but eventually I picked up a job on a local newspaper as a photographer and...,' now it was my turn to pause, '....to cut a long story short, I ended up living back with my parents. I got this job completely out of the blue. Through Geir from my – our – university days, if you recall him? I've taken his place on this trip.'

'I do, your cool Norwegian friend. I am glad you and him are still mates. It is good to know that you finished the course too; I wasn't sure that you would. Are you still in contact with many people from back then?'

'No, not really. Just Geir I suppose. One or two others, now and then, on Facebook and Insta. I can't tell you how surprised I was to see you, when we all sat down for our first team meeting.'

'Yes, me too.'

'I wasn't sure you'd even seen me. I don't think you looked in my direction once?'

'Oh, I saw you, trust me. I am just not going to sit there with my mouth wide open, gawking.'

It had been a few days since the inaugural meeting and I had been wondering when our paths would cross. I had considered searching the ship and digging her out for a heart to heart but, in truth, I'd not really been sure what to say to her or whether she would even want to speak to me after all these years. That, coupled with the fact that when I did occasionally spy her, she seemed to be in the presence of a bespectacled professor-looking type. She had walked out on me back in Amsterdam at a point when I needed her more than I could have possibly articulated. Through friends and friends of friends on social media, I knew that she was a journo and had married an academic Swede. While a kind of personal pride held me back from chasing her down on the boat, I knew, in time, we would inevitably bump into one another. I was less sure how and where our conversation would go though.

'So, what are you hoping to write about?'

'I have to put some passages together for the Greenpeace newsletter and website and I hope to write a few articles that I can sell to newspapers, magazines and campaign groups. Despite the ever-rising number of citizen journalists and bloggers who claim to be authorities on everything under the sun, there is, thankfully, still a demand for trained and seasoned reporters! I will need to liaise from the scientists on board for some of the detail but my plan is to write about how the marine ecosystem is being degraded by contamination from industrial run-off and sewage and, also, on the accumulation of man-made debris in the ocean, particularly plastic. Most ocean pollution actually comes from the land, did you know that? I will also write about the havoc that is being caused by the acidification of our seas. And then a piece on how these issues are affecting the livelihoods of all those people who rely on the ocean - in terms of both poisoning their food source and the impact on tourism. I will also probably write an easy-kill feature about dolphins and whales; these wonderful creatures invariably capture the hearts and minds of the public. Sometimes telling stories through pulling on heart strings gets the message across more effectively than hard facts.'

'Sounds like you are going to be kept busy,' I said, raising my voice as wailing gulls and a strengthening wind threatened to carry my words away.

'She certainly will be! Just as we all will be.' Out of left-field, we had been joined by a third person, who took me aback by his sudden lolloping appearance and, even more so, by slipping his arm around Angelina. I'd not realised that her partner was on board too. The aforementioned studious, bookish type.

'Ah, Jochen dear,' Angelina said, and then, turning to me: 'This is Zach, Zach Boocock, an old friend from……my past, from my uni days. I think I may have mentioned him to you. What a coincidence, eh? I've not seen him for such a long time.…well over fifteen years. We were just catching up. I was telling him about the articles that I intend to write.'

Angelina also seemed to have fleetingly lost her poise by his unannounced arrival. 'Zach will be taking photographs on the trip. Zach, this is my partner Jochen Goldreich; he is an Assistant Professor of Sustainability at the Stockholm Environment Institute. He is one of the experts I will be consulting with when I write my articles.'

I shook his proffered hand: 'A pleasure to meet you. Angelina and I go back a long way. We knew each other at college in Manchester and then, like Angelina said, at university in Amsterdam.' I thought it best to leave it there, not being altogether sure how much Angelina would have shared with him about our past, if anything. Sensing I was in danger of careering down what could be a slippery slope, I shifted the discussion. 'And what are you looking to achieve over the coming weeks?'

My question seemed to flick a switch in him; he was suddenly off on what seemed like an oft-delivered and well-practised monologue.

'Right now, my focus is on water. It is our most precious resource: we came from it, are largely made up of it – 95% of our brains are water - and our survival depends on it. Rising temperatures and population growth are putting increasing pressure on our supply of freshwater. In some locales there is just not enough potable water for people's needs. Future wars will be about it. All living things demand it, indeed, as I say, they are made up of it, just in varying arrangements.

'During this trip, I will concentrate on the ocean. Whilst we call our world Planet Earth, it should really be called Planet Sea. Seventy-one per cent of the globe is ocean and currently – and really quite unbelievably - only 2% of it enjoys protected status. It is only 13 years until 2030, the deadline for us to meet the United Nations' Sustainable Development Goals. To do this, we need to manage our oceans much better - to somehow work them harder in order to produce more from them - yet we need to do this in a balanced and sustainable way. Quite a challenge for people like me. On the one hand we need the sea to provide us with more food, more jobs, good health and more energy. At the same time, we must maintain its capacity to regulate the climate and support biodiversity. Most urgently, we have to fight against the degradation of marine ecosystems and the pollution of the sea. This means fighting a war against anthropogenic climate change, marine litter, loss of habitats and unregulated fishing – did you know that one third of all fish consumed is caught illegally? On this trip I hope to help with the collection of data that will support Greenpeace's campaigning and which I can also utilise in my own work. That is why I am on this boat.'

Pausing only briefly to draw in salty air and perhaps thinking he had not clearly explained to us what he was all about, he continued: 'Three billion people, predominantly in developing countries, directly or indirectly, rely on the sea for their livelihood. For one billion people, fish is their primary source of protein. The UN prognosticates that by 2050, there will be another 2 billion people on the planet, many of whom will also be reliant on the sea.

'As long as the ocean habitat remains polluted,' he continued, 'we run the risk of poisoning ourselves with plastic-laden fish. Already microplastics are in our bloodstream. Yet, unfortunately, whilst we desperately need to save our oceans, we find new and ingenious ways of degenerating them.'

We all stared wistfully into exhibit number one, the expanse of restless and seemingly infinite North Atlantic which rolled out in front of us, as Jochen expanded further: 'Essentially, we hit our oceans in three ways. What some might call a perfect storm at sea. Firstly, through overfishing by huge industrial trawlers, some of them over 100 metres in length with nets the size of football pitches that scoop up vast swathes of sea life. Anything that is not edible or cannot legally be fished or takes the catch over its quota is thrown back in the water, often dead. Depending on the haul, four fifths can be made up of by-product, including dolphins, sharks, birds, rays and turtles and, in some regions, even endangered cod and haddock. This vast wastage means there is less chance of fish reproducing and there will come an inflection point, sooner than we think, when some species simply cannot replenish their numbers. Many of these unscrupulous super-trawlers will, by night, think nothing of turning off their satellite communications and fishing in protected areas. Right now, across the planet, eighty per cent of marine stocks are overfished or are perilously close to being so.

'Secondly, we poison our seas, using them as a dumping ground for radioactive waste, industrial decommissioning, effluents and plastic; not to mention the pollution that comes from nuclear testing, oil drilling and spills.

Plastic does not decompose. Every bit of plastic that has been produced since the 1950s is still on our planet; it just tends to break down into smaller and smaller pieces. People don't realise that ninety per cent of all the plastic in the ocean is so microscopic that it cannot be seen by the naked eye - but it is there and now, as I said, it is in our food chain. Eight million tonnes of plastic waste is dumped into the sea each year. Think about that for a moment. *Eight! Million! Tonnes*! Every year. That is the equivalent, weight wise, of over a million elephants! It has been computed that there are more than five trillion pieces of plastic in the sea. I've been right around this planet and, trust me, there is no beach in the world that does not have plastic on it. And what is scary is that all the predictions are for plastic-production to increase, maybe double, over the coming decades. Very soon there will be more pieces of plastic in the ocean than fish.

'And, finally, there is ocean warming and acidification through our persistent burning of fossil fuels. The sea absorbs about a third of the carbon dioxide that we emit into the atmosphere. This turns the water more acidic – into corrosive carbonic acid as it goes – it is this that destroys coral, which becomes bleached and refuses to grow any more. The oceans also become less capable of sustaining shellfish and crustaceans and microscopic algae called phytoplankton, which form the very basis of the ocean's food chain. Of course, everything is connected. Oceans regulate the climate – rainfall, winds and temperature - and as we know these are becoming increasingly unpredictable. It seems the Greeks were right when they depicted an angry Poseidon blowing up wrathful tempests. Whilst life started in the ocean, right now, it looks like it will end there too.'

As Jochen painted this expansively bleak picture, I found myself slowly studying the dynamic between husband and wife. Angelina looked well, perhaps just the faintest hint of crow's feet but the years had certainly been kind to her. She caught my eye and looked away. I couldn't be certain – especially as we were all lined up resting on the rail and gazing out into thousands of miles of sea - but it looked to me as though Angelina was trying just a little too hard to feign interest in Jochen's soliloquy, perhaps having heard it one too many times. He, in turn, would occasionally throw her a glance, looking for her approbation. Not that he needed it; he seemed to know his subject inside out and despite his singsong delivery and having to reach for the odd word, he had a strong command of the English language. I discovered later that his academic parents had emigrated from the US to Sweden in the late 1970s, disillusioned with the direction that America was heading in.

And then, suddenly, they were gone. Perhaps he had noticed that I had glazed over. Having asked precisely nothing about me, he abruptly announced that he had to get back to his work and, offering me his best wishes for the rest of the day, took Angelina's arm and gently steered her down the deck. For no reason that I could clearly enunciate, then or now, he left me with a feeling that I was indirectly to blame for the state of the ocean.

Chapter 6

7 May 2017

I

A smooth and largely uneventful Atlantic crossing saw us initially veering south, hugging the north-western coasts of the Canaries and Cape Verde, before gradually steering west. The Caribbean, or West Indies as it is sometimes known, comprises some 7,000 islands, reefs and cays, which were fought over and divided up by the English, Dutch and Spanish during the seventeenth, eighteenth and nineteenth centuries. Today there are 13 official countries and numerous more colonies, dependencies and territories which are sorted into three island groups: the Greater Antilles, the Lesser Antilles and The Bahamas.

We were southbound to the Lesser Antilles, into the waters of the Leeward Islands, anchoring around the French islands of Guadeloupe; Gwada to its locals. Christopher Columbus, as far as we know, was the first European to feast eyes on the beautiful archipelago, supposedly bringing back the first pineapples to Europe and naming the islands after the Our Lady of Guadalupe shrine found in the eponymously named town in the Spanish region of Extremadura. The main island's charms have been exploited in the TV series *Death in Paradise* and it certainly lived up to the latter part of this title. Not sure about the death bit. Whilst it has France's highest crime rate and a murder rate akin to that of Los Angeles, it still felt pretty safe. I think most of the killings are domestic and drugs-related. Sitting centrally in the region, it served as a fine starting point for me to first experience the delights of the Caribbean and it proved to be an idyllic location for us to acclimatise while we took some preliminary measures of plastic content in the seawater and made our first tentative readings for a study into coral blanching.

II

A few of us were lucky enough to step ashore for the official opening of a Greenpeace supporters' group in Basse-Terre, the capital on the western side of the island. The clear blue skies, unremitting brilliance of light and slow pace of life were an appealing mix. I was dazzled by the lush verdure and startling primary colours – yellow sand, blue sea and red rooves - of the diabolo shaped island. French was widely spoken and the currency throughout the islands was the Euro, which took me by surprise. Sitting in a harbour café, I assumed, as a European citizen, I could still settle there. If that was the case, I would certainly need to move smartly with the Brexit train hurtling down the track.

Angelina and Jochen were with me and, as we shared a jar of Ti' Punch and watched the terns wheel, they were schooling me in the astonishing lives of whales. They had my full attention as Philippe had tasked me with photographing these formidable creatures once we reached the Turks and Caicos Islands. I think he already had a repository of images and probably thought a few more wouldn't go amiss. The pictures were to support a piece that Angelina was writing on how whales' lives and ecosystems are perpetually threatened by human activity.

My own whale knowledge was rudimentary at best. I knew that the nearest land animal to them was a hippopotamus. I knew that sperm whales have the biggest brain and can make the most noise of any creature on our planet. I knew the blue whale to be the largest creature our world has ever seen and that their arteries were so thick that you could, in theory at least, swim down them. I was aware too, like every schoolboy, that their penis was the size and weight of a small Volkswagen truck. Aside from being such magnificent beasts, few people – myself included until enlightened by Professor Goldreich - know quite how much we are indebted to them.

'We need to look upon the 40 or so different species of whale as eco-warriors of the sea,' asserted Jochen. 'Throughout the course of a year, they will travel vast distances, operating in their own complex social structures - essentially small tribes or clans. I often think that to them, the world must seem a much smaller place. Blue whales can comfortably hear each other up to 1,000 miles away – think of the distance between London and Madrid - or at least they could before human noise and shipping started interfering with their communication channels.'

'How do you mean, eco-warriors?' I asked.

'So many of the things they do keep our oceans healthy. They are essentially living carbon depositories, absorbing the pollutant into their bodies whenever they feed and locking it away for their whole lives – think of them as floating trees! A whale will sequester the equivalent amount of carbon dioxide as 30,000 trees. Different whales enjoy different diets. Some sift large amounts of krill – up to a ton a day for humpbacks - and plankton from surface waters whilst others dive several kilometres to hunt squid. This ensures that they mix nutrients both horizontally and vertically in the ocean, connecting the sunlit surface to the inky depths. As whales travel between feeding and breeding grounds, they often migrate thousands of miles, linking up distant parts of the globe. So, a whale born in warm, tropical seas might potentially feed in the freezing waters of the Southern Ocean. All the time, they are fulfilling the important role of spreading nutrients across vast distances. Whale faeces and urine act as fertiliser, making the sea conditions more favourable for the growth of microscopic plants called phytoplankton that live near the surface and drift on the currents. Like all plants they photosynthesise, using sunlight and carbon dioxide to generate their own food. A by-product of this photosynthesis is oxygen. Scientists estimate that phytoplankton produce between 50 and 85 percent of the oxygen in our atmosphere. So, literally, every second breath that we inhale. As if that wasn't enough, these tiny and ephemeral floating marvels are the basis of all ocean food chains, including that which whales themselves eat.'

'Important work,' I mused. 'And you say they do this for their entire life? How long does an average whale live?'

'They *should* live very long lives. While the blue whale can easily live up to 100 years, others can live much longer; the Arctic bowhead, for instance, can live as long as 250 years. Given that some of these intelligent creatures that are alive today have witnessed the slaughter of millions of their own, I am amazed that they trust man at all.

'As a result of the vast distances they travel, a whale's dead body could end up far away from where it was born. When they sink to the seafloor, so-called "whale falls" become a whole ecosystem in themselves, supporting all sorts of weird and wondrous deep sea creatures, from worms to sharks. Crucially, as I said, they also take a whole load of carbon down with them to their grave on the seabed. This, like you surmise, has been a life well spent, mixing nutrients that keep the ocean healthy and capable of dealing, as best as it can, with the climate crisis. So, let's hear it for the whales, as they go about their business, they make the ocean – and consequently our world – a healthier, more resilient place. And how do we go about thanking them for this?'

It was a rhetorical question that Jochen did not intend me to answer: 'Yes, you guessed it, we hunt them down, of course, with grenade harpoons. This insult is compounded when we add a little historical context. Whales date back some 50 million years, whereas modern homo sapiens are relative parvenus on the block, having been around for just 300,000 years. Interestingly, both species can trace their genealogy back to a tiny shrew-like creature which existed 80 million years ago.'

'Yes, now you say it, I think I've heard that before,' I said. 'I struggle to get my head around stuff like that.'

'What we have done to whales over the past couple of centuries,' persisted Jochen, 'by relentlessly hunting many species almost to extinction, has not only been a crime against them, but actually against ourselves and the planet. Because they grow and reproduce slowly, it takes a long time for their stocks to replenish. This is at a time when we should, of course, being doing all we can to help their numbers recover. If nothing else, more whales means less carbon in the atmosphere. A classic example of how when we harm nature, we harm ourselves and all life.'

Then it was Angelina's turn to weigh in with her thoughts. She had already penned two thirds of her article and was keen to educate me on the threats that Cetaceans – that is whales, dolphins and porpoises – are facing.

'Our treatment of whales has been nothing short of barbaric,' she opined. 'From the 1860s right through to the middle of the last century, intense hunting of whales drove many subspecies to virtual extinction, after which the first efforts were made to curb the practice. Read *Moby Dick* if you want the gory detail. Taking the blue whale as an exemplar of human maltreatment, we only have to go back 160 years to find a quarter of a million or so blue whales in Antarctica alone. Early explorers brought back tales of bays being 'clogged up' with whales. However, after the invention of the exploding spear in 1864 they were hunted to near extinction. Nowadays, estimates of how many are left across the entire world range from 10,000 to 25,000.

'During the 1960s, giant factory ships and ever more efficient ways of catching whales meant something had to be done to stop certain species from disappearing forever. In Japan, whale meat had become a staple part of the diet during straitened times after World War Two. In 1986, the International Whaling Commission banned commercial whaling, yet some countries were allowed quotas to hunt for so called "scientific exploration". Whilst there is so much that I love about Icelandic, Norwegian and Japanese cultures, they have got it seriously wrong on the question of whaling. Each year, between them, they are entitled to legally hunt about 1,500 large whales for "research" although, for some reason, academic papers never seem to materialise. Few people are interested in eating whale meat anymore – be it locals or tourists. In Iceland, less than two per cent of the population eat whale. My research taught me that in Japan, it is now a failing and unprofitable business that only survives because it is propped up by the Japanese government. Sometimes we have to change and move on. Believe me, once you have watched a whale thrash around as it slowly dies, entrapped in a fishing net, you will realise how shameful this practice is - demeaning to both whales and humanity.

'Despite the mid-eighties' moratorium on whaling – you can thank Greenpeace for that - many species, including blue and sperm whales, remain on endangered lists. Whale populations are subject to an array of modern day threats, everything from entanglement with fishing gear, being caught as by-product, collisions with ships, disturbance from industry and the military to noise pollution; not to mention the vast swathes of plastic and chemicals floating around which they habitually ingest. Hundreds of thousands disappear each year.'

'Well, I guess this is where we come in – where we can make a difference?' I thought out loud. 'Through our words and photography, we can help foreground the perils they face. Let's hope we can persuade countries and industries to play their part in ensuring that we give whales not just a chance to survive but all that they need to thrive and to help keep our seas healthy, for all our sakes.'

'Yes, quite. As I keep telling people,' proffered Jochen, as he and I found a rare moment of concord, 'a sick ocean is a sick world.'

Chapter 7

13 May 2017

I

Our evening meals were usually split into two sittings as the whole crew could not be off duty at the same time. After our regular game of darts, Philippe and I usually found ourselves sharing the same mess table as Angelina and her husband. Generally, conversation tended to revolve around what each of us had been doing that day. More often than not, Jochen held court, regaling us with long-winded tales of how busy he was or would be, explaining, among other things, all the tests, research and experiments he planned to run, including scuba diving for specimens, surveying shark and whale migration, analysing coral, monitoring fish populations, assaying changing weather patterns and ocean toxicity, and the subsequent impact on the environment of all of these phenomena. He seemed to have no mechanism for filtering what level of detail may or may not be of interest to the general listener. On occasion, when we were feeling more effusive as a group, we would deflect Jochen's lengthy descriptions of pelagic exploration and consider the woes of the world and how it might be made a better place. It was during such exchanges that Angelina shared with us her growing concern for the planet and a solution for how we might yet avoid apocalypse. Two particular evenings come to mind, although it is possible my memory conflates several other discussions.

II

For most of us, Sunday usually offered a little time off. This meant alcohol flowed a little more liberally on a Saturday evening; people played music and often talked into the early hours. On one such occasion, I recall the whole crew being in a cheery mood after a productive day or two spent in Venezuelan waters. We had trawled the coastline, in seas which were renowned for being poisoned by large oil refineries that had been operating with impunity for 60 years. Of late, there had been increased contamination due to local politics and intensified drilling - a result, ironically, of worries that the world would soon be moving to renewable forms of energy. Our scientists had collected samples and run a number of tests. Unsurprisingly, they detected conclusive evidence of dangerous amounts of heavy metals and hydrocarbon compounds at levels far exceeding international norms. There would be yet more tricky questions for Venezuela, one of the world's largest oil producers, to answer; a place where a bottle of water costs more than a tank of gas. And, as a bonus prize, twenty-four hours earlier, under the cover of night, we had sneaked into port to daub the word 'stolen' in red paint on a large Venezuelan fishing trawler that had over a ton of illegally fished red snapper on it.

Returning to Caribbean waters, we toasted our work with a green barbecue held on the heli-deck; there was singing, dancing, imbibing and laughter. As the soirée drew to a close, instead of retiring to our respective bunks to read as we normally did, Philippe, Angelina, Jochen and I settled in the lounge and opened another bottle of wine. Our alcohol-infused chat had coalesced around the chances of a Global Ocean Treaty ever being implemented.

If I recall, the discussion had begun with Jochen talking about the denigration of coral reefs, something I'd been trying to photograph off the Dutch South Caribbean island of Curacao. After Gwada, our journey had seen us steer south between Cuba and Haiti into the Lesser Antilles, just 40 miles off the north coast of Venezuela. Curacao is renowned for its tucked away beaches and outstanding coral reefs - rainforests of the ocean - rich with marine life. Or, as I quickly came to learn, it once was, before our climate started breaking down.

'No wonder you had problems photographing it,' Jochen sympathised, 'these days, less than 10 per cent of that reef has live coral, whereas just a few decades ago it was 50 per cent. Studies show that more than half of all coral habitats have declined, stagnated or disappeared in the Caribbean since the 1970s. What were once colourful ecosystems teeming with life, are now dead reefs, bleached and petrified like Pompeiians coated in Mount Vesuvius' lava. Unless urgent action is taken to protect them, they'll disappear from our waters entirely within the next 20 years.'

'Just one more reason that we need a global treaty to protect our oceans,' contemplated Philippe.

'On this issue I have a cautious optimism. I believe that in my lifetime, we will secure a treaty that creates a national park in our seas and which may cover as much as 20 to 30 per cent of it. I might be getting towards the end of my days when this happens but I do think it will come about,' said Jochen, painting, for him, a surprisingly upbeat outlook. 'What's more, it has to happen.'

'I am not so sure,' countered Philippe. 'For too long, we debate and argue and protest but very little changes. It is agonising to watch.'

'Philippe is right,' agreed Angelina. 'Individual countries will not choose to do this of their own volition. The way the current international political system is structured simply does not permit this, and for that reason, and many others too, we need to change how the world works. There is a quote from the Norwegian explorer Thor Heyerdahl, who summed the situation up when he said: "Any scientist can tell you that a dead ocean means a dead planet. No national law, no national precautions can save the planet. The ocean, more than any other part of our planet, is a classic example of the absolute need for coordinated, global action."'

'It is certainly going to need international collaboration on a scale that is rarely seen,' Jochen conceded.

'As we stand, it simply won't happen,' asserted Angelina. 'So many of the problems that humanity faces are compounded by the fact that we find it difficult to work together multilaterally – be that reactively or proactively. Despite scientists emphasising the urgency, there is often an obdurate few countries that put their own short-term, self-interests first and block clear, expedient and necessary action. I guess this is why we have a habit of leaving things to the very last minute before we feel compelled to act. Unfortunately, this will no longer wash when it comes to dealing with the pollution of our seas, our forests, our planet; just as it will not work if, one day, we are serious about eliminating other macro issues such as disease, war, poverty, migration and climate change, which are so often inter-linked.'

Gesturing that the platform was hers and always happy to play devil's advocate, I said: 'Okay, Angelina, tell us more. How do we fix all the world's problems?'

'Believe it or not, I might have the answer! Recently I wrote a piece on an interesting, up and coming pressure group agitating for worldwide federal governance. It calls itself the New One World movement or, in short, NOW. It was formed in Copenhagen but I became alerted to it when it began to gain a foothold in the Netherlands. They believe the solution to many of our global problems is through a strong world government. Their view is that the only way we will get meaningful action addressing our oceans and many other issues, including all the economic, political, health, war and climate disasters that afflict our planet, is by bringing nations together into a federalist, international government. Likewise, it is my opinion that while the world's problems are serious, they are not intractable; there are things that we can do to save ourselves, but it is imperative that we move quickly! As Einstein said: "There is no salvation for the human race, other than the creation of a world government." Now is the time to act on his words. Or, more succinctly, as Elvis once said, – and now the Rioja is getting the better of me – "It's now or never.'"

There was a moment's silence as we digested her words and before anyone could frame a cogent riposte, Angelina, the bit between her teeth now, continued: 'As you know, I am not religious but I do believe our sacred texts, once you go beyond the hyperbole, are suffused with much wisdom. If you think about the major faiths, they all carry a key message of believing in a finer place as they talk about reaching a halcyon, promised land - nirvana, paradise, Elysium, heaven, call it what you will. Instead of spending a lifetime hoping and praying to reach some kind of Shangri-La upon death, we should be striving to create our own paradise right here on earth. To me, the path is clearly laid out in front of us. Sticking with the religious allusion, wasn't it Luke that said in his Gospel something about the Kingdom of God being found here on earth and within each of us? Just occasionally in nature we catch fleeting moments – perhaps you have paused briefly and sat calmly, you might have closed your eyes and become mindful of the sound of crashing waves or of birdsong or a burbling stream or soughing wind in the treetops or you may have just laid back and gazed at the starlit firmament? Or perhaps you have awoken from a beautiful dream, half befuddled but still recalling transient moments, snatches or thin slivers of perfection, of what could be? Admittedly, finding tranquillity is easier if you can avoid the low background rumble of traffic that accompanies us almost everywhere we go. If you clear your mind of all our self-created problems and noise, swerve all the incessant rushing and distraction, it is almost possible to imagine you are in paradise. Some people experience these elusive moments more often than others – the young and the old notably - but, in different ways, they exist for us all. For me, practising mindful yoga can take me there.

'However, somehow, as a race, we have chosen another path. The Caribbean itself provides a sobering example of our plight: take the Dominican Republic or Jamaica or even Venezuela, all potential paradises with white sand beaches and azure seas, yet, through human-manufactured problems like drugs and guns, we have found a way to make them dangerous and violent places. One of so many examples of humankind snatching hell from the jaws of paradise.'

'You say white beaches but they won't be white for long,' chimed in Jochen obliquely. 'This goes back to the coral breakdown that I was talking about earlier. The beaches are – or were - predominantly created by brightly coloured parrotfish feeding on the slimy algae that always threatens to smother reefs and excreting it out at industrial rates as sand! However, as a result of overfishing, parrotfish numbers are in rapid decline. In turn, without them feeding on the reef, there are no beaches and the reefs die as algae takes over. This isn't just a Caribbean problem. Globally, 275 million people live within 20 miles of a reef. Aside from their outstanding beauty, coral reefs are biodiversity hotspots and provide food and protection for young fish, which, of course, in turn grow and provide sustenance for other sea creatures as well as for the local populace. The disappearance of coral is made all the more alarming in that while it covers just one per cent of the ocean floor, it supports a quarter of all known marine species. Coral is much beloved and visited by tourists and its destruction also jeopardises this line of much needed revenue for locals.'

Angelina was in no mood for interruptions and, blanking Jochen before he could get going, returned to her own theme: 'Since the 1950s, the world has lived with the threat of annihilation by nuclear bombs hanging over us. Prior to that, we awaited our fate from the four horsemen of the apocalypse and other religious doomsayers. As a species, we invariably find a means to despoil things. For me, it is plain to see we are within touching distance of utopia, yet for reasons I cannot entirely fathom, we choose not to reach it - well, not up until now at least. So far, we have not found a way of organising ourselves to take best advantage of that which has been afforded to us. And trust me, while there are many complicating factors, in the end we have a straightforward, binary choice between heaven and hell: to live in the Garden of Eden that has been given to us or to destroy it and ourselves.'

'So, why do we not choose heaven on earth then?' quizzed a sceptical Philippe; his religious sensitivities nettled.

'I am afraid I don't have a one-word answer for that. If I am honest, our inertia never ceases to surprise and disappoint me. Too many people sit complacently and assume that nothing can be done, believing that society is what it is and that the odds are cripplingly stacked against them in terms of changing it. They do not believe in the power of their own voice. But, if you will permit me, I can give you a few possible theories as to why this might be,' continued Angelina.

'On an individual level, most people are so heavily embroiled in life's Sisyphean struggle - the daily fight for existence, to make ends meet, to pay the rent or mortgage, to put food on the table, to pay the bills or to pay off a car or student loan, or whatever - that they just don't have the capacity or energy to dedicate the little free time they have to political causes.

'For many too, it is down to conservatism with a small "c". A terror of stepping into the unknown, a misguided fear of rocking the boat and losing control of things and of only allowing themselves to be goaded into action when the situation absolutely dictates. Despite all the outward bluster and self-confidence of many people, in reality, most of us are timid, conformist creatures, afraid to upset the apple cart. But this is seized upon by the grasping and insular interests of nation-states, by big business and by a few super-rich opportunists. For them, life is but a game. They play by their own set of rules and the masses are there as their playthings to be manipulated and exploited at will; they work on the principle that, through wily lawyers and accountants, they can bypass regulations and buy their piece of heaven on earth. Whatever they do, they usually get away with. They often own or run the power structures – the media, the legal system, politicians, property, industry – that help maintain them in their lifestyle and the status quo per se. Or they know someone that does. One of the main reasons the world stays as it is, is because it suits those at the very top to keep it that way. Just as many businesses are beginning to do, now is the time to switch from top-down control of our world to bottom-up management.'

'And you honestly believe people, nations will give up their sovereignty just like that and pledge allegiance to a world government?' queried an incredulous Jochen.

'Up until now, people have simply not been educated on the benefits a world government would bring. How can they have been, when each country fights its own paranoid battle for self-justification and survival; has its own biases and writes its own history? Let's face it, in the grand sweep of things, many of the democracies we know today are still in their infancy and remain in the process of developing, defining and asserting themselves. The world has been divided up into countries for less than 0.1% of our history. Until the last couple of hundred years or so, most societies alternated between anarchy and tyranny. In the early 1800s just one per cent of people lived in a democracy. It is easy to forget that in 1942 there were still only eleven democratic nations on the planet.

'Consider some of the most powerful countries on earth, the likes of the US, Germany, Italy, France, the UK, Israel and South Korea. All of them have been involved in struggles to expand or shore up their territorial claims and political systems in the last 100 years or so. Today, still, one third of the world lives under authoritarian control. Even those civilisations that we know to have been around for ever like China, India, Japan and Russia are nursing relatively new political systems as well as often looking to pursue revanchist policies and anachronistic spheres of interest, nearly always bloodily, controversially and quite often fruitlessly.

'What's more, almost all are shackled by their own predominantly unimaginative, myopic, patriotic, jingoistic media who continue to doggedly perpetuate the misgiven – dangerous even - ethos of tribal nationalism. As a journalist, I see how the industry is like a blinkered dinosaur, lumbering clumsily from one cause célèbre to the next, always seeking polemics, infantilising issues along the way. More often than not, newspapers are run by ageing right-wing moguls, patronised and fawned upon by right-wing politicians, conjoined in an unholy alliance which is determined to belittle the left – indeed anything leftfield - in order to serve their own needs. They play upon the fears of those worried about immigration, economic instability, moral degradation and a loss of identity and are always eager to point out to us how poor people – never the rich – are exploiting the system. If you need evidence, just consider the Murdoch dynasty. A media tycoon who has played the insular, nationalist card wherever he has set up office. He has pursued his own political agenda through the editorial support of right-wing xenophobes. In return for his backing, politicians have extended favours to him, allowing him to monopolise news channels and grow his family business. In fact, worldwide, the media is run by a surprisingly small clutch of tycoons, the very embodiment of capitalism; a rich overlord sitting pretty at the expense of poorly paid workers and a duped public.

'Think how newspapers report tragedies such as terrorist atrocities or plane crashes: the first consideration is not how many world citizens have died but how many of our own nationals have perished. I have always struggled to understand all this wrapping yourself in the flag nonsense. I guess such people are searching for something? Solidarity, an identity of sorts? To me, it is a myth sold to you as a child just like Father Christmas. We are all born with the instinct of love, it is only through gradual indoctrination that we learn to start to rank this affection – street, town, county, country and so on – always at the expense of someone further afield. As our world shrinks, this rationale is becoming less tolerable, less tenable. If people need to get behind a banner, I am sure a nice world flag can be designed.

'Sometimes I think our capacity for inflicting misery and suffering on others – and ultimately ourselves - is infinite. Think back one hundred years to the noxious effects of World War One - what a tragic waste of human life that was. Few, on either side, knew what they were dying for. Who gained from this? All in the mad expansionist drive of nation-states, or imperialism as it was known then, cloaked in a nationalistic fervour. Instead of all this destruction, imagine what could have been achieved if people had been working together instead of tearing at each other's throats? Try to envisage how advanced we might actually be by now, a hundred years later, as a society. Talk to any war veteran or even just someone of advanced years and they will tell you that war is the most senseless activity we engage in.

'Some people want to hang on to the past and to not forget those that died for their country. I can understand that, one hundred per cent. Too many ingenuous young men have made the ultimate sacrifice in senseless, horrific wars and they, as brave individuals, need to be remembered. Yet, whilst some people want to disinter the past, others want to bury it. I think both standpoints are understandable. Nations, like people, are not perfect. They have things to be proud of and things to be ashamed of. But, just imagine, if you will, a world living in harmony, without parochialism, where countries did not fear other foreign powers and assume the worst of them; where there was no longer an assumption that somehow "they" don't have the same moral scruples as "us". Think of all the arms races that could've been - and still could be - deflected. Imagine a world where we are all on the same side and we do not need to point bombs at one another. Even now the threat of nuclear obliteration looms over us or annihilation by biological or chemical warfare or hypersonic missiles or cyber-crime or robot soldiers or the premeditated spreading of disease. Many of these weapons of destruction are developed because of a paranoia that this is what the enemy is doing. But stop for a moment and try and imagine a world in which we work together rather than against one another.'

'But surely you are missing the point that people want to belong to something? They want to feel part of a community or a region or a nation, to have some kind of identity?' I interposed.

'Okay, okay, I'll vouchsafe you that, Zac. Perhaps it *is* the case that people need to feel protected and that they belong to something bigger – a network or society, for sure. I don't disagree. But they need to understand that a world government would guarantee, not take away, safeguards and protection of traditions and ethnicities and national borders. It would also offer the ultimate community, a global one. When I recently wrote an article about this, I found it was the actor Peter Ustinov, of all people, who summed things up most succinctly when he said: "World government is not possible, it is inevitable; and when it comes, it will appeal to patriotism in its truest sense, the patriotism of men and women who love their national heritages so much that they wish to preserve them in safety for the common good."

Angelina licked her wine-stained lips and continued: 'Right now, our planet is home to about seven and a half billion people, distributed among 195 countries or so, speaking 7,000 languages and there are more types of religious and personal beliefs than, how do you Brits say, "you can shake a stick at"? So, I grant you, it will not be easy to pull them all together into a single cause. But I believe it can be done; more to the point, that it *has* to be done. Despite warring factions, the human race has, time and again, showed itself capable of unifying – from the formation of city-states through to modern day countries and continent-wide economic and political unions. After World War Two, who would have thought that the European nations were capable of coming together to form a political bloc? But they did. As weaponry and technology become potentially apocalyptic, slowly we make the realisation that we simply *have* to collaborate.

'The transition to a world government will come through the people, through political movement, yes, but not existing political groups. There are very few internationalist and outward looking political entities, quite the opposite in fact, parties are frequently and necessarily insular and short-termist, knowing they are likely to only have a brief tenure in office. They rarely think long-term with regard to domestic issues, never mind on matters facing the planet. Ordinarily, they are focused only on their own success. It is why, for decades, countries have talked big but delivered next to nothing in the fight against climate change. In terms of world governance, we now need a wider outlook and longer term vision. I am sure we could easily agree a common set of values upon which to build a new global order.'

Processing Angelina's words, I asked: 'So, if I have this right, you are suggesting a world federalist government will solve all our problems?'

'Yes, exactly that. It is time for a fundamental rethink of global politics. It all makes perfect sense to me, I have always seen myself as a world citizen. Whether we like it or not, we all are. Some of us have made that realisation and others are yet to. The concept of world federalism is not a new thing; it has been spoken about since the dawn of civilisation – the empires of Egypt, Mesopotamia, China and Japan, to name but a few, envisaged hegemony of "all-under-Heaven". Albert Einstein, Mahatma Gandhi and Martin Luther King, three of the most influential thinkers of the last century, were all World Federalists. Gandhi said war will only come to an end when there is a global system in place to deal with it; something along the lines of "the future peace, security and progression of the world demands a world federation of free nations, and on no other basis can the problems of the modern world be solved" and he talked about a "pooling of the world's resources for the common good of all." Pretty simple really and it is what I stand behind, one hundred per cent.

'I see. A bit like the EU with balls and on a world-scale?' I mused.

'Yes, you could put it like that. Contrary to what some people will think, this is not some extremist plot to install socialism or communism or fascism on the world. Politicians, poets and philosophers have, over the years and across the political spectrum, expounded the benefits of a philanthropic world government. Wait a minute, let me pull up some quotes I have saved; I still have them stored from some recent research I did.'

Angelina ferreted around in her bag and whipped out her iPad. 'Here we are,' she continued, 'I found that so many great minds, having wrestled with how we best run the world, ultimately became advocates of a global federalist system. Back in the eighteenth century, we find the German philosopher Kant speaking about "a federation of free nations" in an essay called *Perpetual Peace*. In the mid-nineteenth century, the poet Alfred Tennyson prophesised: "For I dipped into the future, as far as the human eye could see and saw the vision of the world and all the wonder that would be; until the war drum throbbed no longer and the battle flags were furled into the Parliament of man, the Federation of the World." A little later and Bertrand Russell, another philosopher, summed it up when he said: "Science has made unrestricted national sovereignty incompatible with human survival. The only possibilities are now world government or death." And writer and historian H G Wells talked of: "A federation of all humanity, together with a sufficient means of social justice to ensure health, education, and equality of opportunity, would mean such a release and increase of human energy as to open a new phase in human history."'

'Yes, but the hypotheses of academics and philosophers do not always translate into the real world – that is why they are chimeras, not realities.' This time it was Jochen who cut across Angelina.

'I truly believe we are on the pathway to a world government. It is just a question of whether we can get there quickly enough – in time to be able to proactively manage global crises. If we don't, some Armageddon scenario will force us there anyway. I guess the first tentative steps on this road came after the mass slaughter of World War One. The American President Woodrow Wilson won the Nobel Peace Prize for his part in setting up the post-war League of Nations – the first attempt at a world government, charged primarily with maintaining world peace. A man who understood history; a man with a PhD in the subject and the US's most academic president.'

Reaching for her tablet again, she continued: 'His actual words were: "There must be, not a balance of power, but a community of power, not organised rivalries, but an organised common peace." Something, as we know, it failed at – partly due, despite Wilson's best efforts, to the US never joining and partly because it was never invested with enough authority. Given it never even had its own army, what chance did it really have? We cannot play about with half-measures; a global government will need real teeth. And that might mean militarily, certainly to begin with.'

Before anyone could interrupt again, Angelina carried on: 'Internationally, leaders from all political persuasions have championed world federalism. US President and Republican Theodore Roosevelt talked about all mankind being eternally grateful to the statesman who could bring about a new structure of international society. Prior to him, another Republican, President Ulysses S Grant, who brought the US together after civil war, spoke of the "Great Framer of the World" developing it so that it becomes one nation which can address international questions and whose decisions will be as binding as the decisions of the Supreme Court are on Americans. Democrat Harry S Truman, you remember him, the guy who implemented the Marshall Plan to rebuild Europe after the Second World War, said: "It will be just as easy for nations to get along in a republic of the world as it is for us to get along in the republic of the United States. If we do not want to die together in war, we must learn to live together in peace." Which takes us right back to the Universal Declaration of Human Rights, which demands that: "All human beings....should act towards one another in a spirit of brotherhood." More recently, even Republican President George Bush foresaw a better future. In a 1990 speech entitled *Towards a New World Order*, which envisaged a post-Cold War where the West collaborated with Soviet states in overseeing global governance, he said: "Until now, the world we've known has been a world divided—a world of barbed wire and concrete block, conflict and cold war. Now, we can see a new world coming into view. A world in which there is the very real prospect of a new world order."

'Even war mongers, having learnt bitter lessons first-hand, ultimately come round to reason. US hawk General Douglas MacArthur said: "If we do not devise some greater and more equitable system, Armageddon will be at our door," while John McCloy, Assistant Secretary of War in the US during the Second World War, concurred: "What is called for is total disarmament – universal, enforceable and complete."

'I can cite more. Dante, Nietzsche, Walter Kronkite, once known as the most trusted man in America, the writer Isaac Asimov, the former Russian President Mikhail Gorbachev, the feminist Rosika Schwimmer and the first Prime Minister of India, Nehru, were all world federalists, the latter saying: "I have long believed the only way peace can be achieved is through World Government." And then there is philosopher Albert Camus and his anti-nationalist stance. The list of those extolling a vision of world federalism is long and compelling. For too long, a parochial media has closed off a grown-up discussion of world federalism. As the clock ticks, if we are to survive and prosper, the time to act on these visions is now.'

Angelina had become quite inflamed and clearly wasn't finished. I recalled how, back in the day, once the 'play' button had been depressed, she could talk incessantly and it became like listening to a radio chat show with one speaker hogging the airwaves. She paused momentarily, composed herself by taking a healthy slug of wine and, as we ruminated on her words, surprised us by continuing in a more light-hearted vein.

'And, worry not, the soundtrack to a new one world order has already been written. Just remember the lines from "Imagine", John Lennon's plea for us all to come together: "No need for greed or hunger, a brotherhood of man, imagine all the people, sharing all the world" and "You may say I am a dreamer, but I am not the only one, I hope someday you'll join me and the world will live as one."

So many songs speak of world peace, don't you think? Of living in harmony, about respecting our planet, finding beauty in one another and of love; yet we choose to soporifically sing along to these tunes without thinking about their true meaning or how we might go about realising some of their panaceas. We always have one hand tied behind our back because of selfish national agendas. Remember, the world wasn't created with borders and checkpoints on it. For too long we have been trussed by a patchwork of man-made – and I use the word "man" quite deliberately - boundaries and lines, demarcating both counties and countries, arbitrarily drawn on ancient maps that have been decided by geographical features or long lost wars or at the whim of negotiating apparatchiks. Yet, when you go out into the world and meet people – I mean everyday men and women, the workers – irrespective of what political system or religious creed they adhere to, they are warm, welcoming, have similar basic requirements and strive for much the same goals as ourselves. In short, they are much like us. The fear and distrust of others that we are repeatedly sold is a lie - an unfounded myth that needs to be exposed.'

'Tell me more about NOW. It is just starting to get a foothold in Sweden. Surely it's just another obscure and short-lived political movement; what chance does it really have of making a difference to anything?' Jochen interjected, perhaps sensing that Angelina was beginning to go off-piste.

'NOW has grown out of Freetown Christiania in Copenhagen; specifically it is the brainchild of Candy Kitcatt, a cult transgender popstar cum politician. As you probably know, Christiania has something of a mixed reputation. It is a semi-legal hippie commune in a disused military camp, a mile or so south of the city centre. About 1,000 people live there but thousands more, mainly tourists, visit it daily. Depending on which side of the fence you sit, it is a haven for on-the-run thugs and desperados dealing drugs and weapons or, on the other hand, it is a forward-thinking collective of free thinkers, new age travellers, bohemians, artisans and artists and those taking time out from the daily grind.'

I nodded an acknowledgement, conscious of not derailing Angelina from her account.

'The movement initially formed in order to protest ecological degradation and climate change. Liv Larsen, a twenty-something zealous eco-activist and politician from the Danish Red-Green Alliance party, held several meetings in Christiania's Gay House, one of its many cultural centres, in which she put forward a plan to save the planet from climate catastrophe. As you can imagine, she was preaching to the converted. Her cause quickly garnered momentum and her ideas began to take hold across the city, taking the form of monthly stop-the-traffic demonstrations, which culminated with marches on Christiansborg Palace where the Danish parliament sits.

'However, before long, things started to plateau and there was internal dissent and discussion about what the next steps might be and how these marches were going to make any real difference globally. The Danish government is often regarded as one of the most environmentally friendly on the planet but it was clear that it could not single-handedly change the world. And, as we well know, climate change has no respect for borders. After much debate, it was agreed that the only way significant global change would ever come about would be by altering the thrust of the demonstrations. While green issues remained very much on the agenda, the gatherings began to take on a new, internationalist slant.

'Candy Kitcatt, although a supporter, was one of the most vociferous critics of the early direction of this, up until then, inchoate and unnamed movement. Her star was rising both musically and politically. She persuaded the steering committee that they needed to agitate for more international cooperation through a pan-world government, which, it was felt, was the only way of meaningfully addressing climate catastrophe and other pressing global concerns. So, the marches mutated and started, at least to begin with, to call for an expansion of the powers of the United Nations in order to create a single international authority that could deal with the world's borderless problems. The hoped for endgame being a unified and peaceful world.

'Whereas the initial climate change demos had attracted dozens of people, occasionally hundreds, with the new focus, several thousand demonstrators started turning up each month and the New One World movement took its first nascent steps. Along with the new name and a shift in direction, came the election of the charismatic Candy as leader; Liv, who is still to be found on marches, remains in the Red-Green Alliance party.

'Through its own momentum and a strong online presence, NOW started to take on the form of an actual political entity, not just an amorphous protest movement. It became renowned for dropping erudite and often sardonic video campaigns which, in turn, saw them start to grow their popularity further afield. Before I set off on this trip, they had their first march in Amsterdam and I heard that there are plans for similar demos in Stockholm and Helsinki. While the NOW movement was originally aimed at creating and empowering a world government, there had been no intention for it to campaign as a political party. However, Candy has since put herself forward as a candidate and will represent NOW in the forthcoming Danish elections. She claims it is to give them more legitimacy and profile. If she wins, I can see further candidates springing up like mushrooms after the rain. While its raison d'être is to drive change in how we oversee international politics, it is, of course, built on a foundation of green issues. So, the crusade for a new world order has begun!'

'Really?' I couldn't help myself asking, wearily. 'I can see how the concept might appeal to activists, the intelligentsia even, but the everyday man in the street? Come on, most people are surely too bogged down in their daily struggles or are too conditioned, too fiercely patriotic to consider a world republic?'

'Why should the notion of a one world government be so abhorrent to people? What is it that they think they will be deprived of? Is it their material possessions, their faith, their way of life that they think will be forsaken? Trust me, none of these would be taken away by a world parliament. Or do they think they will be denied a sense of belonging, of identity, of coming together to achieve the best results for the vast majority of people? A world government would be doing precisely that; it would re-create what they strive for on a local or regional level but across the planet. It would give true meaning to the phrase "think globally, act locally". People *are* changing. More and more, we are becoming aware of how our actions are interrelated – the Butterfly Effect; if nothing else, climate change has taught us that.'

'Isn't it the job of the UN to fix the world's problems?' I quizzed.

But my question was left hanging in the void as the last of the stragglers from the deck party crashed noisily into the dining room; Lori Petrucci, our Communications Officer, clutching her acoustic guitar, and Rachel Onions, one of the ship's engineers, clinging manically to two opened bottles of wine. Both were pretty far gone, meaning an end to any serious debate. We all succumbed to another glass or two while Lori, who turned out to be an impressive human jukebox, entertained us by playing all our requests. It was well into the early hours when we pulled the shutters down on the evening, the plonk finally getting the better of us.

I, and I suspect others, went to bed ruminating on Angelina's thoughts. She had certainly raised some interesting ideas which begged further exploration; it was a subject we would return to.

Chapter 8

21 May 2017

In terms of capturing the whale images, it was a necessarily loose brief as we were reliant on sighting a pod of humpbacks, which locals said had been seen in the waters off the island of Salt Cay, where we were anchored for a few days. I spent several afternoons with binoculars trained on the horizon, looking for a glimpse of a characteristic fluke slapping the water.

Having had no luck whatsoever in our daily whale-spotting endeavours, on the final afternoon before we were due to move on, a small group of us took matters into our own hands. Donning diving gear, we slid gently into the serene, azure water in the *African Queen*, one of *Espy*'s three semi-rigid inflatables. We headed out to Turks Island Passage just off East Caicos Island. Angelina, who it turned out was now a qualified and experienced diver, was hoping to pick up some incidental information for one of her articles. For both of us, this was our first time observing and, we hoped, swimming with whales. Patrick from Austria was our lead diver and an experienced whale watcher. Within 15 minutes of having left the sister ship, we were thrilled to see the distinctive tail fin of our first humpback, resembling the wings of an enormous bird emerging briefly and mirage-like from the water. It turned out that what we had seen was an infant whale, a calf, and soon she was joined by her mother as they both playfully circled our craft, getting closer and closer, seemingly toying with us. Patrick advised that the rest of the pod would be deeper in the ocean but nearby.

After twenty minutes or so and confident that I had captured a range of images from the dinghy, including some, what turned out to be, rather impressive underwater split-shots, it was time to take our chances in the water. The experienced Patrick suggested he accompany us one-by-one out towards the pod. As I was determined on capturing a few close-up photos before they disappeared, I plunged in first with him. Generally in life I've found that brandishing a camera is a pretty sure-fire way of getting yourself to the front of the queue and today was no exception. Tumbling backwards over the side of the craft, we struck out in the direction of the last visible circles of splash-water, trying our best not to come between parent and child. Surfacing briefly, Patrick's advice was to remain calm and the whales, being curious and friendly creatures, will come to us. As we dived again and neared our target area, I was taken aback by what can only be described as a continuous loud clicking sound which filled my entire being; this was quickly followed by a series of squeaks, squawks and whistles. Patrick explained that humpback whales are social creatures and that they communicate freely and easily with each other, with each pod having its own distinct dialect or coda.

And then, appearing from nowhere, the mother was upon us, swimming to within two or three metres, surfacing briefly and projecting water 10 feet into the air out of her blow-hole. Her enormity was at first overwhelming and I had to fight my survival instinct, which urged me to swim back as fast as I could to the inflatable. I steeled myself, resigned to fate and the mercy of this leviathan beauty. Showing off her black bulk and white underbelly, she circled me and I swam around her; pirouetting, she exhibited a surprising agility and I had the sense that she was fooling with me as she mirrored my twists and turns. Gradually our gyrations stilled and, I kid you not, for a few moments we actually locked eyes – or more accurately, given the immensity and immediacy of her head, my two eyes met one of hers. I had the sense of a deep, hypnotic connection as I looked into something that seemed to belong to another age, another world even. Its learned eyes carried primeval sagacity.

It filled my vision and I could almost reach out and touch the fifty or so pyramid-shaped lumps, about the size of golf-balls that dotted her black head. These mysterious tubercles, as they are known, are hair follicles or whale whiskers. The jury is out as to what they are for but it is possible that they detect vibrations in the water which alert them to prey or that they can detect low frequency sound waves. I noted too, the preponderance of barnacles that had encrusted her head, back and oversized flippers. Her dorsal fin, used to aid balance, was about two-thirds of the way down her back and sat on a pronounced hump – hence the naming of this particular subspecies. I was in the thrall of this majestic creature and it was a strangely centring and calming experience; exhilaration only came later. After what seemed an eternity, she broke away and, as if offering a final adieu, treated me to another display of dizzying acrobatics, seemingly careful to avoid battering me with her formidable tail fin, before heading back to re-join her offspring.

Hoicking myself back aboard the inflatable, my heart pounding, I was fleetingly lost for words and unable to stop myself from laughing out loud and grinning inanely. Then I was jabbering: 'Angelina, oh my god, that was fucking unbelievable. Jesus wept! Honestly, what a truly amazing experience that was. Do you know, nothing has ever come close to that! What a beautiful, divine moment. I mean, really, I am struggling for the right words, but - don't laugh - I actually felt at peace with the world. I think that might be what is known as a Zen moment; now I know how a blissed out Tantric guru must feel! But, don't listen to me blathering like an idiot, it's your turn; go and say hello to Mrs Whale and her baby!' She needed no prompting and was already halfway into the water, re-emerging briefly some 20 yards away with Patrick as they re-calibrated their position in relation to us and adjusted their trajectory towards the pod.

As I watched them out of sight and gazed at the benign seascape, a distant yacht puncturing the otherwise straight line of the horizon, a beatific calm washed over me. The encounter had chilled my bones and I found my thoughts drifting to the time when Angelina and I had initially met during our first year of Sixth Form study in Manchester.

Back then, I was quite shy when it came to girls and it had been Angelina that had approached me at a nightclub during a Hallowe'en party organised by our college. She had picked me out, stood alone on a balcony overlooking the dancefloor. I had been totally and utterly car-parked, having smuggled in a jam-jar of mixed spirits, syphoned from my parents' drinks' cabinet. We had found a table and talked a while and I shared my potent concoction – in which, in an intensely fought struggle, the taste of whisky just about won out. The homemade cocktail fortified our shouted but only half-heard conversation. We found we had compatible music tastes and danced drunkenly for a while to the likes of The Stone Roses, The Verve and Primal Scream. She asked me to look after her drink, while she paid a visit to the loo, and I told my mates that I'd pulled and they could forget about me for the rest of the night. Half an hour later, at closing time, she had still not reappeared and the club was quickly emptying. Half fearful that she had suddenly had second thoughts and bailed, I made my way over to the ladies loo and asked a girl to check the cubicles to see if they could find a pretty brunette in a black skirt and white lacy top. Ten minutes later, a sheepish Angelina appeared with the girl Samaritan, looking dishevelled and a tad embarrassed. She looked like she could barely stand and said she had been sick. It seemed I had poisoned her delicate constitution with my hard liquor infusion. I literally carried her out of the club over my shoulder to a backdrop of Nick Cave's latest offering 'Into My Arms' and that was that really; we were both smitten.

Over the course of the next 18 months we became increasingly enamoured with one another. Angelina was half Dutch, half English; her family had moved over to England from Amsterdam when she was thirteen. Her strict Dutch Calvinist father Caspar, who worked for PricewaterhouseCoopers in Manchester, we saw little of. When he was 'in town' he spent long days in the office – and I mean long – he would be out of the door by 6.30am and might not return until 10.00pm or later if he was entertaining clients. Most of the time he was on the road, predominantly in Europe but occasionally in the US and Asia. He earnt the money but seemed to have little time to enjoy it. Angelina's English mother, Jasmine, we saw a fair bit of. Angelina adored her and I quickly came to appreciate her warm, easy going and chilled approach to life. She was an artist, a rather good one too, producing paintings that I guess were a kind of social realism. Her work, which mood-wise reminded me of Edward Hopper, was set against a broody and bleak but stylised northern England backdrop. She sold some pieces but not enough to keep her from working in a marketing agency. Her hippy, libertarian approach to life – and the absence of her husband – meant Angelina and I were soon sharing the same bed several nights a week. Angelina's younger brother was Apollo – yes, really – and he was something of a one-off; bi-sexual, louche, vivacious, eminently likeable and totally out of control even in his mid-teens. If I recall, he was expelled from school for selling sexual favours.

Gradually our friendship groups merged, with many romantic couplings – some predictable, others unexpectedly entertaining. I spent increasing amounts of time at Angelina's parents' flat in Chorlton-cum-Hardy in the south of the city. Our fake ID saw us spend a lot of time at a boozer called The Briton's Protection and, later in the evening, at a variety of venues across town including: The Brickhouse, an indie nightclub and formerly Manchester's first all-leather gay disco; Legends, which, when it was known as Twisted Wheel in an earlier incarnation, was famous as one of the birthplaces of Northern Soul; 42nd Street, once called Slack Alice's and opened by the footballer George Best; and The Boardwalk, an integral part of the Madchester scene and where Oasis made their debut.

Whilst we certainly played hard, we put a shift in academically too and took some time to plan our future together and where we might study post-A levels. It was never up for debate whether we would stay together or go our separate ways, the only question was which city suited both our needs. Prior to moving to England, Angelina's family had lived in Haarlem in the suburbs of Amsterdam. As a child, she had always loved her visits into the centre but they had been frustratingly rare. She still had a longing to experience the city in more depth. I had visited once with my parents a few years earlier, still young at that point but at an age when I could detect a buzz to it that I liked and, at 17, I certainly wasn't unaware of its reputation as a freewheeling city where pretty much anything goes. Being something of a larrikin, decadence and libertarianism were my watchwords back then; they still are if I get half a chance. So, Amsterdam it was.

I recalled our anticipation on the ferry crossing from Harwich to the Hook of Holland, an excitement that spilled over into an afternoon of drinking and cocaine and an attempt to join the 'at sea' club, which was rudely curtailed by an over-officious toilet cleaner.

For starters at least, Angelina planned to stay with her grandparents in De Pijp and I'd elected for halls of residence. This allowed me to cultivate friendships with a number of unlikely characters from across Europe. Geir I've already mentioned but there was also Mads from Germany, Zorro a Greek Cypriot, Antonio from Spain and Rowen, a fellow Brit from Cowdenbeath, plus several other peripheral party animals. I certainly thought of Angelina and I as remaining strong as a couple at the time but, looking back, I have to admit that there were a number of cracks appearing;

distractions for both of us, but particularly me. I had started dabbling with nose candy after my A levels and this, along with a penchant for ecstasy, only intensified during my first couple of years in a city that did not offer up many stop signs.

I played back in my mind some of the scenes of Amsterdam carnage that I could actually remember – late nights, all-dayers, monster parties, all-nighters, copious amounts of drugs, drink, nightclubbing, collapsing, falling over, waking up in strange places, vomiting and hangovers. But there were equally memorable, gentler times too: lazy days in art galleries and picnics in parks; walking hand in hand and stealing kisses along the canals; quiet evenings in brown cafes or watching films.

And then my scudding thoughts settled on New Year's Eve 1999. A day that I'd certainly taken to heart Prince's lyrics 'Tonight I am going to party like it's 1999'. The celebration was imprinted on my mind for many reasons. It was pretty wild but not altogether unrepresentative of other set-tos that we enjoyed in those days.

The session had begun early afternoon when I met a close friend, Big H Mi Skoodle, who was over from England for the night. We'd arranged to meet in *Hooters* – his suggestion - a watering hole I was unfamiliar with but it was on the Damrak and would have been convenient for Big H as he arrived into Centraal Station from Schipol; it would inevitably be busy with tourists. H was my best buddy from my college days in Manchester and was currently studying in London. With flights between the two cities taking just an hour, we paid each other regular visits. Today, it seemed he had started early. I had to take my hat off to H. Despite his best efforts and no doubt impeded by his slight frame, he was not what you would call a heavyweight or even a session drinker. Nevertheless, that never stopped him from throwing himself wholeheartedly into the spirit of things. He'd already eaten his customary lettuce sandwich, which, in a somewhat surprising case of long-term planning, he rather oddly believed to be an antidote to the inevitable ferocious hangover that would consume him the following day. In contrast to this cautious approach, he'd already dropped several cans of Special Brew, a super-strength beer, in order to placate his nerves, which, for him, went hand in hand with any social gathering.

Taking advantage of the ample space at the wide, long bar and with beers in hand, we sat at stools, primed for a catch-up. It was still early and it would take a drink or two before I had my bearings; I had only half taken into account that the bar staff and waiting service seemed to be exclusively young, female, attractive and scantily attired. We had barely got through our opening gambits, when there was an overly vigorous rubbing down of the bar counter, followed by a quick drying off and whipping away of beer towels and then, suddenly, in a series of concurrent occurrences, customers drifted back at least 15 feet from the bar, the opening strains of Tom Jones' 'Sexbomb' reverberated out of the stereo system, now cranked up to full volume, and one of the sassy servers vaulted onto the bar itself.

H Mi Skoodle and I were guilelessly left as front row spectators on a striptease show. No doubt if I had been on my own, I would have owned the faux pas and just shuffled away but as we were a pair, we decided to brave it out by remaining coolly insouciant to the spectacle, as if this was our usual perch of a Friday lunch. Except you could not just ignore the floorshow – or should I say bar-show – and carry on your conversation; the volume of the music alone precluded that. Caught in no-man's land, we froze. Meanwhile the perky, lithe dancer had started to make full use of her catwalk, inevitably reserving special attention for H and myself, wriggling her shapely derriere just inches from our faces and awkward stares. An hour earlier I had been fast asleep and now here I was centre stage in a strip joint with, as Big H later so loquaciously described it, a woman's nether regions so close 'you could hear her foodle growl'. And, at that point, almost inevitably really, Angelina walked into the joint. To be fair, she seemed unfazed and walked straight up to the bar, pulled up a stool next to us and took in the show, ratcheting up the awkwardness of the situation just that little bit more. It had been a bad start to the day. Once the act, which thankfully only lasted one song, had finished, I gushed out my explanation and Angelina seemed to half-accept our protracted pleas of innocence. But the incident was to provide one more nail in the coffin of our relationship, which was interred later that day.

Angelina's appearance had been fleeting as she was out with friends who were much more civilised than my crowd, mixing shopping with the odd glass of wine or G and T before heading off home to titivate for the evening which, for them, would begin with dinner in a sophisticated restaurant. I had arranged to hook up with her again late afternoon as she had asked me to give her an opinion on an item of furniture she was thinking of purchasing.

Meanwhile, H and I had a number of Amsterdam drinking tropes to scale and we had headed off to a favourite haunt down a narrow alleyway just off Dam Square, Wynand Fockink. I was on familiar terms with the landlord there and often called upon his expertise in helping me choose a quality beer. More often than not in those days, for me, this was a Belgian ale. With hundreds of years of brewing experience, they seemed to have perfected their art in the way that the French have with wine. The barman told me it was all down to the yeasts found in Belgium, which give their brews distinct floral tones, coupled with their expertise in blending – essentially using a little of the last batch to blend into the next consignment in the same way that you might cultivate yoghurt. They combined this art with a wide range of fermenting techniques to produce strong and complex beers; anything below 5% is not really considered alcoholic in Belgium.

Given we were drinking in an establishment famed for its genevers and liqueurs, we felt compelled to complement our ales with a Dutch gin chaser each, a local juniper-infused spirit. I recall that it was an unusually quiet moment and, chatting to the genial barman, he pointed out that our 9.8% Belgian beers wouldn't even be considered alcoholic in Russia but, instead, would be classified as foodstuff. Anything below 10% is, somewhat amazingly, described as a 'lightly alcoholic sparkling beverage'. Consequently, he informed us, the country walks around in an alcoholic stupor - this, not religion, was what had turned out to be Marx's 'opium of the people'; every morning, he told us, you can see queues at kiosks outside metro stations waiting to buy their first beer of the morning, which they hoped would take the edge off their vodka-induced hangover. The barman went on to tell us how he had once worked for the Dutch drugs squad and had regularly travelled to Moscow. He'd been somewhat surprised to see rounds of vodka habitually served at early morning police briefings.

Our whistles whetted and now with a hankering for Dutch gin, we headed to Café Hoppe, where we could smoke pot and drink a genever and beer in the same glass, known fittingly as a *Kopstoot* or headbutt. And then on to Café de Spuyt and our downfall, the much-celebrated Westvleteren 12, a 10.2% Trappist dark amber brew widely touted as the best beer in the world. Rumour always abounded that this fabled beer, sold in a label-less bottle, was briefly available in certain hostelries across town. Up until this point, it had always remained tantalisingly out of reach for me, a self-proclaimed beer sommelier; as soon as I arrived at a joint, following a hot lead, they had invariably just sold out and then I had to wait for the rumour mill to start again.

The legendary beer has been brewed by Trappist monks at Saint Sixtus Abbey, just outside Westvleteren on the Belgian-French border, roughly midway between Paris and Amsterdam, for over 150 years. Like each of the eleven official Trappist breweries, all profits go into the running of the abbey and towards charity work undertaken by the monks. They have always made the point that they do not live to brew beer, they brew beer to allow them to live the way they do. The monks make three renowned brews – Blond, 8 and 12. Their beer is sold at the door of the abbey in dark brown bottles. People only know which one they are getting by the colour of the bottle top. Green for Blond, blue for 8 and gold for 12. The monks have deliberately avoided selling to pubs, restaurants, entrepreneurs, larger breweries and the like to minimise the stress involved with the process. In theory, you can only get your hands on the beer by queueing up at the abbey gates on specific days and you can only buy one wooden crate of 24 bottles or a small package of 6 bottles in the *In de Vrede* shop opposite if you are lucky enough to drop by on a day when they are in stock. Now that's a pilgrimage worth signing up for.

The Café de Spuyt was my kind of place. It livened up in the evening but through the afternoon it had a chilled and friendly vibe. It was a traditional Dutch pub, known as a brown café, with yellowy brown walls and a pleasing mishmash of artefacts and decorations. Its large chalkboard menu advertised dozens of speciality Belgian and Dutch beers, including Trappist and abbey brews and regular seasonal specialities – including wines and even Trappist cheese for an accompanying snack.

As we were savouring our sweet and malty Westvleteren 12s with – and apologies for sounding like a beer tosspot - unmistakable pangs of fruit and chocolate, I scanned the saloon and made the bitter-sweet realisation that we were sharing it with the infamous Uncle Eddy or the *King of Amsterdam* as he was sometimes known. He was a well-known 'Dam character, a fifty-something degenerates' degenerate who spent his days festered in the pubs of the inner city. A former soldier, he talked in a rich mix of Geordie dialogue, clichés and maxims, which became progressively lewd as he measured each afternoon out in mixed rum highballs. It seemed that we had caught him only half-cut and he was, by his standards at least, in a relatively sane exchange with a well turned out and attractive, middle-aged American couple.

Knowing that Uncle Eddy was never less than entertaining, we steeled ourselves against the pall of sweat which invariably clung to him and settled ourselves on nearby pews. The entrapped Americans stood at the bar and sipped awkwardly on their white wine spritzers, trying desperately to figure out what Eddy was saying, not wanting to appear rude and keen to engage with a local while attempting, unsuccessfully, to edge that little bit further away. I can't imagine how their conversation had begun but it seemed Unc was explaining to them about Amsterdam's fishermen's bars: 'You know mon, it was Hemingway that said if you need a drink in the wee hours of a port you need to search out where the fishing fleet is anchored. Fishermen like a drink, either upon landing their catch or before setting out, just in case it's their last, like. Not to mention all those working in the docks who demand a drink at the end of their physical shift. No-one drinks like a navvy.' Leaning in to them, he confided: 'Sometimes if I need to stay up all night, if like I've lost my key or something and I don't have a scratcha, I head on out to…'

Suddenly there was an unexpected commotion from within his thick but battered winter coat, something it seemed was trying to get out. It was an alarming moment for Eddy – and for us all. He bolted up from his stool, staggering as he did so, grappling with his coat as he span into a frenzied tussle with himself. He had inexplicably taken on the demeanour of a Sufi whirling dervish having a stroke and, having then seemingly imploded, ended up writhing on the floor. Whatever it was - I fleetingly wondered if it was a small cat - it was alive and within his lumberjack shirt and was desperately trying to get out. The scene was electrifying and people were transfixed in the small hostelry.

'What's happening?' said the well-heeled American woman. 'Is he having a fit? For God's sake, someone do something!'

The pro-active landlord was the first to react, vaulting the bar and grabbing Uncle Eddy – who was still prostrate - by the scruff of the neck. No sooner had he done this than Eddy brought everyone up short as he yelled, ashen-faced now, 'It's a baby owl!' And at that very moment, the bird burst free from the confines of his moth-eaten shirt, its piercing eyes glowering and wings a blur of flapping. It was clearly troubled and after a brief halo-like hover in a spot just over Eddy, who was finding his way to his feet, it threw itself headlong into the window and came crashing to the floor. The American woman screamed but then it was back in the air, proper distressed, dramatically wheeling the enclosed space in which it found itself. If this was a baby owl then I really did not want a close encounter with an adult anytime soon. Most of the bar's clientele threw themselves to the ground. Unexpectedly, the male American threw a wild and wayward punch at the bird before the barman's wife appeared with a fishing net, which her husband seized from her and began what seemed like an elaborate and cartoonish butterfly-catcher's dance around the saloon with the orbiting owlet. Drinks and tables went over in the melee, a crowd had started to form outside to spectate through the window and Big H Mi Skoodle and I were on our knees laughing. Then the bird hit the mirror at the back of the bar, taking out rows of glasses and spirit bottles, which re-focused the attention of the landlord and his wife. We noted Eddy stumbling towards the door and we gauged it a good time to take our leave with him. As the pub door shut, the owlet having chosen to leave too, the last thing we heard was: 'You crazy asshole! Don't come back in here, you fucking Geordie nutcase.'

Tumbling down the street with tears rolling down my face, I quizzed him:

'What the fuck did you have an owl down your shirt for?' An obvious question perhaps but I probed further: 'Did you know it was there?'

'Aye man, I'd just forgotten about it,' came the response from a frustrated and disappointed Eddy. 'I slept in a shop doorway last night and when I woke up – it was bloody freezing mon – there it was: a baby owl right next to me. It was half-dazed and radgie and I thought it had a broken wing. It must have been in a fight or flown into something. Anyway, I took pity on it. As they say, a bird in hand is worth two in the bush. I thought my body heat might revive it and then I could get it a glass of milk and set it free. Then I forgot about the bloody thing.'

If it had been anybody else, I might have asked, why did you sleep on the streets in the middle of winter but this was Uncle Eddy and such behaviour wasn't unusual. I might have also pointed out that Hemingway, who Eddy liked to quote, said if you want a clear head for the morning, you need to stop drinking by 8.00pm; advice that Unc might have benefitted from occasionally.

Giddy and garrulous by now, we spread ourselves across the walkway, weaving our way through the pavement cafes of Prinsengracht - literally Prince's Canal - one of the town's finest waterways, built in the 1600s during Amsterdam's golden days when it was one of the largest and most prosperous cities in the world. We were bound for Café Kalkhoven.

On regaining his composure, Eddy began to see the humorous side of the incident, which in turn seemed to energise him and he insisted upon joining us for our next beverage. Bursting through the doors of the subdued Kalkhoven, he drew immediate attention to himself by eyeballing everyone and shouting at the top of his voice, 'Howay man and show me the tuna!' while stirring a huge imaginary ladle in a fictitious cooking pot. I'd seen him employ this modus operandi for entering bars before; he said it was a re-enactment of a scene from the TV series *Bewitched*, although nobody I ever spoke to could quite recall it. It never failed to draw instant attention to him. The barman took one look and said, 'No. Not today, Eddy.' It seemed he would have to look elsewhere for his next rum highball.

We were now ahead of schedule, having landed at our official gathering point. Over the next hour or so a group of a dozen of us assembled. We indulged in the usual Janus-faced reminisces and predictions associated with year-end festivities. The Kalkhoven was another regular haunt, so much so that I kept a large eggcup of banana skins tucked away under the fitted wooden seating. I was enjoying a phase of pipe-smoking at the time and burnt banana skins were a mild and free intoxicant or at least that was what someone had convinced me of. My recollections start to blur from hereon in but I know we were thrown out of this hostelry. I have a vague notion of H, apropos of nothing, careening backwards in an arc which took him inexorably towards the flagged hearth, where he tripped his heels and fell rearwards into the pub fire. There was a seemingly slow-motion donnybrook as time seemed to stand still, H scrambling around in the flames for excruciatingly elongated seconds as he and nearby customers screamed; after several aborted attempts at extracting him from the conflagration, he was finally heaved free with the helping hand of a burly local, his hair singed and his jeans and jacket fire-damaged and smouldering slightly. The proprietor was having none of it, telling us 'you are all going crazy' and to sling our hooks in no uncertain terms. We downed our draughts and, in a petty act of retribution, I slipped a stuffed mongoose into my coat as we vacated the premises hollering that we were never coming back! Whilst we now had our mascot for the evening, I never did get that eggcup back.

Next, we bowled into Bar In't Aepjen, one of the city's oldest brown cafes. One of only two wooden buildings to have survived the city's devastating fire of 1452, it takes its name – literally 'in the monkeys' - from a time when sailors returning from far flung corners of the world would offer their newly acquired exotic pets as payment for food, drink and lodgings. These days it was tourists and locals that over-ran the place rather than monkeys. Our posse had split into two groups by now, which was a boon as this was a bijou bar. It was another boozer that I was drawn to by its fine selection of Belgian beers, although it was fair to say we had now passed the point of savouring our brews. And then I recalled that I had agreed to meet Angelina on Kalverstraat to look at some curtains or cushions or something, I really can't remember. It was the last day of the end of Millennium sales and she had some domestic purchase in mind but wanted my input as we were thinking of getting a flat together for our second year of study. On consulting my watch, I realised I was already 20 minutes late and I knew it would take me another 10 minutes to get there; nevertheless, I downed my ale, took my first line of coke and set off anyway.

    Henceforward, my memories fragment further. I know I stumbled across town as the Christmas lights twinkled, tripping occasionally and bumping into people, but nobody seemed to mind; most people were in good spirits and had already had a drink or two themselves as the big evening drew near. By the time I caught up with Angelina, who seemed very sober, in the moneyed, hushed, brightly-lit and bourgeois setting of the department store, I began to assimilate how far along the drunken path I was. The whole excursion took about 30 minutes or so; once Angelina had seen the state I was in, she didn't want me hanging around. I told her about the Uncle Eddy and H tipping backwards into the fire incidents and offered a few quick affirmatives to her proposed purchases before stumbling off to re-join the group at the aptly named *Amnesia* coffee shop, where I bought a space cake. I think we then took in several more drinking dens before setting out to Mazzo, our chosen nightclub for the evening. I do recall a moment of idiocy en route to the club when I thought it might be rather jolly to rattle off a blast of pull-ups on some builders' scaffolding we happened to be passing. I jumped up, lunging for the horizontal bar which I grasped impressively, pulling myself up with some wired athleticism only to crash my head into the tread boards above, that, inexplicably, I had failed to register. Defying logic, I repeated this twice. The moment provided much hilarity for our group and a split head for me. Using my undercrackers as a swab-come-bandage, I stemmed the flow of blood and soldiered on.

One of my tricks to get noticed and served at a packed nightclub was to pull the front of my t-shirt up over my head and to wave my arms around manically as if having some kind of epileptic fit. It invariably caught the eye of the bartender and, more often than not, resulted in quick service. Not on this occasion though. Even though it was ticket only, Club Mazzo was rammed and it took an eternity to get served. I am not sure why we went to Mazzo, as none of us were House music fans and we were deeply sceptical of an evening which revolved around a DJ's ego. I recall that it did offer some rather cool video and slide projections that kept us entertained for a while. Buoyed by a smorgasbord of stimulants I headed out to the dancefloor and, for reasons that escape me, forced a diminutive girl's head up the front of my t-shirt. I recall her skull jerking around chaotically as she unsuccessfully tried to extricate herself. After 20 seconds or so of being pressed against my sweaty, hairy chest, I lifted my t-shirt and let her out. She blasted me with a tirade of expletives as I grinned back inanely. It was at that point that I noticed Angelina staring at me aghast from the edge of the dancefloor. She must have just landed at the club, having been out with friends enjoying a civilised dinner at a restaurant called G-Spot. I recall little else of the club, no doubt some mock dancing and piss-taking out of people blowing whistles, then kisses all round at midnight before I was triumphantly chaired out by the boys, still clutching the stuffed mongoose, my head clunking against the ceiling, my bloodstained and skid-marked underpants on my head, having fished them out of my jacket pocket, to the strains of Frankie Knuckles' *Your Love*. Welcome to the new millennium. As an aside, I heard recently that the club has been replaced by an Italian restaurant of the same name.

For a 'nightcap' we had decided to head to Soundgarden, a rock dive bar which was a far better fit for us. I was in a real mess by now – as were most of us. Prior to the new century, there had been much worry about the Y2k bug, where computers would not be able to cope with the new date of 01/01/2000 and much time, effort and money had gone into ensuring that planes didn't fall out of the sky, power plants didn't melt down and banking systems collapse. Whilst the world seemed to be operating as normal as we hit 1 January, my own personal world was about to come crashing down.

After spending a long period in the loo, having thrown up and then fallen asleep or blacked out, I recall Angelina's angry words vividly upon my return: 'Zach, enough's enough. I am going home and I would like you to come with me. If you stay out, you stay out on your own. I can't live with your benders any longer. Just today I've found you in a strip joint, tolerated you turning up drunk and late for a shopping trip for our new flat, seen you with a girl's head up your t-shirt and wondered where you were while you'd passed out in the loo! I can't go on knowing this is what I must put up with every time we go out! You either choose me or you choose a life of drugs and booze. You can't have both. But you make that choice right now. Don't come looking for me tomorrow or the day after or whenever you decide to stop poisoning yourself because you are making the choice now. I don't care if you are off your tits, the decision you make right now is final.'

It was late and it had been a long day and, of course, I should have gone home with her. But I didn't and in that moment my world shifted. A sliding doors moment. It was a mix of not wanting to be told what to do, a new wave of coke kicking in giving me a lift and an unexpected purpose of mind, and, I have to admit, a will that I cannot explain even to myself that just urged me on into the night, into the dark. More begets more - a need for excess.

And that was that. As she had predicted, I did go looking for her once I had partied myself out and, like she had promised, in short she did not let me back into her life. As passionately and intensely as we had fallen in love, she fell out - or at least that is how it seemed to me. Looking back now, I can see my lifestyle at the time was unconscionable and I fully accept her reasoning, but at the time I could genuinely not fathom what had happened. Yes, I knew my dissolute ways meant I whooped it up a little too hard at times but didn't all teenagers? Okay, I probably threw myself at it harder than her, harder than most if I am honest but I was never unfaithful and, I like to think, rather good fun on a night out.

I recalled once, years later, meeting Shane MacGowan, the former lead singer of *The Pogues*, in a bar called *Filthy MacNasty's* in Islington, who graciously put down his copy of Jon Savage's *England's Dreaming* and gave us half an hour or so of his time. Amongst many diverting tales, he recounted how he won back his sweetheart, Victoria, after she had caught him in a compromising tableau in his red and white Jockey y-fronts with a couple of groupies in a hotel bedroom. After she left him, he had shaved his hair off, painted himself black, stripped and thrown himself out of a moving taxi on the M1. He had been sectioned, Victoria had taken pity on him and he won her back. Simple really. Now, why hadn't I thought of that?

And then I was back in the present, Angelina and Patrick suddenly in my eyeline, breaking the tranquil waters as they re-emerged from the depths some 20 yards away from the side of the boat. Like me, Angelina, came out breathless, beaming and blethering, ecstatic joy etched across her countenance. 'Wow! Wow, wow, wow. Just ….. wow!' she said.

'Yes, I know exactly what you mean,' I replied.

Chapter 9

23 May 2017

If I recall correctly, it was a week or so later that we returned to our – or perhaps more accurately, Angelina's – little confab on how we might yet save the planet. By which time, we had all had time to mull over her words and the NOW proposition. It was another evening, involving less wine this time, with the same four protagonists retiring to the mess room after witnessing another astonishing sunset.

It was me that dived back in, picking up loosely where we had left off: 'I've been thinking about our little yak the other night Angelina and your espousal of a world government. I mean, surely there already is a World Federalist organisation?' And isn't what you are proposing already in existence in the form of the UN? Surely, it's their job to fix the world's problems?

Angelina seemed pleased to revisit the conversation: 'Having recently written about this, I can tell you that you are right in that world federalism is not a new concept. As you surmise, there already is a World Federalist Movement. It was formed in Montreux in the 1940s; interestingly, it is sanctioned by the UN and has thousands of members across the world. It seeks to create a strong world government with political and legal authority to deal with global issues, while nation-states retain their sovereignty to deal with internal matters. So, the rights of nations would be balanced by, and consistent with, the collective focus of a global community focused on advancing the common good. In an international parliament, no doubt, from time to time, individual nations would need to be brought into line. Each country would retain its own national identity but they would come together, much like the characters in a sports team do, irrespective of whether they get on, to produce results for the greater good.

'There are also several other well-meaning federalist organisations such as the Democratic World Federalists, the Global Oneness Movement and World Citizens. Sure, these groups will be on our side but, let's face it, they've hardly had much success on their own. Most people would not know they exist. It is time to reinvigorate this forgotten political ideology. The only way anything will ever change is when we, the masses, start marching. We may not yet have the power but we have the power to change things.'

Jochen brought her up short: 'Isn't the world just too screwed up, too messy, too polarised, for this neat solution that you propose? You make it sound so straightforward, inevitable even. Yet, in reality, the UN has been incapable of brokering consensus to fight climate change, poverty, war, disease …… all of which rage on and on.'

Angelina was straight back at him: 'I don't agree. I don't look at things quite as pessimistically as you. Yes, there is undoubtedly much to sort out for a NOW government but there is also plenty to build on. We have to cling to the hope that, in the past, we have shown ourselves capable of coming together to deal with global crises. The League of Nations was, as you know, formed after the First World War and then, after the Second World War, we went back to the drawing board and the United Nations was spawned. The OECD evolved from the Marshall Plan to encourage cooperation among countries to rebuild Europe after World War Two. And then steps were taken towards the formation of a European common market, which, as we know, went on to become the EU. The point I am making is that we can, when pushed, come together to better ourselves. What is also clear is that if a NOW assembly had been in place, these catastrophes could have been averted. Being able to see the whole picture rather than being blinkered by self-interest, we could have been proactive rather than reactive. A world government would offer international objectivity rather than national subjectivity. We would wear our varifocal glasses if you like, rather than suffering from myopia.

'However, despite debilitating national tribalism, sometimes our hand is forced. In recent decades, through international collaboration, we have been able to eradicate smallpox, which had been around for thousands of years and up to 1980 had killed half a billion people; we banned CFCs, allowing the ozone layer to heal; we eradicated acid rain and leaded petrol; we have seen two billion people move out of extreme poverty; we have drastically reduced the prevalence and death rates from AIDS; and helped contain infectious disease outbreaks of SARS, MERS and Ebola. The global community came together to steer us through the financial crisis of 2008. It is clear that good can be done when we collaborate. This is evidenced through trade deals and work in the fields of scientific and space exploration. Surely now, in the face of a climate emergency, which threatens our very existence, we can come together again as a human family to save ourselves?

'There are rays of hope. Let us take comfort from the positive work that has already taken place in the battle against climate change, in the war on terrorism, in the fight against people and drug trafficking and in combatting expansionism and warfare. It is a start but, clearly, not enough. And think about this, if we don't move of our own freewill to a one world government soon, then ecological crises or viruses or other existential threats are likely to force us there anyway.'

At this point, Jochen, who had been, unusually for him, on the edges of the debate, could hold himself back no longer, jumping in with: 'The scientific community can and does lead the way on collaboration of thought. As far as I can see, apart from perhaps the Olympics or the World Cup, nothing brings the world together more than science. Consider CERN in central Europe as a fine example of uniting people from all over the world in the pursuit of understanding what the universe is made of and how it works and, of course, it was where the Worldwide Web was born.

'Think too of space exploration. NASA stipulated that every effort should be made in terms of cooperation between nations. Much has been gained and is still to be reaped from countries working together in this field. We have come to better understand the universe and our own place in it. There has been a bigger pot of money and expertise to utilise, resulting in the advancement of scientific and exploratory skills. The endeavour to deliver economic gain and to extend our human footprint has led to improved political civility between countries. If we are to explore new frontiers, we need to ensure that we do so as a united world with a shared outlook, not as individual countries or, even worse, as affluent, maverick businessmen. The US and Russia and Japan and the European Space Agency have all collaborated in space – the international space station is a fine example of this - but, to maximise the chances of success, China also needs to be brought into the fold.

'Antarctica also provides ongoing proof of the possibility of international teamwork and how it can benefit us all. Incredibly, it was only 200 years ago that it was first sighted by humans and, in the early 1950s, it looked like it was set to become another battleground between countries during the Cold War. However, the Antarctica Treaty was signed by several nations and reserved a whole continent, where 90% of the world's ice is to be found, for scientific research and peace. The treaty has now been in place for some 60 years and has allowed for the protection of wildlife and the environment on and around the continent, as well as enabling research into issues that affect the entire earth. Scientists from across the globe work there and it is often referred to as "the laboratory of the world". It has been instrumental in our understanding of climate change and on the banning of ozone-depleting chemicals. We also know that unless things change, Antarctica may contribute more than a metre of sea level rise by the end of the century and 13 metres by 2500!'

'Thank you, dear' Angelina said, interrupting Jochen, who had foolishly paused for dramatic effect, before climbing back on her own soapbox: 'Even on a business level, there are reasons to be cautiously optimistic, signs that we make progress and that we can transition to a better world. It is becoming less acceptable for companies to focus solely on profit – they are having to reimagine how they measure success. They must be seen to be reducing their carbon footprint, paying appropriate taxes, weeding out corruption, upholding human rights through their recruitment of staff and supply chains – to be improving the ambit in which they operate.

'Consumers increasingly want to be assured of a company's environmental credentials and they are becoming more sophisticated at spotting tokenism. Businesses can no longer be just about benefitting shareholders; they now need to consider employees, customers and communities. As companies report on their corporate social responsibility, their public and environmental impact is suddenly as important as their financial results. Despite government inertia, old models are dying as the world strives to become environmentally sustainable and to not betray future generations. Enterprises must now consider how they might reduce to zero their net CO^2 emissions. It is fair to say that a good number of up and coming entrepreneurs have strong social, ethical and environmental beliefs and, moving forwards, some will be genuinely eager to embrace new business models and a new world outlook. At Davos, where the world's rich and successful business people mingle with influential politicians and academics at an annual week-long economic forum, there has been an increasing focus on meeting worldwide aspirations such as the Paris Climate Agreement and the United Nations' Sustainable Development Goals.'

Jochen, however, had his misgivings: 'This is true up to a point. Whereas my current focus is on environmental sustainability, during my PhD years I focused on economic and societal viability. It cannot be denied that even the most hard-nosed businesses are beginning to recognise that if we do not protect our biodiversity - our natural resources, clean air and water – and if we do not have stable and fair societies, then they, along with our economies, will fail. So, consequently, some companies are starting to make efforts to counteract their carbon output, but what is clear to me is that it is too little, too late. For most, it is nothing more than greenwashing. Progress remains constrained as scientists are perpetually let down by governments and politicians who are lobbied by big business and what they refer to as realpolitik. Meanwhile, the pillaging of our planet accelerates and we hurtle towards self-destruction. I can see no evidence to disabuse me of this notion. Call it fatalism - it is certainly depressing, but it is true. I have done my own soul-searching and while I have been a vegetarian for years, I have recently turned vegan, I have ditched my car and wherever possible, which is almost all the time, I travel by train not air. I have to say that I thought long and hard before joining this mission, fretted about the damage that we would cause but, in the end, and as you can see, I decided that the positives generated by our work outweighed the negatives.'

'Your glass really is half empty sometimes dear,' said Angelina. 'But it is certainly true that we need to ensure that the marginal gains of balanced scorecards and such that companies talk about are more than pyrrhic victories. As we know, whilst we can celebrate some things, all is not entirely rosy in our garden. We still have manifest problems: climate change, pollution, rising sea levels, drug smuggling, people trafficking, obesity which has tripled since the 1970s, burgeoning numbers of refugees as a result of never-ending wars, to name just those that spring to mind. And we have not even spoken about the disturbing recent rise in national populism eating away at democracy. People kicking back in what is often a nationalist stance, resentful of increased immigration, high youth unemployment and the gig economy; they have worries about a diminution of tradition, of increasing automation and sophisticated technology and are fed up with political correctness. Often it is about people feeling they are not being heard; of course, these concerns have manifested themselves in the election of Trump and in the UK leaving Europe.

'As we all know, the world remains a far from perfect place. While the global percentage of people living in extreme poverty has fallen to around 10%, the World Bank still estimates that nearly half of the world's population lives on less than $5.50 per day and struggles to meet their basic needs. A quarter of the global population is without electricity. Nowadays, hunger is the biggest killer of humans – forget war, heart failure, malaria, pneumonia or cancer. There is a worldwide aim, ratified by 193 countries in 2015 and one of the UN's Sustainable Development Goals, to eradicate global hunger and all forms of malnutrition by 2030. This will not be easy. A billion children live in penury. UNICEF tells us that 22,000 children die every day from poverty. It is difficult to reach many of those in abject misery as they live in countries that are difficult to access due to war or secretive governments or uncooperative autocrats. One in seven people in the world live in countries that are classed as fragile or volatile states. But it doesn't have to be like that. Oxfam estimates that it would cost $60 billion per annum to bring an end to extreme poverty – this is less than one quarter of the income of the world's top 100 billionaires. And don't get me started on this little club. A recent report cited eight super-rich individuals as being as rich as the world's poorest half and, in essence, to be running the world. Spanning out a bit further, a separate report found that 147 inter-connected institutions, predominantly financial, actually run the world. Perhaps not such a big surprise, but what is dangerous – and what we have already seen - is that we are now at a point where once a crisis sets in, all the markets, and thus the world, tumble through financial contagion.

'The best way of overcoming these problems? Perhaps the only way? You're starting to get my drift. When we are united, of course. As our collective history unfolds and, increasingly, technology and blue-chip companies operate *sans frontieres*, as we recognise how it is impossible not to work internationally to overcome so many issues, we gradually come to realise that if we are to prosper, we must work together. We are now standing at the crossroads. This is our chance for a new beginning. Call me an idealist but I believe humanity is on the cusp of reaching its most advanced stage. At a point where we genuinely listen, communicate and collaborate across nations to create a better world and to move us that little bit nearer to the paradise that each of us seeks. I just hope it does not take some global catastrophe to finally bring us together – or, worse still, tear us apart.'

'You never answered the question about the UN. Can they regard themselves as a success? Clearly, this first attempt at world governance has not worked!' Philippe interjected, his usual phlegmatic self, unshackled as he poured himself his next glass of vino.

Jochen jumped back in, this being yet another of his specialist subjects: 'Good question. We cannot have a conversation about world governance without talking about the United Nations. We could spend a long time debating the merits and de-merits of the UN. I suppose it really depends on what you envisage it was - or is – for. When it was formed after the Second World War, it sought to bring the world together in peace, promote democracy and alleviate world hunger. You could argue that it has succeeded in its primary objective of steering the world away from what would be a catastrophic, nihilistic and perhaps final world war. As the words emblazoned on the wall at their New York headquarters, spoken by the UN Secretary General during the 1950s, Dag Hammarskjold, say: "The United Nations was not created to take mankind to heaven, but to save humanity from hell."'

Angelina couldn't stop herself cutting across with: 'Perhaps it has now done that job and it is time for it to recalibrate with the goal of taking us all to paradise?'

Jochen persisted, oblivious to the disturbance: 'Is it taken seriously across the planet? Well, yes, it's certainly a club that everyone wants to join. In 1945, it comprised 51 nations but that has now almost quadrupled to 193 countries, two thirds of which are developing nations. With the exception of Palestine and Vatican City, that's the entire world! However, what we must not forget is that it has never been invested with any real power; beyond the UN's Security Council, it is essentially an advisory body seeking to promote cooperation between nations.

'Since 1948, one million people have served as UN Peacekeepers, having been deployed on dozens of missions; regrettably several thousand have lost their lives. World War One saw over 23 million deaths and in the Second World War a staggering 69 million lives were lost. The biggest wars since then, if you put the Sino-Japanese War to one side, have seen 3 million deaths respectively in the conflicts in Korea and Vietnam, in the Bangladesh Liberation War and the Second Congo War. In 1988, the UN won the Nobel Prize for Peace.

'It has also played a big and ongoing role in trying to end famine; it oversaw the prosecutions of Charles Taylor and Slobodan Milosevic for war crimes in Liberia and Yugoslavia; ensured that countries like South Africa and Kazakhstan gave up their pretensions at building atomic bombs; and successfully protected biodiversity on the Galapagos Islands. In 1980, the World Health Organisation, a UN agency, declared smallpox extinct after a 13 year immunisation programme. UNICEF, another UN agency, looks after the needs of children and their mothers in developing countries. It has brought new vaccines to more than 400 million children, feeds more than 80 million people each year and has been instrumental in providing clean water to 2.6 billion people. The UN branch for overseeing the safety of refugees, the UNHCR, provides for millions of refugees year after year, giving them security, food and basic shelter. And let's not forget, it was a UN conference in 2015 that shaped the Paris Climate Agreement. Undoubtedly it has been a force for good.

'Less known but of equal importance is its work behind the scenes, where it has overseen and helped write hundreds of international laws in fields such as human rights, anti-terrorism, global crime, refugee entitlements, disarmament, space travel, international trade and jurisdiction over the seas – all of which provide a basic framework for civilised interaction between nations. Much of its successes go under-reported as they do not fit the mainstream media's short-term, alarmist and nationalist agendas. It is the world's policeman, doctor, teacher and protector.

'However, don't get me wrong, there are areas where it has disappointed too – usually as a result of a combination of factors: its need to build consensus before it can take action; its policies of mitigation; and because of what some see as its martial impotency. The world has faced many crises where the UN has been ineffective, usually because of its inability to act quickly and decisively.

'Off the top of my head, there was the civil war in Cambodia in the 1970s; the Rwandan Civil War in the 90s; and the Srebrenica Massacre in 1995 was another low point – the worst mass killing on European soil since the Second

World War. You can also include the US invasion of Iraq where more than a million people have died. A UN Resolution attempted to give legitimacy to the US and UK led invasion, both of which have since admitted, with caveats, that "misjudgments" were made. The invasion arguably paved the way for ISIS.

'And some bloodbaths are, of course, still playing out: the never-ending Kashmir dispute; Israel's ethnic cleansing of Palestinians from a territory which both have claims over; the Somali Civil War; and the Darfur conflict in Sudan, ongoing since it erupted in 2003. The Syrian Civil War, which has raged since 2011, still endures. Russia has used its UN veto on at least a dozen occasions to protect its ally, Bashar al Assad, who initiated the crisis when he launched a brutal crackdown on peaceful pro-democracy protesters. So far, more than 6 million people have been displaced, accounting for one third of the global refugee population. And remember, more than half of all refugees are children. Shall I go on?' he asked. We were by now beaten into submission and nobody spoke.

'You can add to the list, failures in South Sudan, in Yemen and in protecting the Rohingya people in Myanmar; on this occasion, it was China who blocked the UN from helping. The UN has described them as the "world's most persecuted people."'

And then Angelina did, thankfully, disrupt his flow: 'Nevertheless, despite these failings, I still believe in the UN; it is well-intentioned and it is unimaginable to envisage a world without it as we perpetually develop more emphatic means of annihilating one another.

'Over the years, there has certainly been those willing it to succeed and to champion its role as our saviour – and not always who you would expect.' Angelina was then digging out and scrolling through her iPad again: 'The UK's favourite Prime Minister, Winston Churchill, spoke of a world order in which "the principles of justice and fair play ... protect the weak against the strong" - a world where the United Nations would fulfil the historic vision of its founders and in which freedom and respect for human rights would prosper across all nations. He hit the nail on the head when he said: "Unless some effective supranational government can be set up and brought quickly into action, the prospects of peace and human progress are dark and doubtful." Interestingly, he went on, in a speech made in Zurich shortly after World War Two, to call for "a kind of United States of Europe" in what was obviously an augury of the European Union, which is, of course, a significant building block towards a world government.

'Decades later, US President Ronald Reagan echoed Churchill's sentiments when he said: "Our goals are those of the UN founders, who sought to replace a world at war with one where the rule of law would prevail, where human rights were honoured, where development would blossom, where conflict would give way to freedom from violence."'

'Let's not forget the contribution of non-governmental organisations too, all their altruistic endeavours,' Jochen opined.

Angelina concurred: 'That's very true. I think in many ways, several NGOs have been leading the way – canaries in the coal mine, if you will, in terms of delivering an improved world for us. More often than not, it feels like it is a battle between well-meaning campaign groups like Amnesty International, the Red Cross, CND, the World Wide Fund for Nature, the ONE Campaign, Save the Children, the Center for Global Development, Médecins Sans Frontières, Oxfam and the like against the system. Instead of being lauded, you will notice that politicians and press agencies try and pick fault with them. Philippe, you have been with Greenpeace many years, you must have witnessed first-hand the commendable work that it has done?'

'For sure. As we all know, Greenpeace has been a beacon of light in an often dark world,' said Philippe. 'It has been fighting for a greener planet for almost 50 years. Year after year, it has highlighted issues and petitioned companies, banks and governments to adopt more eco-friendly approaches. It has recorded significant successes. In its early days it managed to block nuclear testing in the Pacific atolls. In 1982, after almost a decade of campaigning, worldwide commercial whaling was banned. With a fight, which began in 1985, it has been instrumental in ensuring that Antarctica has become a protected environment. It began a similar campaign, which is still ongoing, to protect the Arctic in 2012. I was lucky enough to photograph it. A crusade against the dumping of radioactive waste at sea led to a moratorium on the practice and to subsequent international laws that now prevent it. Also, back in the twentieth century, it won public support as it intervened to stop the disposal of the Brent Spar oil storage platform at sea and, after this example was set, a general cessation to the dumping of oil rigs at sea was ratified. Rainforest campaigns led by Greenpeace have, to a degree at least, slowed the mass commercial exploitation of forests across the globe.

'Throughout the world, we have many friends and secret admirers. This was shown just a few years ago when Russian troops boarded the Arctic Sunrise and arrested 30 activists, including some of my friends. It looked like they might be sentenced to 15 years in prison but international pressure and condemnation saw them released.

'In Britain, a recent fight against new coal-fired power stations saw six activists acquitted after they convinced a jury that their attempt to block carbon emissions was justified. Soon afterwards, the UK government announced an end to the unabated building of new coal plants. These successes have been impressive given the odds that Greenpeace is up against - a world predisposed to the powerful, greedy and selfish exigencies of companies, their directors and shareholders.'

'Well said Philippe! And it has, as one would expect, been utterly ignored by the mainstream press. We do owe so much to NGOs. They deserve backing by any future world government – in fact they should probably be part of it,' asserted Angelina.

Before she could get going again, I brought her up short, trying to keep the sarcasm out of my voice, when I said: 'As much as your concept of a galvanised world government saving our planet is a lovely idea, how do we actually move to this wonderful panacea?'

'Musicians, poets, philosophers, academics, politicians, artists, seers, even journalists' said Angelina, 'they can all signpost the way for us, but in the end, the route to a new world order will only come from us, the people. I am afraid we cannot rely on politicians and due process to move things along for us. It is too late for that now. We should heed the maxim in campaigning circles that if you cannot gain direct access to the Prime Minister or a Minister, you should take your cause to the streets. A one world government cannot be imposed from the top down, it must be demanded by the public. There is no will to do this from the powers that be and, even if there was, long term it would never work, consider the USSR as an exemplar of why not. Think of Lenin's "Red Terror" and then Stalin's "Great Purges" which killed, at a conservative estimate, 1.2 million people – with over a million more dying in the gulags. Think too of China and Chairman Mao's "Great Leap Forward" which resulted in tens of millions of deaths from starvation.

'A new world order would be different; no longer would countries or systems be competing against one another, it would finally see world citizens moving forward together. Just imagine, for the first time, the human race would be working as one and for the benefit of all. However, trying to force this issue from the top down will inevitably end up in discord. Change must come through the people. I think if we knew that the end of the world would come about on a specific date – I don't know say in 5 years or 8 years or whatever - then that would focus people's minds. However, in all likelihood, this won't happen. What we need to do is to detonate a mind bomb, something which succinctly exemplifies all that is currently wrong with our world. An example of how we, the masses, are manipulated by those with wealth and power. The exposing of a lie - something that shocks and inspires people to get out onto the streets and protesting. We need to plant a seed in people's minds and let it grow of its own accord. The transition to a new one world order must be organic and of the people's own volition.'

'A mind bomb?' I found myself interrupting. 'What do you mean?'

'As I said the other night, the NOW marches are growing in terms of frequency and size. Students and the young in general are embracing the cause. But, globally speaking, we need a catalyst to give critical momentum to the movement and to truly catapult it into the international spotlight. Whilst for me, its focus on promising the most basic elements of Maslow's Hierarchy of Needs - food and drink, shelter and education - is enough, some people will need something more dramatic to convince them, more jolting and jaw-dropping to pull them in. Of course, you would think that there is nothing more arresting than saving the planet but somehow people have become blindsided or blasé; they just do not appreciate the urgency.

'The thing is, we need to get the message out there and, as you know, it is not easy in a world of increasing noise and interference: conspiracy theories, disinformation, fake news driven by fear and paranoia, deliberate miscommunication and self-serving rhetoric. We need some kind of cut through and it needs to be convincing. Something that ultimately makes people sit up and realise that something has to be done and, more importantly, can be done. We cannot go on forever turning a blind eye to the problems of the world. They are catching up with us fast and as our population looks set to grow by another 2 billion people in the next 30 years, our generation has the chance to secure the future of humankind or, through apathy, set us on the road to hell. The next ten years will make or break the planet.

'Without doubt there's a lot of people carrying resentments out there but some are angry about the wrong things. Subjugated people do protest and march, occasionally violently – as Martin Luther King said "riot is the language of the unheard". There have been lots of well-meaning demonstrations protesting climate change, against racism, against war, against austerity, against oppression. It is time now to provide a focus and a purpose, to give shape to these disparate strands. We need to make people aware that there is an all-encompassing solution that can ameliorate all these problems – a keystone to the arch that spans our very existence. Just what it is that will serve as the x-factor or pivotal moment to get the world marching, I do not yet know but I am convinced something is around the corner – it might be through the mass dislocation of people by climate change or an act of terrorism or a pandemic or austerity or the uncovering of an unforgiveable lie – something which affects us all and pays no heed to borders. It is my job, and that of journalists per se, to unearth such a find. I believe some occurrence is imminent which we will be able to use to help mobilise the multitudes. When this happens, we need to be ready with the NOW proposition and philosophy.

'Until then we need to continue to educate. We need to convince a majority of the global population that a federalist world is not only viable but that it is our only chance of survival. Across our planet, we find that there are people of an ultra-right-wing persuasion and those of an extreme left-wing bent and a whole bunch of people, the vast majority I would argue, who sit somewhere in the middle. Let's face it, at the very edge of the spectrum, those with a fiercely partisan outlook are more alike than they would care to admit and it becomes difficult to tell the difference between a fascist dictator like Franco or Mussolini and some so-called communist supremos such as Stalin or Mao or even Putin. It is the people in the middle who want to get on with their lives unmolested, to pursue a career, to earn money, to spend time with their friends and family and to enjoy leisure pursuits, who federalism should appeal to. The problem is that they – the silent majority - are currently fed a diet of insular nationalism; they are stoked to be looking over their shoulder, paranoid of others. For too long, the workers have been fed lies and pitted against each other by a small clutch of manipulative oligarchs. Many people's actual identity is buried deep under social conditioning and other people's opinions, often familial, along with muddled conclusions drawn at an early age about who they are. For those, it will be about trying to remember who they were before the world got its hands on them – a great "unlearning" if you will. We must encourage these citizens to see the bigger picture and to embolden them to speak out and to hold governments to account. It is the age old question of how do you mobilise the masses – people that are either begrudgingly content with their lot or so downtrodden and wrapped up in their everyday struggles that they do not have the will or time or energy to imagine a better world beyond their immediate compass? Let's face it, if we do nothing, we inch towards an actualisation of George Orwell's *1984* with two – or was it three – super-states constantly at war with one another; in our case it is looking like the West, Russia and China.

'Obviously it will be down to Candy Kitcatt and NOW followers as to how they build their movement. I know the intention is to do it without bloodshed. Through the powerful examples of Gandhi, Martin Luther King and the protests in Tiananmen Square, the world has witnessed the effectiveness of non-violent protest. Traditionally it has taken decades to generate momentum but with technology and social media, as we saw with the recent Arab Spring, that process, like life itself, has become accelerated. Campaigns can now be organised online and spread virally.

'No doubt NOW will look to engage the young, for they can usually see more clearly all that is wrong with the world. So much conflict, from all-encompassing world wars to minor squabbles, has been and continues to be about national borders, ethnicity or religion. Slowly we come to realise that lives and peace matter more than these human-made constructs. Technology is breaking down barriers. Many people now see themselves as world citizens. Nowadays, we communicate readily with people across the planet and, through cheap travel, we can visit other countries so easily – in effect, our world is shrinking and we are coming to realise, contrary to what we have often been led to believe, that people are not that different after all. So far, I have lived in the Netherlands, the UK, Sweden and The Czech Republic; I am fond of all these places but I see no reason to align myself to one.

'As our capacity for tolerance, empathy and understanding develops, it is the young and idealistic that are the most likely to show initial support for a new world government. Until, at least, they are drawn into the imperceptible process of being corrupted by the worship of Mammon, by flags, anthems, religious bigotry and xenophobia. All these will, in time, come to be viewed as anachronistic shackles of the old world. Hopefully, in the sweep of history, war will be nothing more than the dying death rattle of a jingoistic past. Likewise, the hydrocarbon industry that still pumps billions of dollars into oil and gas, which destroys our planet. I mean when will they get it? If they do not change their ways and climate breakdown continues apace, soon they will have no customers and no world left to exploit. How long will it take before people understand this? If there is no urgent action, then obliteration lies just around the corner.'

'Engaging a handful of biddable, politicised students is one thing, but the everyday man in the street? I think that will be harder,' mused Jochen.

'Yes, you are right. NOW may well need to initially grow its following through burgeoning numbers of college and university students but, in order to succeed, the movement then needs to quickly permeate out across society. It must be seen as - and actually be - owned by the people. It will need to disseminate the message that it is the poor, of course, the whipping boys of history, that have the most to lose by the upholding of the current system that is so heavily stacked against them. As we all know, since the global financial crash of 2008, it has been the rich that have got richer and the poor, poorer.

'It is true too that whilst people will get behind causes, they more readily get behind people. The NOW movement has a charismatic leader in Candy – striking in both persona and appearance – someone with balls, although in her case not anymore but you know what I mean. Articulate, bespectacled professors of meteorology – sorry dear - don't always pull in the crowds and captivate the world in the same way.'

'Yes but still you have not convinced me of what it is that will rouse the populace? As a political journalist, have you not come across *anything* – a story or rumour – something arresting that might get people out on the streets and give impetus to the NOW marches?' quizzed Philippe.

'Not yet, no. Of course, there's an endless muddle of conspiracy theories out there but most are fantastical speculation not realities.'

'What about the death of John Lennon?' I pitched in. 'If the truth came out about that, then it might just light the fire – something which might, even now, resonate with people, which would turn the NOW marches from just another protest into something that millions of people can get behind.'

'John Lennon?' Philippe asked, puzzled. 'He was shot by a psycho loner outside his New York apartment wasn't he?'

'Yes, to all intents and purposes. However, Lennon was hated by the American authorities and seen as a real threat to the establishment and there is a school of thought that the killer, Mark Chapman, was a CIA-programmed assassin.'

'Sounds a bit far-fetched?' said Angelina, half-interestedly.

'Ultimately, yes, you are probably right,' I replied before continuing. 'It is certainly true that the CIA used brainwashing, hypnosis and mind-controlling drugs to try to robotise or programme individuals during the fifties, sixties and early seventies. No one disputes this. They did this on their own agents and on unsuspecting members of the public, turning them into assassins and accomplices. It was a secretive programme called MK-Ultra, which has subsequently been referenced on the big screen – in The Manchurian Candidate, in Jacob's Ladder, in episodes of the X-files and in the Bourne films. It was an attempt to weaponise minds to help America gain an edge in the Cold War and was driven by a fear that the Russians were ahead in this field and that some US agents had defected as a result of Communist mind-altering drugs.

'The drug of choice was LSD, which they developed and used as a political tool to manipulate minds. Inadvertently and somewhat ironically, the CIA, through a guy called Sidney Gottleib, who headed up the MK-Ultra project, was responsible for bringing LSD to the US, which, in turn, gave rise to the counterculture movement which lionised Lennon.

'The FBI and the CIA are, and always have been, utterly paranoid about communist infiltration – the Red menace – and, as part of its deep state shenanigans, has worked to undermine civil rights campaigners, anti-war demonstrators, activists, the left and any ideologies that they see as "not aligning" with the US. They were worried about the USSR but also European intellectuals and those working in the Arts – Picasso, Chagall and Rothko were all avowed communists. Over the years, many rich and famous people have had files on them and not just artists and long haired rock stars like Lennon, Jerry Garcia, Kurt Cobain or Jim Morrison, but characters as diverse as Liberace, Charlie Chaplin, Tupac Shakur, Norman Mailer, Arthur Miller and Marilyn Monroe.

'We can sometimes forget that The Beatles were *the* cultural experience of the sixties and seventies and that they changed the world. CIA and FBI surveillance of John Lennon for his left-wing tendencies, for his anti-Vietnam War stance, for his pacifism and for his lyrics are well documented. He had the power to rally, radicalise and organise the American youth and was seen as a very real threat to the establishment. He was just a month away from becoming an American citizen when he was killed in December 1980. We know that both the CIA and Hoover's FBI were watching John and Yoko and several of their close friends.

'And then if we consider Lennon's killer, Mark Chapman, things don't quite add up. He was something of a lost soul, bullied at school and nicknamed "Garbage Head," a slang term for someone who would take anything. He quit college at 15 and ran away. Then he found Christ and joined the YMCA, took a job, tried to commit suicide, married, bought a gun and, so the story goes, became obsessed with John Lennon and The Beatles. Yet, given he was not a rich man, it is odd how he unexpectedly turned up in Beirut at a time when the CIA had a top secret assassination training camp there. Another such camp was supposedly in Hawaii, where Chapman also pitched up for a few years. Neither has anyone explained who paid for a round-the-world trip which saw him take in the likes of the UK, Nepal, India, Japan, Korea, Vietnam and China.

'When the police found Chapman outside Lennon's apartment building at Central Park West, he did not attempt to run away, meekly handing himself over; their statement actually said Chapman looked and sounded like he had been programmed or influenced by somebody else to kill. He'd certainly hung around in a zombie-like state, waiting for the police to arrive. Lots of people have suggested he had been hypnotised and was a "stooge" or "patsie". It's interesting that the so-called super-fan did not own a single Lennon record or book until the weekend before the killing. Also of note is the slack police investigation – Chapman was not even tested for drugs, although it appeared to all and sundry that he was on something. He was carrying a copy of *Catcher in the Rye*, which it has been argued was part of his hypnotic programming. Chapman believed himself to be the protagonist in the novel, Holden Caulfield, and to be in a battle against "phoniness". Until the final few files relating to the secret service's investigation into Lennon's activities and his death are released – they are still classified - we will not know the full truth.'

'It's a great story,' Angelina smiled, 'but, as I said, for me, it seems a bit far-fetched. You are right though, if it was true it might just tip the balance; it is certainly the sort of thing that might anger, appal and mobilise large swathes of the public. A world icon assassinated by right-wing fanatics in the American political establishment. A classic example of societal manipulation from above.'

'I thought you might appreciate a good story before bed,' I said, forcing back a yawn. 'So, we must all wait for this mind bomb to go off before we can move to the next chapter in the history of the world? Well, I am in and, from what I have heard, let's hope it's soon.'

'We can wait until we stumble across something or we can go find something. I have one or two ideas on that front,' said Angelina mischievously as we tottered off to our respective quarters.

Chapter 10

2 June 2017

We had worked unremittingly for six weeks or so, occasionally enjoying a half-day off, although I've never really classed photography as a job. Preparing for our return to Amsterdam, we looped back and moored just off Guadeloupe once more; permission was sought and extended to those who fancied a night on shore to spend a few hours in Pointe-a-Pitre, the bustling economic centre of the archipelago on the eastern side of the island known as Grande-Terre.

Ten of us clambered out of our motorised dinghy into the muggy late afternoon, quickly found our land legs and spent our first half hour or so, pottering through the lively market, haggling with friendly and flamboyant purveyors of tropical fruit and veg, exotic spices, bright flowers and colourful apparel.

Shaking off the last of the itinerant vendors, we sauntered through busy side lanes peppered with multi-coloured two-storey French colonial houses, admiring the vibrant street art and pausing briefly to take in the imposing yellow-fronted bulk of the Cathedral de St Pierre et St Paul on Rue de General.

Someone in the group was navigating via their phone, and, escaping the narrow alleys, we skirted the coastline briefly before we fell out into Place de la Victoire, an expansive park, lush and dotted with palm trees and Royal Poinciana, their scarlet blossoms shading us from the still fierce sun. We forewent the pleasure of sitting in one of the sidewalk cafes lining Rue Bébion and headed back into the hubbub, someone having recommended a small restaurant called *Le Petit Jardin*, next to the nineteenth century courthouse. We were ushered straight through and out into the luxuriant – and thankfully shaded - back garden. A live band was playing an upbeat set of Creole standards, accompanied by a sozzled couple, entwined and slowly swaying uncoordinatedly on the dancefloor. A mix of profligate tourists from a recently docked cruise ship and friendly locals, all intent on a good time, had engendered an upbeat conviviality and the joint gave credence to the maxim that Pointe-a-Pitre is the 'New Orleans' of the Caribbean.

Parched, we ordered a round of Kronenbourg Blancs which barely touched the sides. Our party comprised: myself and Angelina; Philippe with his best friend, his camera; Patrick our Austrian diving friend; our popular Indian chef Hiya; engineer and my occasional drinking buddy Miguel from Spain; a couple of marine biologists with academic titles I never knew and whose names now escape me, one was from Germany and the other from what he always referred to as the 'Land of the Long White Cloud', which I took to be New Zealand; the smart and funny Comms Officer Lori from Canada; and our ever-so organised team leader or bosun, as she seemed to have badged herself, Dr Francesca Ballotelli. Jochen had declined the invitation to join us, choosing to make use of the serenity on board the *Esperanza* to write up his research findings.

After a satisfying smorgasbord of seafood and fruit, followed by banana split ice cream sundaes and coffees, for some, people began to drift away, conscious of our now limited time. One or two sought out another bar, others went back to the evening market and the biologists wandered rudderless ahead of our scheduled pick up time of 10.00pm in the harbour.

Having slated our thirst on another beer or two, Angelina and I went halves on a bottle of white wine and I lit up a cigarette, which we shared. The ice had gradually thawed between us over the weeks we had been at sea. The euphoria of swimming with whales had lowered our defences and given us a shared moment of joy; a new experience and a bond had been forged between us, leaving us more susceptible to reminiscing on some of the happy times we had spent together. Our paths crossed regularly, confined as we were to a vessel that was 70 metres long and fifteen wide, and was both home and workplace for us, but there would invariably be other people present. Up until now, tonight had been a case in point. Consequently, it was a rare and pleasant moment to find time and space for just the two of us.

'That was quite an impassioned outburst the other week,' I said. 'You've become a lot more politicised in your old age. How did that happen?'

'I've grown up I suppose. In my line of work you see all kinds of inequalities - random and shitty injustices. People's lives decided by pure whim: the family they were born into or where they happen to be brought up. Lives determined by the hand of fate. Existences torn apart by war or climate change. I am thinking of desperate refugees I suppose. But also bigger picture stuff. If we want to fix our broken world, we have to put national allegiances aside and collaborate. I know a world government wouldn't put everything right overnight but rather than just a pusillanimous acceptance of the ways things are, I am happy to join the fight for a fairer world, a better world. Actually I found my "outburst" as you call it hugely cathartic. And not so much of the "old" thank you.'

'Nice word, pusillanimous.'

Not really in the mood for another attempt at fixing the world and conscious that time alone with Angelina was at something of a premium, I cast my mind back to our days in Amsterdam.

'Do you remember that time when we were walking in Museumplein and suddenly the sky went from a foreboding purple to jet black and it started sheeting it down, sideways?'

'Yes, I do. We'd come out of the Rijksmuseum early because you were bored.'

'Was I? Really? Funny, I love places like that now. I find them so therapeutic. Anyway, if you recall, we were soaked and we ducked into the nearest café, just grabbing the last table before everyone else in the park followed suit. It was there in that bistro, sat by the rain-spattered window with your hair all wet and dripping and your cheeks flushed that I knew that I loved you, that you were the one. Strange at what moments these revelations come to you.'

'Zach, what makes you say things like that?'

'I dunno? I am just being honest. No point lying.'

'I do remember it. I think it was the first time we uttered those three little, big words out loud to each other.' Then, after a pause: 'If it is any consolation, I meant it at the time – things were pretty intense for a while - but it was such a long time ago.'

We sat for a moment or two in silent reflection, entranced by the mesmeric rocking of the drunk couple, who seemed to have merged into one, on the dancefloor.

'What did you tell Jochen about me?' I probed.

'Nothing, well …. not a lot of detail anyway. What we had seems like another life. And we were so young. I did not think it was worth mentioning to him. Who wants to torture their partner with stories about their past exploits?'

'Why did you leave me? You were all I had,' I said. All I've ever had, I thought to myself.

'Zach, you know why. It was the hardest thing I have ever done but I told you why at the time. I know we were in love or at least thought we were but I just couldn't live in your deranged and chaotic world. Surely, having had all these years to think it through, even you've worked it out? You was in a mess - an alcoholic or on the edge of becoming one. It's difficult to stick that label on kids as you hope it will turn out to be youthful exuberance but if you'd been in your thirties and drinking like that, that is what you would have been called. Not to mention a drug problem that was spiralling out of control. I was in constant trepidation of the state you might get in, the things you might do and say.'

Clutching at straws: 'I was never disloyal.'

'No, that's true as far as I know but there was always a third party in our relationship – booze, a fourth too if you include the drugs. I know you loved me in your way and no doubt I was the most important human being in your life at that point but you chose intoxicants and hedonism above me - above us. Your choice, not mine. We had something special and some lovely times together, memories that will stay with me forever but, sadly, the allure of alcohol and pills was just too strong for you. They won, they beat us; they beat me and they beat you. So, don't put the blame on me, put it on yourself.' She'd got quite worked up and paused before saying: 'I am sorry, that was a cruel thing to say.'

She was right, of course, one hundred per cent. My only response was: 'No, you are not wrong. It is …. it was a disease. Once it gets its insidious claws into you, it doesn't let up, not for me anyway. You need that little more each time to reach the same high and, before long, inebriation becomes a normal way of being; it becomes so that sobriety feels alien, like sitting around in an airport departure lounge waiting to take off. Still, I think you could have tried harder. Given me more time to work it through. I could have sought help.'

'Not then, you couldn't. You were too young and headstrong. Maybe a few years down the line. I am assuming you did get help in the end?'

I bowed my head: 'Yes, things got out of control when I lived in London and there came a point when I was on the sauce as soon as I got up. I lost my job and was in debt. Mum and dad bailed me out on the proviso that I moved back north and got cleaned up by going to AA and Narcotics Anonymous meetings back in Bolton. That was a grim few months in a cold, stark Methodist church hall, I can tell you. Enough to drive anyone to drink. Not to mention living with my parents. But I got clean.'

'Sounds like it saved your life,' said Angelina. 'And now? You're clearly not teetotal.'

'No, but I have things under control. More of a dipsomaniac these days. I still enjoy a few scoops now and again but I only drink beer and wine, no spirits and no hard drugs. I think they call it a Californian de-tox? Everyone needs an escape from reality now and then. It could be walking or reading or football or shopping or knitting – mine happens to be through booze. I just find it takes the edge off life……rounds things out.'

'I thought once an alcoholic, always an alcoholic? Like a puppy, it's not just for Christmas but for life?'

'You're right, I do need to be careful. But so far, so good. Maybe I am one of the lucky ones?'

'Mmm, yes, maybe. Come on, let's go explore this place before we run out of time.'

And with that we called for the bill and stepped out into the sultry night; the light was failing now, and being a Saturday, the streets were still bustling with activity. Market stalls continued to ply their wares; the Gwada youth was out in force; couples, old and young, meandered unhurriedly around the harbour; and groups of men fell out of packed bars which were airing the national football team. We picked up a half bottle of rum – yes, yes, I know I said I wasn't on the spirits anymore but this was a special occasion - and headed for the sea. After twenty minutes or so of treading the boardwalk, largely in silence, we paused and stretched out on the deserted beach. I had almost become accustomed to these stunning evening skies; as it dropped below the horizon, the sun's swansong cast a dramatic red and lavender hue that bled imperceptibly into the turquoise expanse where the Caribbean Sea met the Atlantic.

I opened the rum and took a slug. 'I never asked, how is your brother doing? Apollo? I know he was a few years younger than us, but I always liked him; he was just the right side of sane. Do you ever see him?'

'Do you want the official story, the one he tells mama and papa and relatives or do you want the actual truth? Either way, I think, now, he is very happy in his own way and that is all that matters. He had a go at a conventional life. He lived with a girl called Summer for several years in Berlin and took a job as a van driver and they had a child together. Unfortunately the boy died aged five after contracting an infection. His mother was into alternative medicine and tried to treat him using homeopathy, refusing the penicillin that the doctors prescribed. I think it broke Apollo's heart. He split with the girl and lives in Madrid now, where he hires himself out. As far as mum and dad are concerned, he is an actor who supplements his income with bar work; in reality he is a roller-blading porn star cum gigolo. Quite popular with both sexes I believe. Whatever makes you happy, I guess?'

'Wow! Okay, yes, I can picture that; it fits with how I remember him. I bet he's having a blast – and in considerable demand. What about you - are you happy with Jochen?'

'Yes, of course. Why would you say that?' she came back at me, quizzically and perhaps just a little too sharply.

'I don't know. Doesn't he bore the pants off you?' I said, instantly regretting the analogy. 'Isn't he just a bit dull, a bit too bookish and dry? Too wrapped up in his own world, let's say?'

'Not at all. I have great respect for his intellect and his passion for his subject. Just because he's not the party animal and a little awkward in public does not mean he is not interesting or fun to be with. Not everyone needs to get hammered to have a good time.'

I took the hit. 'Touche! A bit harsh but no, that's fine then, I believe you. I just want you to be happy.'

'I am. Don't worry about me. But what about you? Are you happy? Have you not found anyone to be with?'

'No, I suppose I've always carried this monkey on my back – the demon drink that is. Over the years, there have been one night stands and occasionally something that has lasted a little longer. If I am honest though, it has been pretty barren in the last few years. The possibilities and opportunities are significantly reduced once you get into your thirties. It seems nearly everyone is spoken for. I suppose people will start getting divorced soon, so maybe I will have an Indian summer?'

'So, there's never been anyone special?'

'Nope. No one quite like you if that is what you are asking?'

'No, I don't think I am asking that. I just think you need someone. You have love to give and you need to be loved and cared for. I think the right person could make you happy – or happier. I think with alcoholism, it is not always what you drink but why you drink that is important. A loving relationship might assuage your discord.'

'I don't know. Yes, maybe. Perhaps you are right. But, in the end, I always let people down; I let myself down I suppose.'

I passed the bottle of rum to Angelina, who pressed it to her lips. 'Are you trying to get me drunk?' she asked, which I am sure didn't just send my mind racing back to our first evening together, clubbing in Manchester.

'I don't think anyone will force you to do anything. If you get drunk, it will be because you choose to.'

A pause. Then: 'Jochen can be a little unusual. Do you know he only has five CDs on his playlist that he has on constant repeat? He has a theory that only live albums reveal the true worth of a band – are they tight, can the singer really sing and the band properly play their instruments in real time in front of an enraptured audience? Consequently, he has elevated live recordings above studio ones. He explained to me that he had made a scientific appraisal to enable him to settle on the best five. I can't remember his criteria – some guff about length of album, number of sales, position in a variety of influential charts, that sort of thing – and he has finessed it down to offerings by Johnny Cash, Cheap Trick, Nirvana, The Who and Bruce Springsteen.'

'Wow. Yes, that sounds like Jochen.'

After another brief pause, I asked: 'Will you have children together?'

'None of your business,' snapped Angelina. 'That's a very personal question.'

We lay there in silence, contemplating the serene night firmament, now a canopy of muted orange and gold, which stretched across the horizon. A waxing, gibbous moon, impossibly large, its lucidity dampened by wispy clouds, lorded it over coruscating stars, puncturing the black canvas through which they flickered. The heat of the day was finally waning, waves lapped mellifluously, earthy ylang ylang and faint strains of calypso from further down the beach came lilting over us on the soft breeze. Further afield and mingled into the soundscape came intermittent and somewhat incongruous snatches from The Smiths' 'How Soon is Now?' a song we both loved back in the day. I reached out to touch Angelina's hand. I found it and rested my hand on top of hers for the briefest of moments. Then she was on her feet:

'No Zach, you know you can't do that. This cannot happen.' Before I could proffer a floundering explanation, she was stomping off back in the direction we had come.

She took some catching. I drew alongside her in a narrow, practically deserted side street, where we both stopped. She looked teary.

'I am sorry; I didn't mean anything by it. It was just meant as a gesture of friendship,' I said, trying to explain myself while attempting to catch my breath.

'Shut up, you idiot' she said as she flung her arms around my neck and, taking me completely by surprise, kissed me passionately. Then, after perhaps 10 seconds or so but what felt like forever, she broke away and ran off down the street, leaving me rooted to the spot, thunderstruck.

What the hell just happened, I thought to myself as I sat nursing an emergency double in the nearest bar. It was a complete head shag for me. Yes, I had felt it keenly - been devastated even - when Angelina had left me nearly twenty years ago and it had taken a long, long time to get over her. But I had built an existence where she now only fleetingly entered my thoughts; I had virtually exorcised her from my mind. Buried my emotions or, some might argue, drowned them. And then, out of nowhere, there she was again, exploding into my world by sitting diffidently in a workplace meeting. As soon as I had seen her, if I am honest, my heart and head were aflutter. It was hard watching her with Jochen but things were what they were. At least they had been until half an hour ago. In vino veritas, I thought to myself. I ordered another drink. And another and then possibly one more. I was beginning to block everything out when Dr Francesca Ballotelli burst in.

'Zach, there you are! Have you lost track of time? We waited for you for 20 minutes in the harbour, now we are spread out across the town looking for you. Why is your phone turned off? Let me make some calls. What is wrong?

Are you drunk?'

She was right, our carriage, in the form of a dinghy, had been due to set sail from the harbour at ten o'clock.

Francesca fed me a strong coffee and with the help of Miguel and Patrick, who steadied me occasionally, got me down to the harbour where I was shot some steely looks by the rest of the group. Angelina was there, of course, looking a little downcast, her make-up perhaps a tad smudged but otherwise offering a reasonable account of herself. There was a fair bit of fussing around me as I was clearly unsteady and having a drunk on board a small boat is, I suspect, a little unnerving. I found myself saying how sorry I was and babbling an excuse about getting lost in my thoughts and losing track of time. It was going up for eleven o'clock at night now and a hush had settled over the group; most of them were tired after a long day and they let me jabber on. The last thing I remember, as we eased out of the shoal, is singing 'Thousands Are Sailing' by the Pogues and standing up to deliver the line about getting back to my empty room and crying. After that, having misjudged the tug of the ocean, I remember lurching forward, the screams and expletives, then careering backwards, going arse over tit and suddenly the hard thwack of freezing cold water. Luckily somebody had thought to equip me with a life jacket and I spluttered and splashed around in the water until the dinghy turned tail and I was hauled back aboard, sodden, shaking, spluttering and suddenly quite sober.

Chapter 11

I

15 January 2018

I have a love-hate relationship with Hebden Bridge. I have lived here on and off for almost a decade. It is an unexpected outlier, an anomaly, in terms of towns in Northern England. To a first time visitor, it is undeniably attractive, hewn out of millstone grit, set in a steep-banked and lush, wooded valley, dissected by the Rochdale Canal and the confluence of Hebden Water and the River Calder. The river, fed by streams tumbling down the steep inclines, provided the water power to drive the weaving mills and the settlement's subsequent growth as a cotton town in the nineteenth and twentieth centuries. The precipitous slopes and multiple waterways, the exploitation of Walshaw Moor for grouse shooting and the climate crisis, proved a calamitous mix in the devastating 2015 Boxing Day floods. The place wears all the attributes of a former mill town – terraced housing, cobbled streets, disused smokestacks, derelict factories and Methodist churches. However, whereas most other East Lancashire and West Yorkshire towns are no-nonsense, insular, traditional, conservative with a small 'c' and deeply suspicious of alternative lifestyles and viewpoints, Hebden is by comparison something of a bohemian enclave.

The town saw an influx of avant-garde, creative types – predominantly hippies, artists, writers, musicians and conservationists - during the 1960s and 1970s due to the preponderance of cheap housing during the final death throes of the once booming textile industry. There was talk at the time of bulldozing the abandoned mills but locals joined with the new arrivals to fight off this eventuality. During the '80s and '90s, more New Age travellers and free-thinking types arrived and the town gained a reputation as the UK's lesbian capital. The town's quirky character, its renowned music and alternative comedy venue, The Trades Club, the civic owned cinema and theatre, a preponderance of independent shops and regular markets, all combined with its convenient location between Manchester and Leeds to see the arrival of increasingly more commuters – including me in the mid-noughties. It has been voted the UK's best market town, called 'the greatest town in Europe' by the Academy of Urbanism – I know this because they used some of my photos in their article – and was ranked as one of the world's funkiest towns in British Airways' High Life magazine.

All good you might be thinking. However, the town has a less appealing underbelly. Its reputation for tolerance, drugs and counterculture doesn't work out for some. A significant number have succumbed to an ethos of lethal hedonism. I've often wondered if it is not helped by sitting in the bottom of a valley with the steep hills giving you a sense of claustrophobia, of being entombed. Ted Hughes described it as 'a gruesome dead-end tunnel'. That and ridiculously cheap and easy to score coke and heroin. Compared with national statistics, suicide rates are way higher than they should be. Some of the older generation and their offspring have become marginalised by gentrification and it is often in these families where alcoholism and drug addiction is rife. I have personal experience of this, with several acquaintances, caught in eddying, out of control dependencies and despair, tragically taking their own lives.

II

15 January 2018

I'd had too much cocaine, plain and simple. As soon as my local gym opened, I stubbed out my last stogie of the evening, and I was in, disappointed with myself and determined to sweat out last night's excesses before hitting the sheets. A befuddled receptionist greeted me: 'Hello, Mr Boocock, you're making an early start.'

I could smell the not-that-stale booze and cigar smoke still lingering on me and I knew she could: 'Actually, more of a late finish, as it goes.'

Powering away, perspiring copiously on the exercise bike, my mind drifted to the 'night' before. We had actually started early afternoon at some friends' house in Hebden. I had picked up Joseph Squibb en route, a friend of a friend who was a little older than the rest of us, a former Detective Inspector no less, now a teacher in a private school and the not so proud owner of a disintegrating marriage and drink problem. Each of us chose our poison at the offy and pitched up at Nick, Stuart and Neil's house in time to see the Liverpool versus Man City game kick off.

Nick, a lifelong friend from Bolton, was an import-export manager who had been given a crate of spirits of dubious quaff-ability and heritage for Christmas, almost certainly 'off the back of a lorry'. He was away that weekend but, as it was my birthday, he told us to partake of the odd dram. Stuart, or S-Man as he was known, was not really a footy fan but enjoyed nothing more than sitting around drinking, smoking and talking nonsense with his mates. He was someone that Nick had befriended at work. Neil was someone I had known since the year dot, his drug was women and with his chiselled features and easy manner, he never had a problem getting his fix. Ed, had also landed; he'd been brought up in Burnley the poor lad and now lived with his long-term boyfriend in Hebden, he was a pal I had acquired while working at *The Bolton News*. Ten minutes into the match, we were joined by Big H Mi Skoodle, my friend from college days, who, nowadays, was always tired, a consequence of being married with two young boys. He said he'd married a crypto-fascist and was increasingly on the lookout for an excuse to get out with the lads – us lot, not his own.

Without trying too hard, we drank the bulk of Nick's liquor as the six of us watched a thrilling match which saw Liverpool put an end to City's unbeaten run for the season, running out 4-3 winners.

Nicely lubricated and still loudly debating some of the game's dubious refereeing decisions, we trained it into Leeds and bundled down Boar Lane, heading for The Duck and Drake, an infamous real ale drinking den. Not the most salubrious joint in town and certainly not *en vogue*, it was increasingly incongruous in the city centre, surrounded as it was by cool new microbreweries and chic gastro-bars, but it held memories for us. It was still one of the few places in town where the quality of the draughts meant it was not at all unusual to find solicitors and Hell's Angels cheek by jowl at the bar.

We were off to a New Model Army gig at Stylus at the University of Leeds and, knowing how busy the bar would get and how expensive the alcohol would be, not to mention the paucity of choice, we decided to pack a few pubs in before show-time. As was occasionally our want, we decided to add a little spice to the afternoon by having a paired up drinking competition, complete with wagers and forfeits. This meant three teams of two, roughly balanced out by drinking capability, although this in itself was a contentious and hotly debated issue. Such events were taken very seriously and, by the end of the night, often boisterously disputed as to who had consumed what. The earlier consumption of Nick's crate of assorted liquors was a case in point as we had clearly indulged in different strength shorts and to varying degrees. It didn't stop us endlessly arguing the toss about it.

I had been spending a bit more time with the lads since my return from the Caribbean earlier in the year. We were all getting by, some better than others. Gradually turning from angry young men to grumpy old fuckers. Blokes being blokes, we didn't really talk about anything too deep. There was something quite sad about this. It was a common feature amongst northern men – perhaps most men. I think we all probably had personal issues that it might have benefitted us to give a public airing to. And I am sure in the moment of revelation, we would have 100% had each other's backs but, alas, somehow a silly macho adolescent spell still clung to us – each of us concerned about the long-term implications of any such personal reveal. The nagging concern that, longer term, others would now have a stick with which to beat us. And yet, as is common in Hebden, when someone slips into despair we all express our surprise.

Having taken further refreshments in BrewDog, Head of Steam, Whitelocks and The Victoria, we were nicely into our cups by the time we rolled into the Old Bar at the university.

Mid-gig, I felt my phone ping and disentangling myself from the sweaty, bare-chested, tattooed and kilted scrimmage, I saw that Angelina had WhatsApp-ed me. This constituted an event. We did not correspond frequently. In fact, I had barely heard from her since our moment of madness on Guadeloupe. The band was playing some of their more reflective offerings so I resolved to grab a drink from the bar before reading her message. Plastic glass in hand, I was knocked sideways by its content, lacking as it was Angelina's usual sangfroid.

Zach my dear, I have a feeling that everything is closing in on me. In Amsterdam I was sure that someone was following me. I've decided to take some time out and I am staying in a small village in southern Spain for a few months in the hope that things will settle down. Even here, I thought I was being watched the other night, hence this message to you – perhaps it is paranoia but I do not feel safe right now.

You remember me saying on the Esperanza that the NOW movement needed a catalyst to propel it onto the international stage? A mind bomb, I think I called it. Well, I searched and I now have something that fits that description, something that will perhaps sway public opinion.

If anything should happen to me, you must unearth and deliver my story to Candy; she will know how to best utilise it.

I do still think of you and those hot nights in my bedroom in my parents' house.
All my love,
Ange

I was nonplussed and more than a little unsettled by this. Re-reading it offered no elucidation. Sod it, I thought, perhaps it will make sense when I am sober and, throwing my drink down, I launched myself back into the crowd.

We managed, just, to catch our last train back to Hebden Bridge, which meant foregoing the encores. It was then back to Joseph Squibb's where four of us – me, Joseph, H and S-Man - played poker into the wee hours. Things got pretty intense, if I recall. Not with the poker, we were only paying for future IOU drinks, but with Joseph telling us how he was planning to bump off his boss, *The Termagant* as he called her, who was the Headmistress at the school where he worked. He explained how she was slowly driving him – and his colleagues - insane through her obsession with health and safety, rules and regs, and policies and procedures. He cited an example from the week just gone of a photographer trying to come onto the campus to drop off a large framed poster; a gift for the school. He needed a parking spot to avoid having to cross a busy road with his bulky delivery. There were no places available but there were some free contractors' bays – spaces for tradespeople who regularly came into the school to maintain the building. Even though he would only be on site for a few minutes, he thought it polite to contact the Estates Department. On doing so, he learnt that anyone parking in such a bay, had to sign in with them and anyone signing in with them needed to bring with them proof of liability insurance, a Method Statement and a duly filled out risk assessment form. On petitioning the Headmistress about the pettiness of this, she told him he would also need appropriate personal protective equipment sign off and Disclosure and Barring Service clearance. All this for a bloke dropping a poster off. It was, he knew, trivial; but it was just one more example of the sort of incident that tied him up in knots on a daily basis and, coupled with the Head's accusatory, snappy and mistrusting persona, was driving him closer and closer to taking her out. He had even started to work out some of the details, envisaging pushing her over a cliff on a forthcoming field trip to Malham Cove. Three of us spent the next couple of hours talking him down.

Which explains how and why I was first through the door in the gym and powering away on my spin workout when my mobile phone started pinging. Sensing something was wrong, my world came crashing down and time suddenly seemed to take on a new dimension as I read a text from my mum telling me to get on the BBC website – they were saying a Dutch woman had died in a bomb blast in southern Spain. The woman, she said, looked a lot like Angelina.

Chapter 12

9 November 2017

With Scissor Sisters exploding out of his headphones, a taut, roller blading Apollo Estrella deftly weaved his way through the choked early evening Madrileño traffic of El Paseo del Prado. He was a presence. On a first encounter, you were immediately struck by his looks, his dress sense and assured strut. You would be forgiven for thinking he was someone: a footballer, a rock star, a film star, a porn star - take your pick. Cocaine tore through his body and endorphins were still being released from his intensive weights' workout as he looked forward to dinner at *El Restaurante Botin* with a regular, fun and attractive client. In his line of work, this was not a scenario he could always savour. After dining at the world's oldest restaurant, there would be cocktails, easy chitchat and laughter and then he would be remunerated for administering sexual favours in a suite at the five star Palace Hotel. On nights such as this, life was good.

Despite what many would consider to be a depraved and dissolute life that would make the Marquis de Sade blush, Apollo was punctilious about punctuality. The sort of guy who would prefer to arrive one hour early rather than one minute late.

Landing ahead of the assignation meet time, he sat on a stone bench outside the Museo Nacional del Prado, awaiting his companion for the evening. Routinely behind schedule, he was neither surprised nor angry when Talulah Dante appeared, shining, well dressed and well-coiffured, some 20 minutes later. They kissed on both cheeks, she clasped Apollo's hand and they sallied off into the balmy late afternoon like regular paramours.

It was a perfect Autumnal evening in the Spanish capital, clear skies and a temperature still over 20 degrees Fahrenheit, as the pair sought shade under the canopy of 100-year-old sycamores that lined the boulevard. The night air inspired frivolity and recklessness and they made the half hour *passeggiata* to their chosen restaurant hand in hand. Apollo occasionally caught glimpses of them reflected in store windows. They were a striking couple, he with his 6ft 2 inch perfectly toned and tanned physique, Adonis good looks, chiselled chin and flowing black locks; Talulah, a brunette in high heels and a tight fitting power suit that accentuated her curves, sashaying along with a no nonsense, confident swagger. In her early forties, she looked younger, which helped mask her being almost ten years older than him. Only when job titles came into play was their incompatibility truly revealed: he a male escort and she the Minister of Defence and Civil Protection for Switzerland.

Talulah was a regular visitor to Spain – both for business and pleasure. She was currently in negotiations with her Spanish counterpart about the extradition of a Basque national from Zurich, who was wanted for terrorism. She had a little down-time and knew that Apollo was good at what he did; on occasion, she had been known to pay for him to fly to a European city so that she could enjoy his attention.

Escorted to their restaurant seats in an enclave by the unctuous maitre d', the pair ordered a bottle of expensive Rioja. Living in two completely different worlds did not stifle conversation as they enjoyed a dinner of suckling pig roasted in the 300 year old ovens. With Talulah a regular visitor to Madrid and to the arms of Apollo, the pair knew each other well and amicably swapped anecdotes, finding common ground over their rags to riches stories, their love of good food and wine, of cars, clothes, of the Spanish television drama *Money Heist* and of sex. Two hours later, satisfyingly sated after cocktails at Museo Chicote, they taxied it back to The Palace.

And so to the bedroom. Talulah's thing was edging and her own orgasm denial; a practice out of the S and M box of tricks. Apollo would use his body, along with a selection of sex toys and lashings of lube, to deliver slow, tantalising pleasure. Most of his clients, both female and male, were predictably vanilla in their requirements and he enjoyed the challenge of meeting Talulah's unusual demands by dreaming up new forms of exquisite torment and denial. She told him he was her favourite and that she had never found a man as understanding, as skilled and as patient in delivering such a service.

The champagne was popped, glasses poured and Talulah slipped into something dangerous, ahead of what would be a long night for them both. Apollo had brought plentiful quantities of cocaine to fuel the session and they both inhaled their lines deeply before disrobing and rolling onto the bed, leisurely making their first tentative caresses. There were ground rules in place, parameters had been agreed prior to their first engagement and these had been gradually tweaked over the years. Apollo always took on the role of master – or 'Daddy' or 'Sir' as she had to call him - and he would spend at least the next four hours giving persistent, low-level sexual titillation to Talulah until she was tired, nauseous, faint, half-deranged, aching and begging for fulfilment. He would bring her to the very brink of climax time and time again and then at the last possible moment would stop cold, denying her the ultimate release in a process known as ruining an orgasm. Already into a self-imposed fourteen week period of denial, tonight Talulah demanded that Apollo continue to spoil things for her. There was little physical gratification for Apollo other than he loved pleasure – ideally his own but, if this was not to be, the next best thing was to administer and vicariously spectate on it. He'd never been one for partying alone. Conscious that the clitoris comprises eight thousand nerve endings - twice as many as a penis – Apollo was very much of the opinion that one should learn to relish such a wonderfully complex instrument and learn to play it with dexterity. From a young age, he had invested much time and effort in mastering the practice.

Occasionally edging and overstimulation – think of it as Tantric sex - could go wrong and Talulah would tip over into orgasm but tonight she seemed particularly focused on going the distance. As part of the role play, there were rules and regulations, certain phrases and words could not be spoken by Talulah such as 'oh my God' and 'fuck'; these were punishable by incremental time penalties which were added to the edge. Talulah had her safe word too to bring the whole process to a close. With several sex toys firmly affixed to her on suitably low settings, Talulah, eyes half-shut, semi-delirious and trembling, was kneeling on the bed, hands tied to the bedstead, emitting a continuous moan above the whirring buzz as Apollo excused himself and slipped into the adjoining lounge quarters of the hotel room. Tonight he was fulfilling the wishes of two women.

Now for the other half of the job. He had been primed by his sister to search out the Swiss government regulation-issue Hewlett Packard laptop and knew both passwords and precisely which folder he was looking for. It was there on the desk, exactly as Angelina had predicted. The whole process from powering up the laptop to copying the files across to a flash drive, logging out and then closing the lid took less than four minutes, including wiping it down and precisely returning it to its original location. Talulah was in exactly the same position and state when he returned to the bedroom, seemingly oblivious to his brief disappearance. They were two hours into their play and Apollo decided it was time they both had another line of Charlie. At 6.00am, his work complete or, more to the point, successfully incomplete, he crept quietly away from The Palace with his roller blades and bag of 'tools' slung over his shoulder.

Chapter 13

31 January 2018

As we touched down at Schipol and the passengers cheered, already nicely lubricated and relieved at having safely navigated some strong headwinds that at times had left us juddering and helpless, I pushed back my third red wine – KLM had added a rather rich and palatable Cabernet Sauvignon to their collection. It felt good to be back in my old manor. I had read Angelina's email over and over, trying to decode it or find a hidden meaning, something that might offer up some answers. Whatever it was that she knew was clearly incendiary and I found it hard to believe that she would not have kept physical or digital copies of her find. Whilst I was here for the funeral, it also seemed appropriate that my search should begin in the 'Dam. I was booked into the Hilton alongside the central station, the one where newly-weds John and Yoko held their famous 'bed-in' for peace back in the day. After a quick stiffener in the lively roof-top bar, I headed out into the murky winter evening on Shanks's pony across town to Oud-Zuid where Angelina's parents, Caspar and Jasmine, now resided. I had not seen them in over 15 years.

'Hello Zach, it's been a while,' Caspar answered in his unmistakable, saturnine drawl which filtered through the video intercom as he buzzed me in.

Their loft apartment, converted from an old Amsterdam canal house was something to behold – a triumph of interior design. I could sense that the artistic hand of Jasmine had been at work. All white painted floorboards, exotic house plants, turquoise shutters, wicker fan chairs, distressed furniture, wooden beams, floaty gossamer curtains, large Arabesque lanterns, flickering candles, low tables, colourful throw cushions and even an uncaged, exotically coloured cockatiel. The overall effect was arresting – intoxicating even - and warmed the bones, an evocation of a tarty Moroccan caravanserai on acid. I knew Apollo would approve. A life given to PricewaterhouseCoopers clearly had its rewards in terms of financing boho home decor.

Angelina's death hung in the air, suffocating us all and stultifying conversation. Jasmine, usually the more vivacious of the pair, sat morose, staring at a fixed point somewhere in the past. 'I am so sorry for your loss and to intrude at such a time,' I said, 'but, like you, I am trying to make sense of Angelina's death.'

Caspar responded bluntly: 'You won't make sense of it, because it cannot be made sense of.'

'Yes, that's probably true,' I agreed, hugging my Lagavulin single malt, which Jasmine had silently proffered. 'However, that's not going to stop me trying. Did Angelina visit you much here?

'Yes. Well, occasionally,' Caspar responded, before adding: 'She paid us a surprise visit back in early December and insisted on staying the night. We were delighted, of course. She had a sherry or two and it got late and she didn't fancy the walk back to her own flat. She said she was probably heading back to Sweden for the festive period, so this was our little family celebration, although Apollo was missing of course. We see so very little of him nowadays. Angelina told how she had visited him in Madrid over the summer and said that he was well and still keeping afloat, making ends meet from his acting. Anyway, I know we shall see him tomorrow.'

Thinking out loud, I said: 'Shortly before….well, shortly before the explosion, she sent me a WhatsApp message in which she seemed genuinely fearful for her life. She knew she was in real danger.'

'What did she say?' was Caspar's rejoinder.

'It wasn't too expansive and it didn't always make sense but she did say that she was on the verge of breaking a news story. One of the things she said, incongruous with the rest of the message, was "remember those hot nights in my bedroom in my parents' house?" Now, as it goes, we never did have any hot nights in your house ….. well not this one anyway. Is a bedroom still made up for her? Could I perhaps take a look in it, just in case there is anything in there that jogs my mind and helps us understand this whole mess?'

'Have you shown this message to the police?' returned Caspar. 'If she was about to break a story then this could be an important lead.'

'And how are you Zach?' Jasmine finally spoke, 'I know it did not – could not - work out between you two but I know Angelina was the love of your life. Whilst we cannot always do the right things or even find the right words and although we cannot always love ourselves, sometimes the love of another is all that we have.'

I took a moment, letting her words land. 'To be honest, I am in shock. I know I am not in a good place right now. I might, just might, be able to find a little solace if I can find out who did this and why.'

'Well, be our guest, go take a look in her room; you know where it is, you will find everything just as she left it…..' Jasmine's voice trailed away.

I drained my malt and slowly hauled myself to my feet out of the low-lying Maharaja chaise longue. As I made my way to Angelina's bedroom, out of left field I felt something give under my foot and at the same moment there was an unearthly, high-pitched squeal and a lightning fast streak of furred animal, the shock of which sent me flailing sidelong into a carved Moroccan screen. That dominoed but, thankfully, its and my collapse were cushioned by a bed of Mediterranean houseplants, resulting in a spillage of soil but not blood. The unseen cat had been sparked out on its back, just behind the divan; not surprisingly really as it was tropically hot in the flat and I was sweating profusely. It scarpered off smartly, thankfully still with us but noisily airing its disapproval. The cockatiel, who I had been keeping a wary eye on throughout, watched on impassively. I was surprised and relieved not to have broken anything.

'Jesus, I didn't see it! Well, I kind of did, out of the corner of my eye at the very last moment; I didn't know cats could lie like that, I thought it was just a patterned rug. It's very thin. That scared me half to death.'

Caspar looked at me accusingly as I brushed myself down and said: 'Scared us all half to death, especially poor Mata Hari.'

Jasmine smiled for the first time since I had arrived and asked: 'Can I pour you another Scotch?'

My glass charged, I limped, dishevelled, into Angelina's old room and, instantly overwhelmed, sat on the bed perspiring. Her parents had moved back to Amsterdam after we began studying there. They had set the room up as Angelina's even though she remained with her grandparents before taking student digs, although I believe she did stay with them for a period during her Master's study. The boudoir had not changed since then, even though it was now used as a guestroom; it was thickly carpeted and sparingly furnished. Her single, quilted bed; an expensive looking and matching chest of empty drawers and wardrobe, walnut or mock walnut; some small framed posters of European cities hung on pink walls; a dinky little dressing table where a small family of cuddly toys lived, watching over a collection of mouldering make-up; and a few shelves of teenage novels and school books. Incongruous with the Moorish living room, this was a shrine to a life once lived. I took out my phone and re-read her last message to me for the umpteenth time.

The only line that offered any glimmer of a clue and seemed relevant to this specific room was the reference to hot nights and, as I said, there had been none of those. Could she have somehow been referring to the temperature in the room? That certainly seemed possible but, again, didn't offer up any answers. And then, there it was, staring me in the face. Sat on the windowsill, the curtains not yet drawn, was a slightly weary looking chilli plant. This was what the oblique 'hot' reference related to, surely? And her line saying *"you must unearth and deliver my story"* that fitted too. I had to pull the plant and its roots out of the soil but, in doing so, my heart skipped a beat as I lay my fingers on a tiny memory stick encased in a plastic wrapper.

'Nothing,' I heard myself saying, upon my return to the lounge where Caspar was sweeping up the last remnants of soil debris.

'Oh dear, I am sorry. Still, I am not surprised. What next in your quest?' asked Jasmine, with perhaps just a tinge of sarcasm.

'Not sure really. I will speak to Jochen at the funeral. Between us we might be able to piece something together. He might know if anything had been found on her electronic devices. Well, if you think of anything else, I am staying in the Hilton by the station for a couple of days. Oh, one last question. I don't suppose you have a key for Angelina's apartment? No doubt the police will have been all over it with a fine tooth-comb but I might just see something, a clue or something that could help.'

Jasmine said she didn't think I would get in as it was a crime scene but slipped me a key anyway and we bade one another adieu until the morning. I felt enlivened as I stepped back out into the biting winter nip and away from the oppressive mood and heat of the flat. My mind raced as I hacked across town through the encroaching fog. What was on the memory stick? Could it help explain Angelina's murder? Would it light the touch paper that would change the world?

Back in The Hilton, after an interminable wait for my laptop to fire up and a frustrating issue with the hotel wi-fi, I inserted the memory stick only to be left deflated to find a single file on it with just these words: 'In Christiania you will find Mad Lizzie, she is wiser than she seems.'

Chapter 14

1 February 2018

The first thing that struck me was how many people were at Angelina's funeral. I knew her to be well-liked wherever she presented herself and to be a highly respected journalist but I was still taken aback by the throng that met me when I stepped out of my Uber, which had delivered me straight from The Hague's Central Station to *Escher in Het Paleis*, a museum dedicated to the life and work of mind-bending Dutch artist M C Escher. I wondered about the small, raggle-taggle bunch that might, if the weather wasn't too grim, assemble for my own funeral.

Angelina's parents were lapsed Catholics; Angelina herself was of no religion. The Netherlands is one of the least religious countries on the planet, which seemed to suit Angelina, perhaps even had helped mould her. Apparently she had mentioned to Caspar and Jasmine, in what seemed like a moment of idle conversation when she last saw them, that when her time came she would like her ashes to be scattered in Tyresta National Park, just outside Stockholm, and, if there had to be a ceremony, she would prefer it to be a Humanist one. I believe Caspar had enquired about holding the memorial, or should I say celebration, in Amsterdam's Rijksmuseum in the room with Bosch's *Garden of Earthly Delights* but, having been knocked back on that, had more luck in hiring out the Escher museum, which lauded the life and work of one of Angelina's favourite artists, a man famous for his nonsensical take on perspective. Given Bosch was a devout Christian, the Escher choice was perhaps apposite.

I had been dreading this day. In life generally, I always had the sense of teetering on the edge of making some terrible social faux pas and funerals ratcheted up that worry to another level. So, feeling decidedly raw and brittle and having realised en route that I had forgot to send flowers, it was both cheering and refreshing to see such a swathe of humanity and colour. The wake comprised people of all creeds and hues, of varying nationalities and sexual persuasions - a testament to Angelina's rich life. I'd assembled a screwball selection of black clothes, having borrowed an oversized suit and dark tie from my dad and some brogues from Joseph Squibb, but had clearly not had the email about dress code as most people were colourfully arrayed in vibrant sartorial garb.

What remained of Angelina had been cremated at Zorgvlied, her ashes inurned in an ornate Delft casket, which now sat atop a table alongside various keepsakes: photographs of her at different stages of life; several framed copies of favourite poems and excerpts of writing; postcards of her favourite works of art; and a video of her as a young child running artlessly around with her brother and laughing in some towering sand dunes. I found it difficult to peruse but, at the same time, could not tear myself away and took a furtive nip on my hip flask to steel myself. Nick Cave's 'Nobody's Baby Now' played, barely audible in the background.

'It is difficult to watch, no?' I was jolted from my catatonic reverie by an instantly recognisable twang. It had been well over fifteen years; he had thickened out a little and now sported a heavy stubble but I recognised him in an instant. Tall and still easy on the eye; sanguine, swarthy and, today, dapperly attired as a gunslinger. The only disconcerting incongruity from bygone times was – and I took it to be the occasion rather than age – an air of sobriety and solemnity. He also looked like he had been up all night, which there was every chance he had.

'Apollo, my man. Good to see you, although how I wish it wasn't in these circumstances. Yes, you are right, it is painful to watch but beautiful too. It looks like the pair of you could play in those dunes forever. I am not sure where or how or why we lose such innocence?'

'I have made a life of trying not to,' he replied with an anaemic smile.

And then a female voice joined our conversation: 'It is rare for our child spirit to remain untethered. Many of us spend our adult years unknowingly floundering around trying to recapture that wonder and purity. Sometimes, later in life, we can make the reconnect.'

Apollo was accompanied by - I was shortly to learn - a voodoo priestess or mambo. She certainly wasn't in mufti. To say she stood out from the crowd, which wasn't altogether easy, was an understatement. Strikingly attractive, her skin positively shining and with extraordinary things happening in her hair – coloured beads, plaits, clots, dreadlocks - she was attired in an ornately brocaded, crimson dovetail coat, what looked like a black satin shirt, ripped black jeans, leather boots and sleek top hat, lending her an overall height advantage over Apollo; oh, and just to complete the look, a sturdy-looking cane with a silver skull handle. She would have cinched the best-dressed award at a Sisters of Mercy gig.

'This is Sylvenie from Queens, New York. She is my friend and has been over in Europe for a few weeks now.' And then, addressing her: 'This is Zach, he and Angelina were teenage sweethearts. He is a good man,' and, turning back to me, 'we must go for a drink together after this terrible ordeal. I will need reviving, I really don't like funerals. They make me dwell on all those that I have lost.'

Knowing the circles in which Apollo liked to move, I suspected he had indeed witnessed the passing of a fair share of friends and associates. Sylvenie had become distracted and moved off to put her arm around a beleaguered looking Caspar, who had been standing alone, glassy eyed, completely absorbed in his own world. She looked to be whispering what I assumed, to her, were words of consolation in his ear. Unusually for him, he looked a little flustered.

And then we – there must have been getting on for 200 of us - were directed to our seats in a large function room adorned with three-point perspective Escher lithographs. Out of instinct, everyone rose when the celebrant came in but he immediately gestured us all to sit back down and launched himself straight into his spiel: 'Today we are here to celebrate the life of Angelina Fontana. Life is precious, the most incredible gift, which we must cherish. Today, let us not talk about how Angelina died but how she lived and her legacy…..' he began. He wittered on about how our time on earth is short but priceless and delivered some lines about random incidents in Angelina's life that her family must have fed him. I took another surreptitious hit from my hip flask; the coffee and cake hadn't quite been doing it for me. There were several speeches to endure: Caspar spoke calmly and lucidly about his daughter's journalism, her rigorous pursuit of truth and of her quest for a fairer, greener and finer world; Jochen told of his wife's beauty, of her external features but more importantly of that which was within - her kindness, her humour, her relentless pursuit of justice and equality; a favourite aunt read a poem which talked about the importance of the dash between the date of birth and date of death, for that, the ditty explained, is where our lives are lived. Unaccountably, these lines stuck in my head: 'For it matters not, how much we own, the cars, the house, the cash. What matters is how we live and love and how we spend our dash.' Between them, they came close – perhaps as near as words can come - but none of them truly captured Angelina's spirit. The reflective music was The Beatles' *Let it Be* but the ceremony provided no catharsis for me. I was sympathetic to the Humanist aim of making this a joyous affair and, maybe if Angelina had died of old age, it might have worked but the fact was her life had been unnaturally cut short and there was neither music nor words that could compensate that.

As we filed out in silence to the muffled strains of REM's 'Everybody Hurts', I cast an eye over the assembly. Jochen seemed to have brought a posse of Nordic academics with him, presumably some of which were Angelina's friends too, along with his parents and siblings; Caspar and Jasmine were being consoled by their brothers and sisters and their nieces and nephews, Angelina's cousins; there was a good sprinkling of women, some of whom clearly knew each other, who I took to be journalistic colleagues; and also a small group of what I think were old university friends, acquaintances made after our split. There were one or two Greenpeace members that had sailed with us on the *Espy* but no Philippe. After that I was struggling to identify a good number of the mourners: friends accrued over the years, pals acquired at night classes or down the gym, one or two characters in raincoats who I took to be either police officers or reporters, after all we were dealing with a murder case here. And was that Candy Kitcatt, now an elected member of the Danish parliament and leader of the NOW movement? Very possibly, I thought. She was tall and elegant and moved effortlessly through the gathering, seemingly drawing people towards her, convivial even at an event like this.

Purely by chance I pitched up next to Jasmine as we shuffled out of the rows of seats. We acknowledged one another and for want of something to say, I asked: 'Who chose the music?'

'Ah, that was me,' she replied. 'It's not too macabre, is it? Some of it I know Angelina liked; some of it I like. Despite what the celebrant said, upbeat music did not seem right to me. Anyway, I don't care what people think; it was my daughter.'

'I think you've nailed it,' I said, just as Velvet Underground's 'All

Tomorrow's Parties' started up.

'Will you stay for more coffee and cake?' she asked. 'I would like that.'

'Yes, absolutely but first I just need to get some air and have a wee smoke.'

On finding egress, I discovered Apollo and Sylvenie and one or two others had already set up a smokers' corner.

'Zach, join us,' called Sylvenie, waving her clay pipe at me and clutching her top hat with the other hand as the wind gusted. 'That was so well done, don't you think? A really touching tribute to what I think was a very special woman. Upon death, our soul immediately enters the spirit world but it does not go far from the body for at least a week. She was with us Zach, in that very room; I could feel her. Such a vigorous spirit.'

Apollo was deep in conversation with one of the rain-coated men, who seemed to be grilling him about something. 'Get to jiggery fuck!' he shouted or at least that's what it sounded like. 'Get out of here you fucking jerk-off,' Apollo suddenly exploded, pushing his tormentor square in the chest. A few mourners jumped in, restraining Apollo and guiding his inquisitor firmly down the street.

Apollo returned to our group and was visibly shaking. 'Wanker. Come on, let's find a bar, I need to get fucked up,' he pronounced.

'I'll be right there,' I said. 'I just need to grab a word with someone.' We swapped numbers so that he could text me their whereabouts.

On re-entering the museum, I was fortuitous in finding the two people I wanted to talk to, Jochen and Jasmine, together. I made a bee-line for them.

'Jochen, my man, I am so sorry for your loss. I can't believe it, can you? What sort of arseholes would do this?'

'I have my suspicions,' was his curt reply.

'Who?' I demanded.

'When I last visited Ange in Cómpeta, she told me she was on the verge of breaking a story that would reveal the true nature of our warped world. My money is on the Americans, although there is just an outside chance it could be the Russians. Both are reactionary states led by ruthless megalomaniacs and are propped up by the corrupt corporate cultures of the anachronistic fossil fuel industry; both also have expansive spy networks that miss nothing. Whatever Ange had unearthed, clearly they knew about and it certainly had some powerful people very worried.'

'But enough to assassinate her? That seems insane but….then….you might be right. Someone clearly decided she must go. She must have found something pretty incendiary if it had the potential to unbalance the current system? I suppose we could be looking at any country? Did you not get a sense of what her discovery might be?'

'No,'

'And the police? Nothing from them?' I pursued my questioning, 'what is their theory?'

'I believe they are keeping an open mind; which, in other words, translates as they haven't a clue,' was Jochen's mordant response. 'As the killing took place in Andalusia, the Spanish are leading the investigation, although I know the Dutch police are also assisting. Would you believe it but, between them, they have mislaid Ange's laptop? Both blame each other. You couldn't make it up, could you?'

'What about the message you received from Angelina just prior to her murder? Did you show it to the police?' Jasmine offered up, somewhat unhelpfully.

'Nah, zilch,' I dismissed quickly, attempting to move the conversation on. 'No clues at all then Jochen as to what her find might have related to?'

'Nothing yet but I have not finished going through all her papers and files. The police have seized so much. I think she knew that what she had uncovered was dynamite and she did not want to put her loved ones in immediate danger by sharing her find with them. Both the Spanish and the Dutch police have been glacially slow in unlocking some of her remote accounts. One thing is for sure, when I do uncover whatever it is we are looking for, I will be straight on the phone to Candy Kitcatt. While I did not share my wife's revolutionary tendencies and fervour for a new world order, I shall honour her memory by sharing her find with those that can make the most capital from it. Somebody has to bear the consequences for their actions.'

'Bravo. That's the spirit,' I encouraged, finally warming to something that the cold academic said.

'But what is this communication from Ange to you that Jasmine talks of?'

'She sent me a WhatsApp message saying she felt worried about her safety because of a story she was working on. Nothing more than that,' I lied. 'But look, Angelina meant a lot to me and I am as determined as you to find out who killed her – and why. Let's swap mobile numbers just in case we can help each other out at some point.'

With contact details traded, Jochen said he would call on Caspar and Jasmine but now he must thank Candy Kitcatt for attending and glided off in her direction. I turned back to Jasmine: 'Will you join us for a drink?'

'Caspar and I need to stick around a little longer, let's see how we feel after the wake,' was her response. 'These days, I find social events so draining and Caspar isn't much use, he hates them more than me. Whilst my mind soars, I find myself trapped in this aging body. But I would like to see some more of Apollo and his partner; I am not sure about her yet, I've not really had chance to speak with her.'

'Ah, yes, Sylvenie. Not partner, just a friend,' I corrected.

As Leonard Cohen's 'You Want it Darker' took things down a further notch, I judged it a good time to leave. I checked my phone to find out where Apollo and Sylvenie had decamped to but really just needed to follow my nose. They were in a nearby small bar, *Discordia*, just down the road from the museum. Hands-down it won the award for the most sepulchrous element of the day. The pair seemed to have stumbled across the prototype gothic steampunk café – replete with ornate mirrors, black carpeted walls, flashes of exposed brickwork, velvet curtains, sputtering candles, wooden floor, dusty shelves buckling under weighty tomes and flourishes of decorative wrought iron.

Before I was half way through the door, Sylvenie was on her feet, beckoning me over. Given there were only a dozen or so customers and the place wasn't much bigger than a tennis court, this struck me as somewhat dramatic.

Clutching my double malt, I joined them. 'How did you find this place?' I asked.

'Pure chance. It's great, isn't it?' was Sylvenie's riposte.

'It suits the occasion,' chipped in Apollo, who, with a Death in the Afternoon cocktail of absinthe and champagne in hand and – I suspected – line of coke snorted, looked marginally uplifted.

'What was the fracas about?' I asked him.

'No se. I am not sure. Some low life - a reporter I think, possibly a Private Dick or actually, in his case, a very public dick - asking me questions about Angelina. What was she doing in Spain? Was she involved with organised crime gangs in Malaga? What story was she working on? I am afraid I lost my patience with the little fucker.'

'So inconsiderate, completely amoral. The spirits will have their revenge on him,' echoed Sylvenie.

Deciding I didn't want to reignite Apollo's ire, I held back from posing the same questions as the reporter and, turning to Sylvenie, gauchely asked her if she was religious.

'Yes I am,' was her reply. 'I am a servant of the lwas or, in your vernacular, a priestess of voodoo - although the correct pronunciation is bo-du, spelt v-o-d-o-u or sometimes v-o-d-u-n. Do you know anything at all about my religion?' she asked, rhetorically. She clearly – and quite rightly – suspected that I didn't and, even if she thought I did, I think she was committed to offloading on me anyway. It filled what could have been an awkward silence.

'You must be familiar with some of its stereotypes – voodoo dolls, curses and spells, animal sacrifice, possessions, black magic?' she continued. 'Don't worry, I understand this. Our practice is often regarded as primitive but that is because it is the religion of slaves, the oppressed and the poor. We have never had money to build extravagant cathedrals, synagogues and mosques, nor do we have a sacred text or hierarchy of leaders. On the positive side, this means we are not run by men for men. Belonging to the people, vodou has not been tainted by compromise, by committees and synods and ecumenical councils, by academics and new ways of thinking; it remains visceral, untainted and a direct link to ancient times.'

'Is it a popular religion? I mean are there many followers around the world? I asked, genuinely curious. 'I have noticed how you never see voodoo temples in cities.'

'That is so true. Ideally, our ceremonies take place outdoors in nature but often in cities you will find our temples in basements and back-rooms. It is the weather that drives us indoors. Vodou is an animistic religion that is practised by 60 million people across the world and is amongst the very oldest of faiths, stretching back 6,000 years. It originated in what is now Benin in West Africa and is the national religion there. Today it is big in much of Africa – in Ghana, in Togo, in Nigeria - and also in the Caribbean, especially in Haiti, where my family is from and, to a lesser extent, in the Dominican Republic and Cuba. It spread around the globe when our ancestors were transported as slaves from Central and West Africa in the 1600s. Now, as the black diaspora has extended, it is also practised in Brazil and across the US where New Orleans is its capital. It is a private faith – followers often have altars in their own houses – but it can be found in most large cities across the world. Last night I led a small ceremony in Amsterdam. It is why I am so tired today. In New York, there are 300,000 people from Haiti or of Haitian descent. Our numbers swelled after the 2010 earthquake; there are many more prayer circles since the disaster, they offer the opportunity for my people to support one another and to rebuild bridges to both Port-au-Prince and to our forebears.

'Like all religions, ours is a syncretic faith, built on African spiritualism but drawing on Christianity. This is true too of our language, Haitian Kreyol – a mix of African tongues and French. Both our religion and language were born of struggle. Many of our festivals coincide with the Christian calendar, this is a consequence of our predecessors having to mask their true religion from their owners; it offered them a form of refuge and liberation. Ever since 1791, it has been markedly discriminated against after a ceremony inspired the Haitian Revolution which saw my people rise up and overthrow their French captors. By gaining our independence, we became the first country in the Caribbean to be emancipated from our European oppressors. Not many people know, but we are the second oldest republic in the world, behind only the US.'

'So, what do you actually do as a priestess?' I asked.

'Firstly, I am very much part of the Haitian community in New York and I must make myself available to help in any way I can. Essentially I am a healer. When I moved to New York at the age of 17 from Haiti, my mother and father had already taught me the ways of vodou; I had learnt all about the history, the botany, the healing, the dancing, the drumming, the singing and rituals.

'Contrary to popular belief, what I practise is not black magic, it is not the creation of love potions or maledictions and dolls – it is white magic and helps my people reconnect with Africa or Ginen as we know it, the land of our spirits. We commune with one God – known as Gran Met or Bondyé – but he is aloof so we achieve this through worshipping over 1,000 potent but sometimes erratic spirits or lwas as we call them. If it is easier for you to understand, think of Gran Met as God and the lwas as angels. Each holds sway over its own domain – such as love, morality or death. As I say, Gran Met does not engage with us mere mortals but the lwas, his children, will. They serve as go-betweens. We are very much in touch with the spirit world, our ancestors and nature. I can connect with the healing spirits through sacred dances, animal sacrifices, through snakes and through chanting and music – they will enter my body and to the audience it appears like I am in a trance. All I see is pure light; it feels to me like I am going home. Sometimes I can reach them in dreams too.'

'What sacrifices?' I instinctively asked.

'At the start of the dance or ceremony, if possible, we like to make a sacrifice to the lwas – usually a chicken, although it can be other animals such as a goat, a pig or even a bull. They also like vegetables, fruits and grains as well as rum and other libations. Last night there was much healing to be done. There were many spirits with us, much more than there were people. I brought with me authentic Haitian rum, the lwas like it. They were in good spirits if you will excuse the pun; it was a perfect evening, the moon shone, we were unmolested in a quiet park and our sacrifices were well received.'

'What did you make of it Apollo, were you there?' I asked, leaning over to the big guy.

'Yes, yes. It is an intense experience for sure, it makes you feel……alive. It is like being transported to another age, no? Another world. Sylvenie was magnificent, so powerful. Every eye was on her; it was spellbinding and we were all completely transfixed. I thought for a moment that she had passed the point of no return, her body thrown out of shape and overrun by the lwas. It was distressing and exhilarating at the same time. You have to witness it once Zach. Perhaps one day you and I will visit Sylvenie in New York and see her in her parish?'

Sylvenie smiled beatifically and said: 'Just for fun' as she suddenly - and without asking my permission - flipped out some cards, drew one, looked at my hands, studied me, all in thirty seconds or so, and proceeded to tell me about myself. I have to say she wasn't too far off the mark although I wasn't altogether comfortable with her advice that I must fight my demons that were encircling me and strangulating my true nature.

And then, thankfully, before we could probe any further into the murky depths of my psyche, Jasmine and Caspar arrived, looking altogether incongruous in the Gothic crypt in which we were entombed.

Quickly furnished with a glass of Rose and a filter coffee, the pair joined us. They looked utterly drained. Angelina's death seemed to have aged them both by ten years.

'Thank god that's over,' said Jasmine, collapsing into the space made for her on the low level black leather sofa. 'Fortunately no-one hung around too long. One of my sisters said she would join us here – Zoe, the chatty one - but otherwise most people have drifted away now.'

'How was that for you Apollo?' asked Caspar.

'It has been the worst day of my life.'

'Yes, mine too, son' agreed Caspar. 'Still, no surprise there.'

'My dear, it feels like I have not seen you for so long. It was such a shame that you could not visit at Christmas – I hope it was a well-paid job that kept you in Madrid? I don't think we saw you at all last year?' said Jasmine. 'Now you are all I…..I mean we…..have left.'

Ignoring what I perceived as a Freudian slip, Caspar chipped in with his own line of questioning: 'Perhaps you will think of coming back to Amsterdam now?'

Sensing that Apollo was in for a grilling and that I was encroaching on family time, I excused myself saying I was leaving town early the following day and still had travel arrangements to take care of. Apollo bade me farewell with a dramatic wink, saying: 'Be good Zach and if you can't be good, don't get caught.'

As I was leaving, the garrulous Zoe, who was on her way in, waylaid me, allowing Sylvenie to catch up with me, who insisted on accompanying me outside to smoke her pipe. Before I escaped, she impressed upon me: 'In vodou, an ancestor is just as alive as a living person. Just remember Zach, death is nothing at all. Angelina has only slipped away to another dimension, into another room if you like. Nothing has changed; everything is as it was. You must laugh and cry as before, as you always did with her and talk to her often. Her name should be used freely; life goes on as it always did. The line is uninterrupted. Out of sight, yes, but not out of mind, Angelina will always be with you. She is very near and you will be with her again more quickly than you can imagine. Go my child, dance and greet the spirits.'

'Thank you,' I said. 'I didn't know how I was going to get through today but you and Apollo have helped enormously.'

Chapter 15

2 February 2018

I'd never been to Copenhagen before and, having assumed it to be a large but rather sleepy town, I was instantly taken aback at how cosmopolitan and busy it was, frenzied even. On stepping out of the city's Central Station, I walked into a smack of raw Arctic air and a wall of blaring police sirens as half a dozen black, unmarked cars with sirens throwing out jagged blue light went speeding past. And then I stepped into my first bike. My fault, I was obliviously in a bike lane and I realised I had to switch on a sixth sense otherwise this could become a recurring theme. The whole place reminded me of Amsterdam on speed and I'd not even seen my first canal yet. Nothing was cheap and the wallet of a humble photographer only stretches so far, so I had checked into a spit and sawdust place near Norreport Station, which, this being Denmark, still cost me an arm and a leg. Forewarned is forearmed on the cost of alcohol and I took a small tincture from my hip flask of Talisker before heading out into the already fading light and across town.

Having crossed Knippels Bridge, taking me out of the city centre in a south-easterly direction, I followed my instincts and nose to Freetown Christiania. I stepped over the threshold, through a wooden archway welcoming me to the alternative enclave and past a huge seated, carved wooden giant with the words 'The World is in Our Hands' above his head – a suitable epitaph for Angelina's grave I thought to myself. I found myself on Pusher Street – yes, literally - and was immediately propositioned by a teenager trying to sell me first weed and then, when I deferred, upping the stakes to crystal meth. Politely declining his offer, I needed to keep a clear head, I asked him if he knew of any Lizzies. Drawing a blank response, I added in the adjective *Mad* Lizzie. This seemed to help. 'Well, now hang on. There are plenty of crazy people around here but I don't know all their names. What do you want from her? Let me think. Come on, I will walk with you. I can think of several strong possibilities.'

While Christiania is not a big commune, home to nearly 1,000 people and maybe the size of six or seven Trafalgar Squares, it made sense to pick the lad's brains over a beer at a long, outdoor wooden table, while he smoked a fat one, rather than zigzag haphazardly around the squat. As he regaled me with stories of a number of colourful characters that might answer to the name of Mad Lizzie, a mate of his joined us who, for the price of another beer, said he could lead me direct to the door of the woman I was looking for. First though, they had to vet me; not all visitors to Christiania were welcome. There were regular police raids and undercover operations in the avant-garde cooperative. The bohemian community had its own set of rules, including no violence, no hard drugs, no motor vehicles, no guns and no stealing as well as a set of minor rules, including having fun, no photography and no running as it causes panic! Ever since it declared itself independent of Denmark in 1971, when hippies took over the old military barracks, there had been run-ins with the authorities. Residents now paid massively reduced taxes and there was a begrudging tolerance of one another.

Once the boys were reasonably convinced I was not an undercover cop, they necked their beers, thought better of accompanying me to Lizzie's door but told me to head out past the colourful mural-daubed barracks depicting trolls, fairies and dragons and over the Dyssebroen bridge to the other side of the canal, into the Amager zone where an eclectic mix of eco-houses and carbuncles, fashioned out of the debris of modern life, nestled amongst the rushes and reeds of the canal bank. I did just that, presenting myself to a young man sat outside a square abode made of window frames, a large greenhouse in effect, who, when he began talking, I assumed could not be a local resident as he responded in such a pukka British accent: 'Mad Lizzie, you say? Do you know, I rather believe I do? Although I didn't know she was called that – there is a ghastly German woman lives just over the way. I don't think you'll be able to make head or tail of her now that the sun's over the yardarm.'

'Why? Is she a drunk?' I asked.

'Hard to say really, given all the other shit she pumps into her body but, almost certainly, among other things, yes. The best time to catch her – the only time really – is first thing in the morning. I've had one or two half-lucid conversations with her then and, on occasion, she has even shown signs of amicability. There seems to be a ritualistic pattern to her behaviour – she starts her day early by meditating outside her house, whatever the weather, and then she takes a yoga class for a few odds and sods, deadheads mainly. I've occasionally seen her reading and walking in the mornings too. She'd probably be best off going back to bed at that point but I guess her body or her mind craves some kind of release from whatever it is that is tormenting her. I don't know if she is schizophrenic, she certainly seems to have a Jekyll and Hyde personality. She seems stuck in an endless struggle between her perfectly respectable morning persona and her demonic, wanton sister who, over the course of the day, possesses her. By mid to late afternoon, she has become a different person. Drunk on red wine and high on drugs, she quickly spirals into ranting incoherence and oblivion. There has been a number of occasions when I've gone round to check if she's okay after hearing these unearthly caterwauls, which rise above the Joni Mitchell, Holly Near, Jefferson Airplane and Cat Stevens shit she always plays when she's at the peak of her bender. To an extent, the ferociousness of her afternoon and early evening sessions are determined by the strength of the LSD she has taken that day.'

'Wow,' I said. 'She sounds like my sort of girl. Can you introduce me?'

'Okay, let's walk round and see what sort of state she is in,' the gangly youth suggested somewhat gingerly who, as he rose to his feet, introduced himself as Tim. Just as he was explaining how he'd flunked Cambridge and was presently discovering himself in Christiania, much to the chagrin of his father who was an MP and lawyer and his mother who was a Headteacher in a Surrey prep school, there was an unexpected commotion through the trees. A skirmish seemed to have broken out in front of a dilapidated charabanc in which an apoplectic, ashen faced grandma was being wrestled to the ground by three crusty-looking stoners, while making an indescribable and arresting wailing noise, a kind of human rendering of the whirring police sirens I'd heard earlier in the day. As Tim and I approached, the old lady wriggled free from their half-hearted restraint but one of them grabbed her ankle as they slithered along the ground: 'Get off me, you silly fucker!' she screamed. Her mud splattered white leggings were inching down her legs, her flowered frock had ridden up above her waist, revealing her soiled underwear and skeletal features.

'Hey, what's going down?' asked Tim.

Against the psychopathic screeching which had started again, the female stoner shouted: 'This woman is crazy. She came over to our house and started shitting on our doorstep. No warning, not a word, I just found her squatting out front. She's off her fucking head.'

'Until you stop your fucking dogs fouling all around my bus, my home, then you'll find me shitting on your doorstep every afternoon.'

Our presence seemed to bring a modicum of order to the fray and the old woman was released but the insane shrieking did not relent. I wasn't sure how such a fragile figure could generate such an awful and ear-splitting sound.

'Who the fuck are you?' Lizzie asked in a clipped Germanic burr as we attempted to escort her back to her bus. As the saying goes, she looked like she had been set on fire and put out with a golf shoe. 'I know this streak of piss,' she said gesticulating at Tim. 'Are you his sugar daddy?' And that was about as much sense as we got from her, she then started flailing her arms about and, seeing something that we could not see, started screaming: 'They're coming, they're here again! Keep them out of my fucking house! I won't let it happen again!' She freed herself from our company and half-ran, half-stumbled back to her wheel-less coach, turned momentarily so that we could watch her dramatically drop a pill down her neck before she flicked a switch somewhere from within her abode and suddenly the strains of 'Big Yellow Taxi' filled the late afternoon air.

Well, I'd found Mad Lizzie but I knew I would not get anything out of her in the state she was in. I wondered how on earth - or if - this mad woman could shed light on Angelina's death? Angelina had said she is wiser than she seems, so I could only hope she was right.

I'd resolved to return early the following day but Tim invited me into his glasshouse to chill with some herbal tea. The interior was warmer than I'd imagined, the heat being generated by a wood pellet-burning stove was supplemented by double-glazing of a sort and thick blankets. Some properties, Tim explained, were now harnessing geothermal heating from the nearby lake; his was on the waiting list. He told me that concrete was the second most consumed material on earth after water and he and his partner, Randi, would rather work with nature than try to tame it. Nearly everything had been salvaged and re-used; it was a perfect off-grid eco-home that he shared with his Danish girlfriend, who was away for a few days at her mother's. He explained how there was no ownership in the commune and that Christiania properties belonged to all and no-one. Randi was a friend of his sister and it was through her that he'd been able to access the community; demand to join far outstripped the availability of space. I offered to share my whisky with Tim but he told me he was teetotal. After we'd eaten lentil curry in a nearby café, I took him up on his suggestion that I bed down there for the night, thinking it would save me an hour or so in the morning of trekking across town. With negligible 'street' lighting and now Mad Lizzie had worn herself out, things went dark and quiet quickly. I turned in early for once. Another reason to stay over was not being able to entirely trust myself on my own; after all I was still nursing a broken heart.

Chapter 16

3 February 2018

After the best night's sleep I'd had in weeks, I was up later than I would have hoped the following morning, brought to by a thick black coffee. Having thanked Tim for his hospitality and promising to keep in touch, I found a transformed Lizzie clutching a mat and with a bag of coloured plastic blocks and bricks slung over her shoulder. She'd already taken her morning restorative yoga class and was heading home. She shot me a curious glance as I flagged her down, as if only half remembering me from the day before. I decided to not beat around the bush.

'Hey, can I have a word? I am here because a good friend of mine, Angelina Fontana, told me that should anything happen to her, I should dig you out. Something has happened to her, so here I am. Does her name meaning anything to you? Can you shed any light on why somebody would choose to blow Angelina up in a Spanish village? Is any of this making any sense at all?' Listening to myself, I realised how deranged and desperate I sounded.

The old woman looked me up and down as if still trying to place me and then her vacant gaze was suddenly replaced by a glint in her eye and she smiled. 'Come on,' she said. 'You should have mentioned Angelina yesterday. She said you might come. Let me filter some coffee and we can talk.'

The interior of her vehicle was surprisingly well furnished and tidy, so much so that I took my shoes off before entering. Whilst the windows were blacked out, the interior was covered with Buddhist wall hangings, Tibetan thangkas and colourful mandalas. At a glance, the living quarters comprised a battered shabby chic sofa which I sunk into, copious plant foliage, a speaker system, a bookcase and a well stacked wine rack. What more do you need, I thought to myself?

Armed with our strong beverages - I resisted the temptation to ask her to make it an Irish coffee, fearful of where this might lead - Lizzie told her tale.

'I remember Angelina well and was appalled to hear about her murder. Another senseless death. She was a lovely woman and I owe her so much. She came here before Christmas in quite an agitated state; I still don't know how she found me. I thought I'd covered my tracks and cut myself off entirely from my old life.'

'Your old life?' I questioned.

'I've not always been known as *Mad Lizzie* – yes, I know my name. I used to be Dr Elisabeth Benvido; I still am I suppose, on paper at least. My doctorate was in Medicine. I was married to Professor Christoph Benvido; we met at university and we lived together for over 40 years in Geneva.

'My husband worked at CERN and was an accomplished physics academic who, along with his colleagues, helped create the conditions for the vacuum for CERN's particle accelerator. Whilst this was an incredible achievement, his fame could and should have been for an even greater discovery. Using the technology that he had invented, he took the same principle to develop his own incredibly efficient solar panels, enabling them to jump from 10% to 50% efficiency. Potentially, this could have changed the world forever and for everyone. I spoke about all of this with Angelina.'

Pausing briefly but resigned to telling her story again, Lizzie continued: 'Christoph first began his work on solar panels in the 1970s when the world was struggling with a series of petrol crises and the management at CERN had to seriously consider other sources of energy for their project. They turned to the sun and, whilst progress was made and a relatively efficient prototype solar advantage of his panels, he told me, was that they were not totally reliant on direct sunlight and that they could also capture diffused light, an important consideration in central European countries like Switzerland where this makes up at least 50% of the light. In 2005, he retired from CERN, so he had more time to go back and further finesse his invention and to find an investor. He convinced the airport in Geneva to install 300 of his panels and enough energy was produced to heat and cool the buildings all year round. Most people would have settled for this and started to consider the possibilities of mass production. However, Christoph was a perfectionist and he looked to learn from the airport rollout to see how he could increase efficiency even further. He was working up enhanced plans when he inexplicably stopped work on the project. It took me a little while to realise this; it was his withdrawn and sullen mood that I picked up on, along with his being under my feet in the house more.'

Lizzie set down her coffee mug and took a moment, her countenance turning ashen. 'Then there was an electrical fire. We went to bed quite early as usual – early to bed, early to rise was Christoph's philosophy, certainly in later life. It began in the garage sometime after 2.00am; the fire report identified old and faulty wiring as the cause. Everything went up, including the new blueprints; his life's work was in that garage. It was Christoph who woke first, smelling the acrid fumes, of course it goes without saying that the silly smoke alarms didn't work. He roused me from my slumber and there was blind panic. The fire was well entrenched by now. He insisted on opening the bedroom door, I screamed at him not to but he wouldn't listen. He headed off downstairs with me wailing at him – that's the noise you might have heard me making yesterday afternoon, I am sorry about that. I think he was heading to the garage to see if he could salvage his work. I never saw him again. Well, not alive anyway, only his charred remains. I knew it was insane to head off panel developed, the oil problem subsided and there was no longer a need for an alternative power source. Christoph's first love was, of course, the CERN project and he was more than happy to give that his full focus. However, in attempting to find and maintain a perfect vacuum in his solar panel – and thus increase their efficacy – he inadvertently found a means to perform this function in accelerators. My grasp of the science is far from perfect but as far as I understand, it boiled down to something called "getters" which he described as molecular flypaper, extracting particles from the atmosphere and thus leaving a purified vacuum. The molecules collected by the getters, when heated, could be diffused out into the atmosphere enabling the getters to continue to work indefinitely. It transpired that these getter things were perfect for use in the Large Electron Positron Collider, the precursor to the Large Hadron Collider. They were cheap, easy to install and very efficient and they were so beneficial that the electron positron collider ended up with 14 miles of them. Later they were ingeniously incorporated into a coating for use in the hadron collider, where there was even less space.

'Thirty years later and early this century, my husband was approaching retirement when he went back to his solar panel drawing board. The challenge was always that flat solar panels are much harder to seal than cylindrical ones that are used in the particle accelerator. Christoph managed it though, not perfectly but very, very well and miles ahead of any other solar panel on the market – then or since. He was a modest man but I do recall him coming to bed late one night, having been working in the lab he'd set up in our garage and whispering to me: "I may have just solved the world's energy problems."

'The following day, he explained to me how the vacuum that he had created between the glass and the solar absorbers now gave the panels incredibly efficient thermal insulation. While snow might be lying on top of the panel, within, the temperature could still be as high as 80°C. Another into the thickening smoke and, although our bedroom was on the second storey, I focused my efforts on trying to get out of our bedroom window. It wouldn't bloody open, the lock seemed fixed or maybe the window had buckled under the heat. I needed something to smash the window with. I threw a lamp at it but to no avail. Then I recalled Christoph kept a golf club in the wardrobe in case we were ever confronted with intruders. The last thing I recall is repeatedly swinging a nine iron at the window with diminishing strength and gasping for air as smoke filled the room. The glass wouldn't break and I passed out.

'Miraculously, I was rescued. Apparently, firemen immediately target the sleeping quarters in domestic night fires. They'd whipped their ladder up, broke the glass and found me collapsed next to the window, still clenching the club. I spent two months in hospital, suffering with smoke inhalation and superficial burns. Christoph was dead, the house was razed to the ground. It seemed to me, my life was over as I left Geneva's University Hospital. And it was; certainly the life I had been leading.

'Of course, once I had received the house and life insurance payments and a proportion of my husband's pension and put that together with our savings and my own pension, I was rather rich. We had no children. I went travelling for a few years and thought about how I wanted to spend my twilight years. I discovered this place while on a trip to Scandinavia and I was immediately drawn to its spirit and its sense of being removed from the real world. It seemed like the perfect escape for me to live a hermetic life and it echoed my own resolution to enjoy the simple things and to pare back on possessions. Shortly after I arrived here, there was trouble with the Danish authorities – there so often is - and the government insisted that the community either purchase the land we are on or be bought out. Remember this is prime real estate. Not wanting to be uprooted again, I threw a fair amount of money into the project which saw us effectively sell shares in the place and enabled us to take out a mortgage on the land. Mainstream society had not been kind to me, so I could not think of a better way of spending my money than on supporting an alternative way of life.

'And even though I thought I had put my past life behind me and dropped off the radar, I could not disappear off the planet. As I said, at the back end of last year, Angelina paid me a visit and pretty much recounted to me the story I have just told you. I couldn't refute anything she said. She also brought news that I had long suspected and for a time had tried to tell people – but my claims had been dismissed as the paranoid ranting of a grief-stricken and demented old woman.' Her eyes had glazed over and her voice had become tremulous; she paused, steadying herself: 'If you want me to continue, I am going to need a proper drink.' She was on her feet in a flash. 'Can I offer you a glass of red? I am afraid that is all I have.'

'It's a bit early for me,' I lied, desperately hoping she might reconsider. She didn't. She uncorked a half finished bottle – from the label it looked expensive and French - and poured herself a healthy measure in a large glass: 'You sure?' she said. Tying myself to the mast like Odysseus, I nodded. Frankly, after yesterday, I was taken aback by how cogently she talked and was busy trying to assimilate all that she had said.

She threw back a generous slug as if it was Ribena, licked her lips and continued: 'Angelina confirmed to me that the fire had not been an accident. She said she had a copy of a secret CIA file, which proved that the blaze had been set deliberately with the intention of doing away with Christoph and destroying his work. The CIA had extracted a confession from a Bosnian assassin, Bogdan somebody or other, they had arrested on suspicion of carrying out several targeted hits for the Russians. The file reported on him confessing to a number of killings, not just ones commissioned by the Soviets, and Christoph was one of them. For our hit, he claimed he had been hired by a couple of smart looking business types with American accents but that was all he could or would reveal. He also proved biddable; his confession was expansive in return for the US promising him clemency as they persuaded him to become a turncoat and work for them. No doubt the goons who hired him would have been working for someone else. Probably the Americans, quite possibly a rogue CIA cell acting on behalf of a senior politician, but, equally, it could have been that he was engaged by the Russians or an oil company or representatives of the oil industry; the likelihood is that we'll probably never know.

'If Christoph's enhanced solar panels had made it to market, they would have changed our world beyond all recognition. They would have utterly disrupted the energy sector, wiping out a large percentage of the US' GDP in one fell swoop and no doubt sending financial markets into a downward spiral. There are a lot of powerful and greedy people who depend on the petrodollar and who would stop at nothing to protect their own interests and those of shareholders. They would not think twice about hiring someone to do their dirty work. Angelina told me that they had gotten to Christoph a few weeks before his death, not threatening him directly but reminding him how dangerous it was for his wife to be driving on the wet, dark country roads around his house; this had been enough for him to temporarily desist in his work. At this point, she said, he confided in a work colleague, telling them how he had been threatened and passing them copies of his sketches, workings and notes for the new solar panels. I don't know who this was but it seems they were the person who alerted Angelina to Christoph's work. She said she thought it was a man that called her but could not be one hundred per cent sure as the voice had been put through a modulator. After the warning, Christoph did down tools; as I said I remember at the time wondering why this was. But, having thought it over or assuming whoever it was that was threatening him had gone away, he eventually went back to work. The rest, as we know, is history.'

'Did Angelina say where she had she got the CIA file from?' I asked, desperately trying to process some of this.

'She said she got it from the Swiss Minister of Defence and Civil Protection, Talulah Dante. Not that Madame Dante just handed her the file. Angelina told a funny story. She said her brother was a male prostitute in Madrid and he, acting on Angelina's behest, had copied the file while "entertaining" Talulah. It seems she had headed up a governmental review of Christoph's death, following an anonymous tip-off. After all, Christoph was a Swiss national and it was supposed to be her job to protect citizens. I know governments like to hold secrets and intel against each other and to sometimes use them as bargaining chips. I think she said the Swiss government had engaged a hacker to access the CIA files, which, as I said, clearly revealed a contract killing on my dear husband. And now perhaps you can begin to understand why I feel the need to get off my head day after day. It is now nothing more than muscle memory for me.'

'And how did Angelina know that Talulah Dante had such a file?' I found myself asking.

'Well, she's a journalist, or was; isn't it her job to dig out such information? My best guess is that whoever tipped Angelina off about Christoph's invention also told her about the enquiry and may have even tipped off the Swiss government in the first place? Angelina said she had been sent a pre-paid phone on which, a day or two after receiving it, the informer rang her. They said they would call her back to arrange for her to meet someone – possibly them – who would be able to give her a copy of Christoph's schema and notes on how the new panels would work. I don't know whether she ever received that second call. Since she has died, I have given a great deal of thought to who the person could have been who called her. I did not know all the ins and outs of my husband's work but after a lot of deliberation, I narrowed it down to three people that I think it could have been. They are probably all retired now and may no longer be living in Geneva or even alive. If it is not one of those that have the plans, then the chances are one of them would know where to find them.' She was on her feet again, pulling a copy of Don Quixote from her bookshelves, standing over me and then dangling it by its spine, letting a slip of paper slowly float into my lap.

I glanced at the notepaper and her scrawled hand. I could decipher three names, two professors and a doctor. Worth following up, I thought, before secreting it away in my wallet and finding myself thinking out loud: 'Yes, I can see how she would have been interested in a story like this. If these super-efficient solar panels had been introduced to the world back in the mid-noughties, just imagine how different the world would have been and what it would be like now. I know there are lots of ifs, buts and maybes and, without doubt, there would have been the fossil fuel companies to do battle with but, just imagine, our homes could be using these panels, our hospitals, our transport systems, our schools, our industries, whole nations. By now, we would have doubtlessly learnt how to increase their efficiency further, working out ways to shrink and play about with panel sizes. I am no expert but surely this is the equivalent of being able to generate five hours of solar energy for the cost of one? By now, energy may even have become free? We would certainly be living in a greener world, allowing what were up and coming countries at the time, places like China, Brazil and India to develop rapidly without adding to the climate problems that now ravage our planet. How many lives could have been saved? We might not be teetering on the edge of environmental breakdown. How much more affluent would many third world countries be? Would the world be?'

Surely this was the 'mind-bomb' which Angelina had been looking for? The telling info that would provide the pivotal moment in altering the public's conception of how the world actually works. A moment of truth, an exposé illustrating how greed corrupts and how politicians and businessmen in hydrocarbon companies put their selfish pursuit of profit ahead of improving the livelihoods of every man, woman and child on the planet. Corporate culture's crushing of the individual. That it was unclear as to whether the killing had been sanctioned by the US or Russia or the oil industry was inconsequential, indeed in many ways it helped illustrate the universality of corruption. But all I had was the word of a half-crazed squatter. Surely Angelina must have had more than this? Where were the CIA files that she had seen? Would one of the three names that Mad Lizzie had given me provide answers?

Now it was time for a drink.

Chapter 17

5 February 2018

As a newly elected member of the Danish parliament, it had been far from easy arranging a meeting with Candy Kitcatt. Her officious PA, Wongbee Lee, had me down as just another groupie and tried to fob me off, suggesting I attend one of Candy's surgeries as her diary was weighed down with meetings, pressing constituent matters and foreign travel. In the end, playing the 'close journalistic colleague of Angelina' card, I was told she could spare me 10 minutes in a waterside restaurant in Nyhavn, pre-meal and post-speech that she was giving at a rally in Freetown Christiania.

Having genned up on Candy online and knowing that Angelina had held her in such high regard, I made a point of arriving in good time at the Grey Hall in Christiania in order to secure myself a prime spot to take in her address. As I approached the venue, I was surprised to find that it felt more like a rock concert than a political rally. There was an unmistakable buzz as hundreds of young people milled around, drinking beer, smoking pot, talking animatedly, laughing and enjoying a few shafts of pale evening sun, while vendors weaved their way through the crowds selling both NOW and Candy t-shirts, scarves and badges. On entering the hall, I was relieved to receive reusable ear plugs which promised to translate the address into English and several other languages. Slick, I thought. A marker that this was a movement with international aspirations.

As show-time approached, a couple of thousand people, predominantly younger than me, squeezed in, mostly standing in the mosh pit with a few seated on the balcony. Heavy bass music pulsed out into the largest auditorium in the commune, which I was impressed to learn had hosted a wide range of musical luminaries including Bob Dylan, the Manic Street Preachers and Rage Against the Machine. Swerving the pricey bar, I took a nip on my hipflask and started jostling my way as far forward into the crowd as I could.

After an interminable but I suppose obligatory wait, the lights lowered, Sam Cooke's 'A Change is Gonna Come' boomed out of the speakers and dry ice swirled slowly and evocatively across the blacked out stage. The crowd whistled and whooped in heightened anticipation and a frisson of excitement rippled through the hall. Presently, the smoke fell away and a statuesque, sinewy figure swaggered slowly but purposefully across the stage, guided to the microphone stand by a single Super Trouper spotlight. She was taller than I remembered and elegantly robed in a red, vampish full length dress, sleeveless with a plunging v-neck and side cut-outs exposing flashes of a lean, toned and lightly tanned physique. With her long black, shiny hair, fuck-me red lippy and silver eye liner, it looked like we were in for a night of burlesque rather than serious political discourse. I was just surprised that she wasn't wearing suspenders and garter but, hey, enough of my hang-ups. The applause and shrieking from the crowd gradually subsided as she removed the mic from its stand and began pacing the stage, working every inch of it, scrutinising her transfixed audience as she did so. There was a palpable energy in the hall. Spectators were at the same time illuminated and blurred in the hazy light from the sea of mobile phones. Finally, having seemingly weighed up her audience, she began her address, her husky tones translated through the thickly accented interpreter in my head-set. There was no auto-cue, this was from the heart.

'Let me get straight to the point: the apocalypse has already begun. The world as we know it – or knew it - is over. It's done. Without changing what we do, now and completely, there is no future for the human race. Einstein wasn't wrong when he said insanity is doing the same thing over and over again and expecting different results. But I am here today to give you hope…….to remind you that it does not have to be like this……..to offer up solutions.'

Then, switching into a more reflective gear, she asked: 'Do you ever look at the world and think to yourself, where are we going? You may, on a personal level, have considered this big question, but what about humanity? Who are we? What is our purpose? How will we be fulfilled? Surely the point of our being is not to toil for a lifetime in order to enable a tiny percentage of super-rich individuals to have a ball at our expense? Surely the human race's destiny is something greater than that? Now is the time for us to evolve to our next level.

'Yes, we are nursing our final nightcap in the depths of drinking-up time at the last chance saloon, for sure, but, instead of walking out into a gunfight in which we all die, we must see the bigger picture, lay down our weapons of selfish ambition, embrace one another, let love in and collaborate in order to save ourselves and our world. We are now in a race against time and tomorrow no longer offers the promise of salvation. Let us make the shipwrecks of our past be our seamarks as we set sail for a new horizon, a new dawn. We must change, we must be brave and re-set. We can no longer live in a world of "us and them", of "me, me, me"; our future demands that we come together and that everything becomes about the "we, we, we". Now is the time for an empowered New One World cosmocracy to move us to our next evolutionary stage, to guide us through treacherous but not unnavigable seas. This is our carpe diem moment.'

The crowd could hold themselves back no longer and broke out in spontaneous applause, whistling and hollering. This is what they had come to hear. The promise of a near and brighter future. I didn't doubt for a moment that the whole event was being recorded for further dissemination across the internet.

'As our world becomes increasingly interconnected, it is blindingly obvious that we need international cooperation, organisation and direction to fix our burning issues -insuperable problems that individual nations cannot fix on their own. Of course, a world government could not remedy everything immediately but it is our last remaining hope for fixing border-blind crises.

'Let us start with the basics. Yes, there is much for a one world government to get its teeth into and it, not me, will quickly decide what the most pressing issues are. Our problems are not intractable. We need to keep things simple and address three fundamental issues, after which, if they are dealt with effectively, many of our other problems will become easier to untangle.

'Three things.

'How do we feed the world?

'How do we power the world?

'How do we eradicate disease?

'Implementing ethical and sustainable solutions to the first two concerns, we start to address the third, giving ourselves a foundation on which to level up living standards across the planet. By addressing these three questions, we start to ameliorate other difficulties such as ecological crises, poverty, pollution, crime, corruption and war. Many of these issues are intertwined; it will be the job of a NOW administration to carefully unravel and resolve them. When we pool the earth's collective resources with humankind's brainpower and indomitable spirit, the possibilities become endless. When we develop into the best version of ourselves, we will find we are an amazing species.'

A brief pause and then: 'Food, glorious food! There is nothing more fundamental to our existence than food. The big challenge for the world's scientists is how to provide a sustainable and healthy diet by the middle of this century for a world population of potentially nine billion people. How can we ensure the green growth of all countries, particularly developing ones, while simultaneously feeding the world? While climate change and irreversible degradation of biodiversity are threats to global security, so too is the risk of massive food shortages. Finding a balance will require the scale of thought and effort that, when pushed, we commit to international disasters. This is a global problem demanding international cooperation and alliances – particularly with, and for, developing countries, for whom the threat is most stark.

'Universities and government laboratories house food scientists, world-leading experts in plant science and genetics. When this expertise is brought together, expanded and properly utilised, we can start to enhance the life chances of the world's rising population without destroying the wonder and beauty of our natural world. It is going to require advances in farming techniques, improved irrigation, reduction of waste, better transportation and a change in our diets. In our hearts and minds too. Continuing to review and procrastinate over matters every few years at a showpiece UN COP conference will not be enough.

'Besides driving more planetary focus on the issue of food, there are simple adjustments that we can all make. Each year, the demand grows for more land to cultivate soy or soya. While it is used in many food products, from cooking oil to chocolate, it is predominantly used to fatten up cattle for slaughter. If we do not address our carnivorous diet over the next decade, we will need extra land covering the size of Hungary to grow soya for use in animal feed alone. Some efforts are being made to farm it sustainably, but still large swathes of the Amazon Rainforest continue to disappear, replaced by fields to grow the soya bean. Amidst this increasing demand, supply chains are difficult to trace and, as it is such a profitable business, desperate farmers are happy to go off the radar to cultivate the crop; for some, growing soya is now more profitable than growing heroin.

'So, the biggest issue that we need to confront? It is staring us in the face! Our consumption of meat. We need to eat better!' Again, the crowd broke out into spontaneous whistling, feet-stomping and cheering. At the same time, huge LED screens slowly lowered behind Candy, depicting emotive imagery of trees being felled and animals being slaughtered. Film clips and soundbites were adeptly choreographed across the whole of the evening, providing a visual backdrop to Candy's speech - scenes of flooding and forest fires, of war, poverty, sickness and famine but, also, where the narrative allowed, footage of hope – of thriving coral reef, of wind farms, lush vegetation, fields of solar panels, beautiful sunrises, majestic waterfalls generating hydro-electric power, pristine Arctic landscapes and crystal clear oceans populated by huge shoals of colourful fish.

As the yelling abated, Candy continued: 'And so I am going to say the thing that cannot be said! Across the world, we need to eat less meat. If the human race was to become vegan, we could change our destiny overnight! Eighty per cent of global farmland is currently dedicated to meat and dairy production; think of a land mass the size of the US, Europe, China and Australia combined. All this land given over to growing foodstuffs for animals not humans! All this terrain that could be forested and soaking up carbon. The impact is enormous. One sixth of all greenhouse gases come purely from livestock rearing.

'Yes, there will be those that say veganism is no perfect panacea. It is true that it too demands some soya production and almond cultivation, which entails large usage of water, but studies tell us that if we all went vegan by 2050, eight million deaths would be avoided. Is that not reason alone for every one of us to change our eating habits today? Are you prepared to change your diet to save a life?' Another rhetorical question, answered by whistles and hollering.

'Stopping eating meat is, of course, the ideal solution, both for our own health and our planet's. However, I am not naïve and I know this won't happen overnight. If people cannot give up meat, then they should at least cut down on their consumption of it; it is incumbent on us all to encourage people to eat less meat. Around the world, we are gradually seeing the emergence of vegan Mondays or vegetarian Tuesdays. All these little wins count. No-one can have a diet forced upon them but we need to explain to carnivores how their habits are killing us. For those that must eat animal flesh, then chicken rather than beef consumption is kinder on the planet. We need to be pragmatic but we need to stop brushing this question under the carpet and making excuses. Remember, it is always later than you think.

'Over a quarter of our planet's ice-free land is given over to cattle. Of all the mammals on earth, 60% are livestock, 36% are human and just 4% are wild. Take the US, where 41% of land is reserved for beef production - that's nearly half the country! The negative effects of cattle grazing are manifold. Aside from its devastating impact on our climate, which is the same as that of all cars, trucks and planes combined, forests are torn down, endangering plant and animal species and causing a proliferation of diseases transmitted to humans; water quality is compromised, polluting local rivers and accompanying eco-systems; and, regularly, cattle urine and faeces permeate our drinking water.

'To those that say a change in our food intake will never happen, I say they are wrong and that it is happening right now. Around the world veganism, pescetarianism and vegetarianism are growing rapidly! Estimates say 8% of the world is now vegan, vegetarian or following a largely vegetarian diet. This is certainly not being driven by any government, the transition comes from the people who realise what we need to do to live a healthier life and to save ourselves.

'Gradually things *are* changing. Even in the US, people are starting to embrace veganism. In 2014, just 1% of American citizens professed to be vegan, that figure now stands at 6% - that is a 600 per cent increase in a handful of years! In the US, veganism has always been interwoven with the American civil rights movement and black Americans are much more likely to be non-meat eaters or flexitarian than whites. I stand behind the words of Dick Gregory, a comedian and actor, who said: "Because I am a civil rights activist, I am also an animal rights activist. Animals and humans suffer and die alike. Violence causes the same pain, the same spilling of blood, the same stench of death, the same arrogant, cruel and vicious taking of life. We shouldn't be a part of it." Things are changing but not fast enough.'

Stopping briefly to catch her breath and to take a few circular steps to gather her thoughts, Candy then readjusted her microphone stand and moved on to her next point: 'So, secondly, how do we sustainably power our world? In the second half of the last century, we faced the threat of mutually assured destruction by nuclear weapons. Although that threat has not gone, the imminent danger now is environmental breakdown, caused by our usage of fossil fuels. If there's one clear reason for strong world governance, then surely it is to save our planet? The climate crisis threatens to undo us all. We should be on a war footing. If we are serious about reversing its devastation, then a NOW assembly is our last remaining hope. It is time, through directed global management, to rebalance our relationship with nature, ensuring measured utilisation of the world's finite resources.

'I don't need to preach to anyone here about how fossil fuels have been, and still are, wreaking environmental disaster. However, continents where the population is set to grow significantly this century, such as Africa and Asia, will need much more energy as they develop. Their per capita demand will increase and there will be 2 billion more people in these regions in the next thirty years. By the end of the century, five of the top ten most populous countries in the world will be in Africa – namely Nigeria, Tanzania, The Democratic Republic of Congo, Egypt and Ethiopia. It's the trajectory of CO_2 emissions from these countries that is of critical importance to our planet. Quite simply, there is not enough land and resources on the earth for everyone to enjoy the same diet and livelihood as Western nations have done. If everyone consumed at the rate that Americans do, we would need five worlds to sustain ourselves. Highly culpable too are the likes of Australia, New Zealand, Canada, Argentina, France, Italy, the Republic of Ireland....I think you get the picture. Up and coming countries cannot be allowed to develop in the way that much of the West has. We must ensure that their growth is far greener than that of the first wave of industrialised countries and that we act, globally, on lessons learnt – they cannot be allowed to rape and pollute the planet all over again.

'Our continued reliance on fossil fuels is killing us. A properly functioning world government would be charged with addressing how we all live. Currently, millions die each year from pollution and from extreme weather, which, in turn, increases the spread of infectious disease as temperatures rise, and engenders food insecurity as arable land degenerates and disappears. As we know, some countries are beginning to set themselves the target of reducing net carbon emissions to zero, some even by 2050. But it is not enough. In the coming years, it is likely that the demand for electricity will double as it is needed for electric and hybrid vehicles and for electrolytic production of liquid and gas fuels such as hydrogen, methane and kerosene, which we will need for aviation fuel. All this is on top of an ageing population that is living longer and alongside a need to decarbonise existing electricity generation from coal and gas. What we desperately need are new ways of extracting more energy – with less wastage – from sunlight, wind, rivers and tides, as well as more efficient ways of storing it. And we need it now! The technology is there or almost there. It has been the choice of governments to underfund and underplay green technologies. They now need to step up to the plate. A NOW assembly would urgently oversee the pooling of scientific expertise, enabling us to supercharge our understanding and deployment of clean, renewable energy. If I had my way, this – and the devastation wreaked on poorer countries - would be paid for proportionately by those nations and companies that have polluted our world. That seems only fair.'

My God, if she only knew what I knew, I thought to myself.

'And there you have it – the two overriding problems threatening our planet – too much meat eating and our reliance on hydrocarbon fuels! Overcome these two issues and we start to deal with so many other problems.'

Again, spontaneous whooping from the assembled.

'When we sustainably feed and power the world, infectious diseases will be pared back. If we are intent on destroying nature – and it currently seems that we are – nature is going to fight back. It is already doing so. Man is not an island. It's pretty simple really, if we trash nature, we have no food and we destroy ourselves. Already we are seeing an increase in the rate of pandemics – think SARS, Ebola, HIV, swine flu and Zika. These are just warning shots and scientists predict, if we do not address the problem, we will see even nastier viruses and to an increasing extent. So far we have been in a game of Russian roulette – there have been several blank warning shots from a loaded gun but, as yet, we have avoided the bullet. New strains of diseases are multiplying, already at a rate of three a year, most of which we never hear of. If we continue as is, there might be as many as five serious ones per annum within the next decade. Many of these pandemics originate from our increasing proximity to animals. One more downside of deforestation: as we destroy natural habitats in order to graze cattle or grow soya for livestock, so we come into closer contact with wildlife. Animals that once lived exclusively in and off nature are increasingly turning up in urban areas, dislocated and in search of food. Faunae carry many diseases – three out of every four new infectious diseases found in humans come from animals.

'And, once a disease is established, it can spread like wildfire - proliferated by a progressively mobile world populace, which increasingly lives on top of one another in pullulating cities. The climate crisis exacerbates the problem of flooding, affording breeding grounds for mosquitoes, fleas and ticks that carry vector-borne disease. You can look upon the abundance of new viruses as nature delivering us an SOS. By changing our diet and reliance on fossil fuels, we would eradicate so many life-threatening epidemics. If we do not change our ways, ultimately, nature may have no choice but to send us an apocalyptic plague to expurgate us from the planet.

'We also court disaster through the selling of so-called exotic animals as pets or for traditional medicinal purposes. They are sold in wet markets or wildlife markets, environments which are notoriously dangerous, where stressed animals in stacked cages are likely to scratch or bite and humans can be contaminated through their faeces or urine or even just from the litter in their coop. Pangolins are exploited for their scales, snakes for their skins, tigers for their bones, rhinos for their horns. So many species are threatened - baby crocodiles, porcupines, scorpions, golden cicadas, sun bears, elephants, it is a long list. Sickeningly and unforgivably, sometimes these creatures are slaughtered in front of the paying customer.

'And so,' with a rapt audience hanging on her every word, Candy continued, 'when our diet and energy needs are catered for and we have started to address other issues, how will we be able to judge if we have been successful? We can do that through the psychologist Abraham Maslow's Hierarchy of Needs - often depicted as layers in the form of a pyramid.

'Firstly, as a basic staple and at the foundation of the triangle, humans require their physiological needs to be catered for, so the basics - food and clean water, clothing and shelter. Once we have this, we can start to think about our personal security and health, getting a job and maybe building up our resources, buying property even. At the next level in the pyramid, we seek out love and friendship and a sense of connection to the world. It is only then that we can enter the realm of self-esteem, of status and recognition. Finally, if all our other needs are satisfied, we can ascend to the pinnacle and aspire to be the very best that we can be, what Maslow referred to as self-actualisation and transcendence. A NOW government would ensure that every world citizen can lay claim to achieving at least the first three levels of the pyramid. After that, well, it can't work miracles; then it will be down to the individual!

'Hey presto – all our problems solved and less than half of my allotted time used up! What else can I talk to you about? Oh, I know,' said Candy, teasingly, 'shall I explain how we get there and how we can all become happy in the process?'

Shouts, cheers and whistles of encouragement.

'We get there by peaceful worldwide protest and by spreading the word about the NOW proposition, through the adoption of world federalism and by then moving towards the Nordic model of egalitarian capitalism. Let me explain.

'So, who do we need to convince, fight against even, to get the overwhelming majority of people on our side? As the aphorism goes, the only thing to fear is fear itself. Once we explain and disseminate our message, we will quickly have the young with us and the intelligentsia and all those well-meaning, righteous activists that have been campaigning and demonstrating for decades: the green campaigners; the anti-fascists; the anti-racists; the anti-war protesters; those marching for human rights and freedom and against austerity, nuclear bombs, corruption, inequality and oppression. People like you! Your time is coming! Our numbers are growing rapidly and NOW marches are proliferating – in frequency and size - in cities across the globe. My election as a Danish MP is just the beginning. Soon we will hold World Unification Day – simultaneous strikes and demonstrations across the planet and on that day everything will come to a stop. The world will not have seen anything like it. It will make the 2003 anti-Iraq war marches look like a gathering on a street corner. Without the workers, the world stops. At that point, politicians will look up and acknowledge us. Once the financial markets start plunging, our issues will be addressed quickly enough!' A huge roar filled the auditorium.

'Of course, not everyone will be on our side. Right now there are many obstacles and blockers inimical to our campaign. Those in protected high positions, which they have often achieved through foul means or pure luck: the good fortune of being born in the right part of the world, in the right country, in the right town, often in the right part of town and into the right family. These privileges, inherited through birth, mean a select few end up with the best upbringing and diet, a superior education and the right connections. For these people, the current system works just fine, some even salve their conscience by sporadic benevolence, charity and altruism. And these people are so well entrenched, so well defended, it is virtually impossible to knock them off their golden perch. Money talks as they buy security, eminent lawyers and the best accountants to cook the books in their favour. I've always found it perplexing how so few privileged people can so effectively subjugate the masses and run the world. They have sold us a lie and it needs exposing. Trust me, these people are not going to relinquish their power, their grip on things, without a hell of a struggle. Why would they?

'But we will do this peacefully, in the tradition of Gandhi and Martin Luther King. We still need to galvanise those people that fear change, that worry about losing the precious little that they already have and are shackled by inhibiting nationalism. Those under the thrall of right-wing parties, for sure, but also we need to battle against those that are lost, a disaffected generation that have become removed from reality and, having been virally fed dangerous misinformation, jump from one crazy conspiracy theory to the next. Studies tell us that 50% of Americans think like this.

'And while we are talking conspiracy theories, we need to battle too, the paranoia of religious extremists. Those who talk wildly of secret Luciferian sects plotting a new world order – oh wait a minute,' Candy permitted herself a wry smile, 'wouldn't that be us? Those that believe there is a long line of connected and hidden societies agitating against the Christian God and against their precious, man-made religion. Did you know, they even attempt to trace this as far back as ancient Babylon and the story of the building of the Tower of Babel, when man defied God and tried to assert his governance on the world? Their story tells how Pantheism was kept alive through recondite lineage - by the Philosophers, the Kabbalists and the Gnostics and then, so they say, the reins were taken up by the Knights Templar and subsequently the Rosicrucians who passed it on through Freemasonry, right through to the esoteric Illuminati today. An Illuminati that is rumoured to have been responsible for the French Revolution and to have included, at one time or another, such members as Galileo, Goethe, Thomas Jefferson, Percy Bysshe

Shelley, Mary Shelley, Karl Marx and Leonardo da Vinci. Modern day members supposedly include – and please don't laugh - Donald Trump, Barack Obama, Justin Bieber, Lady Gaga and Madonna. I do so hope they are right, it makes for such a wonderful story! When they start saying I am a member too then I will truly know that I have arrived!

'Sometimes I am asked the question, can world federalism actually work? I always answer with a resounding yes; of course it can! We are reminded of this every day through extant nations such as Germany, Canada, the US, India, Brazil, Switzerland, Russia, Nigeria, Australia and many, many more. Countless countries around the world are actually made up of distinct regions, states or counties. And in many cases, these regions govern themselves with a fair degree of autonomy and success. Let's consider the United States as a prime example of how federalism can work over a continent-sized area and against the odds. Despite opposition from anti-federalists who said it would never work, the constitution was agreed upon in Philadelphia in 1787. Granted, it has had its ups and downs since gaining independence from the British – the sacking of the Capitol in 1812, the Gold Rush, the American Civil War, a couple of World Wars either side of the Great Depression – but it still endures. Central government takes care of the big issues and individual states their own local concerns. Many governments around the world successfully operate using this model.

'Two hundred years after Philadelphia, Europe followed suit when the EU formed, out of the ashes of the EEC. The collapse of the Soviet Union and the flattening of the Berlin Wall in 1989 paved the way for European Monetary Union, for East Germany and then other former communist countries to ally with the rest of Europe. The implosion of the USSR reminded us how very much not to do it - that you cannot successfully run a federalist bloc in perpetuity through a dictatorship over vassal states. Power needs to be disseminated equally amongst constituent parts. The EU, whilst it has its imperfections, is making a much better stab at federalism. The UK's decision to leave will prove a costly mistake. The narrow vote was won by the old – those with their head in a world that no longer exists and most likely never did. The young wanted to remain in Europe for they can see the future and how the world and its people are merging. In time – and after some considerable pain to the poorest - the UK will choose to re-join, of that I am quite sure.

'So, working on the federalist model, we will scale up; our planet will be our country and nations will become the world's counties. Each will retain its own political system, although I would hope that there will be a gradual transition towards liberal democracy. Studies show that countries where there is more government involvement and a strong welfare state are the happiest nations on earth. People live more prosperously and contentedly in nations where they are insulated from the ups and downs of the market economy. With politicians having to think internationally, they will need to have half an eye on the bigger picture and to consider longer-term planning; they will no longer be constrained by short-termism and narrow party tramlines. No doubt there will always be amoral candidates seeking office and occasionally they will be catapulted onto the national platform but NOW will ensure their influence on the global stage is much more limited than currently is the case. I am confident it will give rise to a nobler politician, weeding out those that are in it for the power and money and to further their own interests and profile - those who look to retire into a life of after-dinner speeches, lobbying and consulting sinecures with blue chip companies.

'Each and every day I thank Buddha that I have the honour of guiding the NOW movement, the first pan-world political group, and of being its first elected representative. As we continue to grow, I know we will see many more of our members take up office. Whilst priority number one is the installation of a federal world government, we will, of course, continue to press our own party agenda. One of the key tenets of which is the eradication of poverty. Something that would make a lot of people happier.

'There is no magic bullet for solving poverty but a world parliament would be uniquely positioned to mitigate many of its drivers. It would be able to hold to account those nations that do not provide adequate infrastructure such as education, healthcare and social welfare. Funds would be freed up for these areas, when, as a result of moving to green energy, money is no longer being spent on dealing with the devastating effects of climate change. Likewise, the poor would benefit from a new world order's focus on combatting infectious disease. So too, from its battle against crime and corruption. These matters need a global approach; they cannot be fixed unilaterally. We must work together today in order to secure a better tomorrow.

'We know from the past that the world can come together for the common good – think about the ending of World War Two, the suppression of smallpox and the reduction in the size of the ozone hole. For the last twenty five years or so, it has actually been the case that, globally, extreme poverty has been reducing. In 1990 there were 1.9 billion people in dire straits. Since then, despite the world population growing by more than 2 billion, the number in destitution has fallen by two thirds and now stands at 689 million. However, in the last couple of years, this decrease has slowed – and in some areas it is reversing. Why, you may ask? A major reason is conflict - 40% of the world's poor live in war-torn regions. Take, for example, North Africa and the Middle East, where poverty has doubled in the last two years as a result of conflicts in Syria and The Yemen. A strong world government would take decisive action to deal with such situations and, as a consequence, to reduce poverty.

'We can also help the destitute by adjustments in macro-economics. In the coming years, we will need to temper the excesses of our current economic system if we are to reduce inequality and save our planet. The cracks in the capitalist model are already showing. Its overarching problem is its reliance on the insatiable consumption of the world's finite reserves. Oil is set to run out within my lifetime and our supplies of fresh water and minerals are dwindling. If we are reliant on a system that means we need to buy more and more items, whether we need them or not, at an ever-increasing rate every year, then the system is broken. We need global governance to protect our limited resources and international collaboration to develop new ways of thinking, of production and, as I have already said, of delivering sustainable energy – in other words, to create a regenerative economy.

'Right now, if the economy does not keep growing - and growing quickly - then some very tough times are ahead of us. Capitalism relies on the notion that we are all working for a rosier future but these dreams are beginning to tarnish as wage levels stagnate. For the first time in history, it increasingly looks less likely that our children will enjoy a better life than ourselves, and we are depleting, to the point of exhaustion, our resources. Not to mention, careering blindly into climate catastrophe. The tipping point is now.

'Friends, let us consider capitalism for a moment. Allow me to play devil's advocate and say that it was just what we needed to jolt us out of thousands of years of living short and precarious lives, first as hunter-gatherers in tribes and then in serfdom. Capitalism was, of course, made possible because of the industrial revolution and developments in mechanisation combined with improved maritime capability and weaponry which allowed nations, the Dutch and British particularly, to start trading routes around the world and to create stock exchanges and, well, the rest we know.

'One of the ways that the Dutch financed their expeditions was by selling "shares" in their companies. The bigger your investment, the larger the share of profits you were entitled to. If you thought a company was going to make a big profit but it had already sold all it shares, you could still buy them from people who owned them but probably at a higher price than their original value. If the company ended up not doing so well, then you could try and sell your shares but, chances were, this was going to be at a lower rate than what you bought them for. The trade in company shares led to the setting up of exchanges across Europe. And so it began. A system was put in place that we are still trying to understand today. I heard an academic say recently that whilst we spend billions on researching the origins of the universe, we still do not understand the conditions for a stable society, a functioning economy and peace. Sir Isaac Newton, who lost a fortune in the first financial crisis with the bursting of the South Sea Bubble, famously said that whereas he could understand the motions of heavenly bodies he could not fathom the madness of people.

'Even though modern capitalism was up and running by the start of the nineteenth century, for many, life had not changed dramatically and a Greek or Roman would still have been able to recognise large parts of society as late as 1900. However, this was all about to change with the advent of the twentieth century. The world exploded in a dizzying kaleidoscope of new contraptions and we were propelled forward at an unrelenting rate into the modern era: cars, aeroplanes, ocean liners, skyscrapers, trains, radio, TV and film, leisure time, space travel, the nuclear bomb, the pc, antibiotics, pop music, the internet, mobile phones, social media, disinformation and a million other things.

'And there has been a gradual acceptance of capitalism – but in many different flavours. Think of all the countries in recent history that have moved over to this economic system, partially or wholly, or who are in the process of doing so. I am thinking of the likes of Russia, China, East Germany, Hungary, Poland, the Czech Republic, Afghanistan and so many more. It is not that long ago that one third of the world was under the spell of Karl Marx. We do, however, have something of a paradox on our hands. There was once a widely held belief that for capitalism to work, you needed to be a democracy, but China and Russia have shown this not to be the case. Russia is now the most unequal nation on earth. A statistic to impress any die-hard capitalist.

'Right now almost 60% of the world's countries are democracies, the highest percentage it has ever been, and only 13% are outright autocracies – but it is worth remembering that a third of the world still lives in authoritarian or semi-autocratic nations. Since 1970, the global economy has grown four-fold, while international trade has increased ten times over. Yet, whilst some people have prospered under capitalism, many, many more have suffered. Across the planet, there are vast disparities of wealth and these are escalating.

'As capitalism races along at a breakneck pace, occasionally, like in the case of Isaac Newton, we are reminded that it is an imperfect system as it implodes due to a lack of regulation of the markets or excessive debt or over-optimism. This boom and bust cycle has accelerated and been punctuated by a number of disastrous troughs in the last 100 years: the Wall Street Crash, which triggered the Great Depression back in the 1930s; Black Monday in 1987; the Dotcom bubble burst; and, of course, after the 2008 financial meltdown.

'We have extricated ourselves from recent crises by pumping trillions of dollars, euros and yen of cheap credit into the system. Before the bubble bursts, we need the next big thing to come along to fuel the flames of abundance of the capitalist fire. The pressure is on our scientists, engineers, inventors and entrepreneurs to come up with something fresh, perhaps a new discovery in AI or bio- or nano-technology that will create new industries, markets and wealth. Something to back the make-believe money created by banks and governments.

'Recessions are increasing in regularity; speeding up like everything else in the world. We await the next one. And, given how all the world markets are so inter-linked through technology, such collapses are more dangerous than ever; something that was first witnessed in the meltdown of Black Monday. Today's world is even more networked and is controlled by surprisingly few "players". A recent report computed there are about 43,000 transnational corporations. These businesses have many shareholders but, essentially, when we start to boil things down, the world's top 737 shareholders control 80% of the revenue of these transnationals. The top 49 companies were exclusively banks, insurance companies and financial institutions with the one exception being Wal-mart. So, not actual producers of anything, just people that push other people's money around. It seems the old saying that money makes the world go round is indeed true. In separate studies that tell a similar story, Oxfam found that 8 individuals own the same amount of wealth as half the world. A NOW government would, I am sure, seek to redress such unjust imbalances. Only the most diehard of capitalists could baulk at this.

'But then this cuts to the very heart of capitalism; it has always meant that whilst there will be a handful of winners, there will be many losers. Now is the time to move beyond this mentality. We must all be on the winning team. Don't get me wrong, I am not advocating a world communist state, let's face it, it has not proved a utopia for the USSR, China or North Korea. But I do think it is time to adopt a much more egalitarian approach. It is time to recognise that it is much better to bring everyone along with us, rather than leave "the weak" behind. The only way to police the squandering of natural resources and potential global conflicts is through a collectivist, unified world government. The critical factor in all of this is that this central body is not a dictatorship, each country or state, has to elect its own representatives. This is not Communism or Fascism or Totalitarianism. As my friend Bono once said, "We are one, but we are not the same."

'It is clear that capitalism is going to need reigning in; a steady hand on its tiller. Ultimately, I can't help thinking that once good governance is in place, globally people will come round to the progressive notion of more state intervention. The world federalist administration will, hopefully, take inspiration from Scandinavian countries where there is slightly more, rather than slightly less, involvement from government. These are nations that place a high value on education and vocational training, that operate generous welfare programmes while offering high standards of healthcare and nursery facilities, cheap leisure and sports facilities and good pensions for all. They are largely corruption-free and are not run for the 1%. And, just for good measure, they also lead the world in terms of the percentage of gross national income given over to foreign aid spending. It is no coincidence that the five Nordic countries plus Switzerland and The Netherlands are always ranked highly in league tables based on factors such as lifespan, health, happiness, life-satisfaction, belief in democracy, wellbeing and safety.

'Of course, the question of how much the state regulates is a thorny one and defines many of the political parties across the world. Absolute capitalists are only interested in profit and have no interest in social good or caring for the environment – indeed they espouse keeping spending in these areas in check as much as possible. They champion Adam Smith's construct in *The Wealth of Nations* that egoism is altruism - that the selfish streak of man drives him to make more profit, which in turn benefits others. However, thankfully, all capitalist economies are tempered by varying degrees of state intervention that deal with the worst excesses of free market economies. No country in the world as ever achieved a full-on free market economy. Governments must provide a welfare state preventing absolute poverty, they need to collect taxes for infrastructure, education, policing and healthcare. They must, in theory at least, introduce legislation which guarantees workers' rights and guards against environmental pollution.

'There is growing evidence that, in terms of stability, managed capitalism, or what used to be called welfare capitalism, triumphs over the market capitalism that became fashionable after the likes of the UK and the US adopted it when Thatcher and Reagan came to their respective helms in the 1980s. Putting some historical context on this, from 1950-1973, the world did not have a single year when economic growth was less than 3%. There were no depressions or bust periods. From 1980 onwards, there have, according to the IMF, been five global recessions. In the UK, the lowest ever unemployment rates, at 1.6%, came under managed capitalism during the 1950s and 1960s. Ever since the '80s and the introduction of market capitalism, both the US and UK have suffered from a lack of investment in research and development and in fixtures, fittings and machinery. These are the hallmarks of a laissez-faire attitude to capitalism. Likewise, this century, social mobility in both these countries has virtually stalled.

'Capitalism is also driven by a belief in perpetual economic development and we have certainly seen exponential growth over the last 250 years. But, ultimately – and it is now becoming alarmingly obvious - this logic flies in the face of everything we know. Our resources are virtually used up. When we set out on a camping expedition, we only have a certain amount of provisions and we know that we need to make them last for the entire excursion, we cannot just have a mad binge on the first night and leave ourselves nothing for the remainder of the trip. Likewise, the materials and energy, upon which capitalism depends, are finite. What is the world going to do when we run out of reserves? How are we going to deal with the chaos of climate change and pollution that unregulated capitalism is creating? Because the world's economy is inextricably entwined with our ecological breakdown, it must change.

'For too long we have been driven by the ideology that we can only make progress through perpetually competitive capitalism. It is now clear that, going forwards, this is not a sustainable model. We need a holistic approach in order to avoid international social, environmental and economic collapse. We need a plan in place for how to manage the transition to another way of living. We cannot promote consumerism indefinitely. It is time to wave bye-bye to a buy, buy ethos. There is a maxim that says that you can only make sense of life looking backwards but you can only live life going forwards. Well perhaps now is the time for us to challenge that saying, to pause and take stock: to assess where we are at, how we got here and where we want to go as a species? How do we shift to a new world through a planned strategy predicated on decarbonisation? How do we manage the world's resources in a manner that benefits us all, not just a few rich industrialists in a handful of countries? Rampant capitalism is not our end goal, it cannot be; it was merely a stepping stone to take us to a properly organised, diverse, fair and philanthropic world.

'Study after study shows that there is a positive relationship between welfare state policies and happiness. This is what, as nations, we need to strive for. Individually too we can make changes. The pursuit of wealth and "keeping up with the Joneses" does not make us happy. Contentment is found in helping others, through friends and family, in nature and exercise and in health. Long term, intellectual pursuits are mentally more rewarding than making money. We have come to learn that the extremes of free-market economies, pollution and materialism inflict misery on us all.

'Otherwise, what? What is the natural conclusion? It is staring us in the face, personified by a vain, greedy, self-serving, morally bankrupt clown running the most powerful nation on earth. A grotesque caricature of capitalism. A vitriolic racist who denies climate change, is incapable of empathy for others and is capricious and dilettante in his policies, which he chaotically rolls out on Twitter.

'The USA, where there is much less government intervention, serves as an instructive counterpoint to the Nordics. Its infrastructure is gradually disintegrating. Roads, bridges, airports, schools, power lines, tunnels, water pipes, dams, inland waterways, all need fixing. Four in 10 Americans face material hardship, pitiful amounts are spent on social care, half a million are homeless, suicide rates increase each year, public transport is lacklustre, 25 million people don't have broadband access and up to a quarter of the population are delaying their healthcare needs. A recent UN study found that the US ranks 24th in the world in terms of meeting its wellness goals; last year, 27 million Americans went the entire year without any health insurance and, as a result, 45,000 die each year while Trump continues to pare back Obamacare. America has a huge problem with drug abuse; 70,000 people died last year from the ravages of it and even Trump declared the opioid addiction a shameful national emergency. There is rampant crime in many cities and their gaols are overrun with more people in prison per capita than any other country in the world; 5% of all Americans will spend some time incarcerated and right now 0.7% of the entire population is locked up! This is a capitalist dystopia - a living exemplar of what stares us in the face when we permit unregulated free markets. We cannot let our world become like this!

'And of course, the US is riddled with another of capitalism's big problems – corruption. Essentially, the world is run by legislators who are lobbied by institutions and wealthy individuals, who buy favours from them. Cronyism arises as politicians so often have stakes in companies or sectors. Again, back to America, the so-called land of opportunity but actually one of the most corrupt of first world nations. If you need evidence that profit comes before people, think only of the gun lobby and the US's inexplicable inability to see the link between regular mass shootings and gun laws. Think too of the billions of pounds that have been spent by the oil and gas industry on lobbying political figures and marketing their so-called green credentials. This is an accepted and everyday part of US life. The mess that America is in, and the thrall in which capitalism holds it, could not be better illustrated than the fact that, unbelievably and deeply disturbingly, one third of the US Congress denies we even have a climate crisis. This is a nation that has pulled out of the Paris Climate Agreement. A nation that has somehow equated being green with being un-American!

'We need to save America from itself and, right now, the world from becoming like America. It is clear that their problems begin at the very top of the pyramid. Excuse me while I go off-piste and get this off my chest but a man like Trump should never have been allowed anywhere near governmental office. If the disreputable behaviour of some statesmen give the whole industry a bad name then Trump truly is the epitome of this and is everything that we abhor in our politicians. When you run a nation properly, the idea is that you try to do so on behalf of all its citizens, but Trump runs it for himself. And then we wonder why, in so many first world states, more than half of people do not believe their country is being run for the benefit of all? He is the ultimate archetype - a narcissistic, manipulative, duplicitous, dishonest, infantile, shape-shifting, mendacious, egotistical, cold, corrupt, vengeful, fatuous, xenophobic bully.' Candy was forced to halt, drowned out, as the audience exploded again.

'The very fabric of democracy is being emaciated as he appoints friends, family and sycophants to critically important roles. Here is a man who openly lies and gets away with it. Certainly those Americans that elected him need to take a step back and ask themselves some serious questions; meanwhile, the rest of the world needs to consider how countries can work together to deal with, work around and surmount crooks like Trump. The only positive that I can see is that he is, inadvertently, bringing the rest of the world together in their loathing and ridiculing of him as they try and decipher the US' unhinged and inconsistent foreign policy. He is the personification of how not to run a country, the very last person you need in charge of the world's most powerful nation as we strive to create a better world. America is gradually surrendering its position of supremacy. His presidency is a rude slap in the face - a wake-up call for us all.

'Right now, and bear with me on this because it is hard to believe, despite all its human rights abuses, China is seen to conduct itself with more dignity and diplomacy on the world stage than the US. At a recent Davos gathering, President Xi Jinping made a speech championing Chinese global leadership which was surprisingly well received. This is where the world is heading, I think we all know that. It accounts for one fifth of the world's population and social mobility is much more prolific in China than the US. Over the past 30 years, the wages of the least economically prosperous half of the population in the US have stagnated; in China, over the same period, wages and prosperity have grown at the highest rate at any time in the Common Era. Whilst China spends heavily on infrastructure, the US procrastinates. As China grows alliances, networks and friendships, the US continues to behave erratically, showing itself unwilling or incapable of leadership or even as a reliable ally, friend or trading partner. Anti-American sentiment in Europe and the Middle East grows, not to mention Latin America, Africa, where Trump referred to countries as "shitholes", and Canada. Across the map in South America, the US is roundly hated for its history of behind the scenes propping up of right-wing dictators and drug kingpins in its paranoia of socialism and communism. Last year there was the first drop in student visa applications to the USA this century, including from their largest suppliers, China and India. And, let's not forget, China, for all its problems, is racing ahead of the US on developing green technologies.

'So, what has gone wrong in the US and how do we put it right? Well, let's not give up hope just yet. Wasn't it Winston Churchill that said after trying every other alternative, Americans can always be counted on to do the right thing?

'The point I am making? Please, when we transition to a world federalist government, let's work towards it being one based on the Nordic model rather than the laissez-faire capitalism of the US.

'My people, hear me, we do move incrementally to a New One World government! It is the blindingly logical next step in our evolution. No longer can we afford to say that it will never work, we must now ask how do we make it work? Our time of competing against one another is drawing to a close. Long term, does a business or government or any enterprise work best with all departments at each other's throats or when there is synergy as they support and encourage one another? Likewise, it is rare for a sports team to be at their optimum if there are internal tensions. As a football fan, I always remember France, despite having wonderful individual players, imploding at the 2010 World Cup because of disagreements in the squad. Too many individuals doing their own thing does not allow for the best results. It is the same in world politics.

'Only a NOW administration will allow us to deal with looming existential crises. If this does not happens, then we will be the species that started off as cave dwellers and ended up there too. Even now, with seven and a half billion people on the planet, there *is* enough food, resources, raw materials, infrastructure and knowhow for us all to live well. Only when individuals come together and work as one, as a slick, efficient machine will optimum results be achieved. Imagine the heights we can reach when scientists, engineers, law-makers, inventors and countries cooperate and work together and do not have economic, personal or geo-political tensions to blindside them. It is then that we will start to fix our problems of hunger and disease and of generating sustainable energy. With the basics in place, an empowered world government can start to bring an end to war and famine and help resolve the refugee problem. It will oversee our transition to a liberally democratic cosmocracy.

'The future will be a place where we realise the importance of *every* life and care about *every* life. Our planet is a lot smaller than we imagine and all life really does matter. Earlier, I said that the number of those in destitution had reduced to 689 million, as if this was an achievement but, given our capabilities, this is a catastrophe! Somehow, as we have watched wars break out and humanitarian tragedies unfold on our screens, we have become inured to this! We have learnt to deal with it by pretending that these pictures are from another world, not connected to ours, and that somehow these people are a sub-species. We need to throw off the blanket of lethargy that enshrouds us now is the time to reawaken our collective sense of empathy and caring. We do not have to put these things out of our mind. In fact, the opposite is true - they need to be at the very forefront of our thinking. These disasters are just a few hours' flight away and involve real people that are often in desperate situations that could have easily been avoided by foresight and better world governance. It is pure happenstance that means it is "them" not "us".

'The time is over for negativity and reluctant acceptance of how our world is. Things do change - even if people think they don't – and, believe me, we are going to ensure they change dramatically. Yes, we are in the final days of the old world order, about to jump off into a better, enlightened, richer, fairer and more peaceful world. It is not a question of if but when; we truly stand on the precipice in terms of climate change. We humans have a tendency to put things off - a mañana approach on both a personal and macro level - but the time for change is upon us, not hundreds of years away but now! Right. Fucking. Now!'

More raucous feedback from the crowd before Candy began her final summation: 'Let us make sure that we are not the generation that lets the world slip through its fingers. We kid ourselves that from the baby boomers onwards we have been the lucky ones, untouched by war and constantly progressing but, all along we have been quietly presiding over the destruction of our planet – death by a thousand cuts. It can't be that no-one is to blame so that makes us all culpable. Everyone is either part of the problem or part of the solution. Ask yourself now, where do you stand? Whose side are you on?

'Our planet's problems are just too big for individuals or solitary nations to solve. A new global parliament will embrace all countries and the rich spread of humanity. World Law will bring justice for all and help maintain a peaceful, sustainable future. Local problems can be dealt with at a local level, we will not impugn the sovereignty of any nation-state. But, of course, even local actions must be balanced against the interests of the planet.

'And, longer term, be big and imagine a borderless world, ultimately perhaps one currency and one language, who knows? One World Assembly, one army, one legal system, one progressive educational system - united minds focussing on development, diet, sustainability and combatting climate change. Imagine a quick and coordinated response to natural disasters and disease – a world where people don't go hungry or thirsty. A world where aggressors are no longer tolerated. A world which would be better placed to explore the solar system and, if the need should arise, to defend ourselves. Imagine what we could truly become with us all pulling together in the same direction.

'As I said, it is a long way to the light but I do believe that we edge there, crisis by crisis, experience making the collective human mind just that little wiser.

'Trust me, we have everything we need in abundance on this planet to make meaningful and pleasant lives for us all, yet somehow we conspire to snatch defeat from the jaws of victory. If we do not have the intelligence nor will to arrange our matters propitiously then we are doomed and we get all that we deserve.

'But, ultimately, I am an optimist. Yes, as a species we can sometimes underestimate ourselves but I truly believe humans have the potential to be incredible. When we finally all come together, we will find that the possibilities are endless. These are extraordinary times; as night ends, a new dawn is emerging.

'Are you with me?' Candy demanded of the audience. She paused and judging by the whooping and yelping, they were.

'Are you with me?' she asked again, the inflection in her voice rising further.

The crowd upped its response as a huge acquiescent roar went up.

Spent, punching the air and exiting the stage, her last words were: 'This is our moment. Go out there and spread the word. March with NOW and help change the world. Remember, the human race is bigger than cultures, ideologies and races. Our fate is on a knife-edge; it is being decided right now.' The reverb had been turned on so that the word 'now' boomed out repetitively into the auditorium.

The rhapsodic audience, like a football crowd, chanted something in Danish along the lines of: 'We want a new world government. When do we want it? Now!' and our mobile phones, like echo chambers, were flooded with love hearts and NOW soundbites.

And then, much to my surprise, the homily was over and the gig ended with Candy performing three of her hits; I'd momentarily forgotten that she was a rock star too. The crowd loved it and was soon bouncing but I was decidedly underwhelmed and took refuge at the bar while the walls shook, the floor pulsed and the auditorium sweated. I'd never seen anything quite like this, it was a political rally like no other. Pop stars taking over the world, whatever next? Candy, of course, performed the obligatory encore, an emotive cover of Patti Smith's 'People Have the Power' and once she had left the stage, the crowd fell into an exhortation of: 'If not now? When?' Even the lights coming up could not dampen the febrile atmosphere. As Fat Boy Slim's 'Right Here, Right Now' played as the outro music, people seemed genuinely invigorated and excited as they poured out into the cold Copenhagen evening.

Chapter 18

5 February 2018

I had arranged to meet Candy later that evening, post-gig, in the touristy Nyhavn or New Harbour district, where brightly painted canal-side restaurants and bars offered snug, *hygge* sanctuary from the biting wind and slate skies. Candy did not know me from Adam. I thought it unlikely that she would recall me from the funeral but I had referenced our both being at it and, for ease, claimed Angelina as a journalistic colleague and friend. I explained that I had important information relating to Angelina's death and that it might also benefit the NOW cause; this bought me the chance of a brief drink with her.

I arrived early at *Cap Horn* and nursed a ridiculously expensive malt, gradually thawing out by the roaring fire and perusing the maritime memorabilia. Moving to the bar, I glanced the tempting menu of seasonal, homemade, organic offerings and fresh fish and flicked through a free English magazine depicting a myriad of visitor attractions and diversions. Hoping to remain low profile, I had purposely not announced myself on arriving. I had a notion that I might go and visit Geir next and was just contemplating an advertisement for ferry trips to Oslo when, out of nowhere, the middle of the magazine erupted in flames and I stepped backwards, expleting as the young waiter floated over with a glass of water to calmly extinguish the fire. It turned out I had held the gazette over a tray of t-lights on the bar. So much for not drawing attention to myself. As the kerfuffle subsided, attention turned away from me to a small commotion at the door of the restaurant as an animated Candy Kitcatt and entourage of three arrived. Several people seemed to recognise her and heads started turning, a mark of her growing notoriety I suppose. I was about to stand up to greet her as my phone pinged. I glanced down just in time to clock that it was an email sent by Angelina entitled: '*I Hoped I'd Never Have to Send This*'. I swear my heart stopped. How could this be? We'd only buried her a few days ago. Reeling, needing to take stock and moments from having to introduce myself to Candy, I threw back my whisky, upped, hoping now she wouldn't recognise me from the funeral and walked straight past her, head down, and out into the sub-zero iciness. Solvitur ambulando, I thought to myself, solvitur ambulando.

As a post-script to my Copenhagen visit, a week or so later Mad Lizzie was found dead of a suspected overdose.

Chapter 19

7 February 2018

I was surprised at the high-profile rendezvous they had proposed: *Harry's Bar* in Venice. They'd paid for my flight and accommodation and were now standing the drinks at this world-renowned bar, which had served luminaries such as Ernest Hemingway, Charlie Chaplin, Woody Allen, Alfred Hitchcock and George Clooney. More impressive to me was that Evelyn Waugh had used it in *Brideshead Revisited* as the 'English Bar' in which Charles Ryder and Sebastian Flyte had spent a lot of their time. There was a perverse logic, I suppose, in that such a glaringly obvious venue provided a kind of unexpected cover. No better place to hide than in plain sight and all that. And, well, at least its windows were frosted out!'

With Bellini cocktails in hand, what else, we – that is me and two middle-aged, male, faceless and rain-coated American banker types - found ourselves a quieter corner in the unexpectedly small but effortlessly elegant bar. The sedate, timeless ambiance - all dark wood, leather seats and Art Deco trim – lent gravitas to our hushed conversation. I never did catch their names so let's call the Yanks, Laurel and Hardy. I couldn't help thinking I had seen one of them somewhere else.

'Well, Mr Boocock, I assume you have been to Venice before?' said Mr Hardy, the more portly of the two coiffured goons.

'As it goes, no I haven't. It's quite a place isn't it? Few places live up to their hype but, so far, this does.'

'Sure does. Well worth an evening climb to the top of the Campanile as the sun sets to take it all in from 100 metres.'

'Yes, I might just do that. I've already stood with the bronze horses and watched the world go by from the balcony of St Mark's.'

'Ah, yes, do you know their story?' chipped in Mr Laurel. 'The ones on the balcony are replicas; I trust you saw the originals inside the church? They were made in Greece, taken by Nero to Rome and then installed in Constantinople by Constantine when it became his and the Roman Empire's new capital. Venetians brought them back to their city after one of the crusades and they were placed above the main entrance to St Mark's Basilica where they served as a totemic backdrop to the incumbent Doge's speeches. Six hundred years later they were conveyed to Paris after Napoleon took a shine to them before, finally, being returned to Venice after he succumbed to the British at Waterloo.'

'Yes, a fine example of how the world keeps turning with one civilisation superseding the next and often appropriating and reinventing much of the former's buildings and cultural capital. As Echo and the Bunnymen once said "Nothing Ever Lasts Forever".' I wondered if they might bite at my bait of a subliminal allusion to a new world order.

'Echo who? Okay, never mind, let's get down to business. I trust you have the files of Talulah Dante, which, no doubt, you have viewed but, I hope, not made copies of?' Hardy's cadence changed as he sought to get things nailed.

'I have. And your side of the deal? Is that all in place?'

'Of course. As soon as you hand over the memory stick, I press a button and your annual tax free payments of $75,000 begin. You will be paid monthly into an offshore Isle of Man bank account, just like a salary if you like, $6,250 per month, inflation-linked, until the day you die.'

'And my house?'

'Well, that is for you to choose of course. Funds of $350,000 will be transferred into the same bank but a different account. That should buy you a nice little semi-detached in, how do you say it, Heb-den Bridge?'

'All good. I just need to know one thing before I hand over the USB stick.' After a brief, hanging silence I asked: 'Who was it that killed Angelina?'

'Ah yes, I believe she was somewhat precious to you wasn't she? In life, there are certain places that you simply should not poke your nose but some people just don't heed this truism; Angelina was, I am afraid, one of those people. Knowing what she knew about Benvido's death doomed her. The truthful answer as to who killed her is that I don't know. At least I don't know names but rumour has it that it was some local hoodlums – all brawn, no brain - hired out of Malaga. Who paid for the hit? I really couldn't say; someone above my pay grade would know that.'

'And blowing her up? Wasn't there a less conspicuous way of going about things?'

'Yes, that wasn't well-judged. I don't think that was the plan. Malaga, positioned where it is, is a drugs crossroads with dozens of gangs competing for turf there. Members tend to be younger and younger these days and come from many nationalities, so it is easy to hire brute strength and hitmen; they are cheap and difficult to trace but they don't always come with subtlety or brains. I believe the powers that be were none too impressed by how the Malagueños went about their business. That said, the killing looked so cockeyed, so damned amateurish it deflected suspicion away from it being state sanctioned.

'And so, if you will hand over the flash drive, I think we can conclude our business here and we can all….' Hardy's voice tailed away as the uber-slick, white tuxedoed and smiling waiter floated over to our table.

'Can I get you another round of drinks gentlemen?'

'Yes, same again all round,' I instantly batted back. May as well squeeze the Americans for all I can I thought to myself. Besides, I could never afford the drinks in here of my own accord. Well, at least I wouldn't have been able to up until the striking of the deal a moment or so ago.

'Okay, there you go,' I said placing the stick on the liveried napkin.

Hardy flicked open his iPad, opened an app and in the clicking of a couple of links made the first payment into my new offshore account. He passed me an envelope with all the banking accoutrements I would need and smiled: 'Now we have a deal. I know you won't backtrack on it or do anything silly. I don't think I need to spell out the consequences of that.'

The Americans had left by the time the waiter returned with the drinks. I savoured mine, contemplating what I had done, before quaffing theirs like pop. Things were going to get messy.

Excerpts from Jochen's Journal Part One

Chapter 1

I

3 February 2018

I had my worries about Zach from the very start. I had, of course, seen him several times aboard the *Esperanza* before I actually learnt who he was. I'd noticed him, from a distance, as he always looked as if he'd had a drink or two the night before; dishevelled, shiftless, a little beat up by life, shall we say? There was a slight stoop about him but he was still taller than me, possibly six foot if he took the trouble to straighten himself out. His face spoke of a hard life; it was pallid, lined and gaunt and his once black hair was now grey-flecked, making him look closer to forty than thirty. That said, he dressed quite well, if a little crumpled and looked in reasonable shape; no doubt he would have been alluring to some women – if they were attracted by the Rolling Stones kind of look. His slovenly disposition always brought to mind the Bob Dylan lyric: 'when you ain't got nothing, you got nothing to lose.'

When Ange did introduce him, I could immediately see that he was enamoured with her; physically recoiling when I slipped my arm around her. Up until the point I found them on deck together, Ange had remained puzzlingly silent over his presence. He gave me a limp handshake and was incapable of looking me straight in the eye – although that was partly because he couldn't avert his gaze from Ange. He clearly had no interest in me, my research or field of work. I found his explanation of how he came to be on the expedition a little spurious. As far as I could ascertain, his curriculum vitae didn't quite match his posting. However, I reasoned, it was unlike Greenpeace to not perform due diligence so I initially let the matter slide. Over time, it became clear to me that he was what the Americans might refer to as suffering from *moral turpitude* and was indeed a drunk. I can only assume he brought his own stash of liquor with him as alcohol was carefully rationed on the trip. I know – through personal experience – that in the galley he had an infantile trick of sneakily turning up the toaster so that it burnt people's toasties and triggered the fire alarm, resulting in them having to buy a round of drinks in penance. This sort of summed him up. Previous to the Greenpeace expedition, Ange had mentioned him but only fleetingly, telling me their relationship had become untenable while at university due to his addiction to opiates and drink. As far as I could surmise, he had not changed much.

II

Before we set foot on the *Esperanza*, I had become aware of Ange's growing regard for the NOW movement and I knew she had been searching around, with scant reward, for a catalyst or scoop that might bolster their cause. She had firmly come to believe that the only way we were going to save the planet was through world federalism – through some kind of international government with strategic intent and ballast. All the evidence, for her, demonstrated that our present system was broken or at least unequipped to deal with the Gordian Knot of global issues that now faced us and the ineluctable changes that would need to be made to untie it. Too many governments, if not all, in her view, were too insular, only interested in their own immediate concerns.

However, the nights when we discussed the Global Ocean Treaty and the NOW proposition were nevertheless instructive. Prior to this, I had not realised quite how advanced Ange's thinking had become on the installation of a new world order or how passionate she was in her support of Candy Kitcatt. Up until then, Ange's world vision and my own had broadly aligned.

While there is logic to a new one-world government, I cannot see us ever getting there. It is very possibly where we need to go, but, for me, it is a race we are doomed to lose. The world is already riven by conflict – socialism versus conservatism and capitalism against communism; not to mention geopolitical disputes over migrants, resources, religion, nationalism, ethnicity, borders. My view was that the installation of a NOW government had the potential to further tear the world asunder, either in the struggle for its implementation or through the dissension that would inevitably follow. Countries or protest movements would be forever denigrating such a central authority, claiming their history, identity and national sovereignty were being compromised. Historically, humans, in the end, have not reacted well to totalitarian regimes. Despite all Ange's protestations, in my opinion, humans are just too individualistic, too wilfully contradictory, to fit into one neat, single political entity.

I will spend my lifetime advising on how to better create circular economies and how to protect our natural environment, after all as a Professor of Sustainability that is my job. I know it is the right thing to do but, if I am honest, inside, part of me is already dead as I deem it to be a battle we are destined to lose. It is sad, I mean can you imagine the infinitesimally small chance of the conditions existing as they do to provide us with life? What are the chances? And do we exult in this? No, quite the opposite, we set about destroying our wonderful planet. It is beyond words really. Perhaps it is that I am too near the data, that I know the facts, but my prognosis for the future is becoming increasingly bleak and my thinking now is that it would be cruel to bring children into a world that is dying. Ange and I might get to live out our lives but I feared the worst for the generations to come. Ange felt differently and we argued about the issue of progeny.

Chapter 2

8 June 2017

I knew something was amiss as soon as the group returned from Point-a-Pitre. They were late for one. I had been on deck, hypnotised by the dancing lights demarcating the shoreline, the gentle threshing of the sea occasionally interrupted by snatches of deep bass beats along with shouts carried on the unusually erratic trade winds, when I noticed the RHIB emerging from the inky foreground. As the *African Queen* was winched aboard, I detected an unexpected silence overhanging the party as they disembarked; I noticed too that Zach was shivering and soaked to the bone. Having spent a few productive hours posting my research findings, I had been looking forward to the gang's boisterous return and had rather hoped to have a glass of wine with them as they regaled me with stories about their afternoon on the island but, alas, everyone filed off sombrely to their quarters. Ange did not seem herself at all. She professed to being tired and gave short shrift to my questions. I asked her what had happened to the bedraggled Zach but she batted me away by saying he had perhaps had one too many and had stumbled into the water. She put the melancholy of the group down to them having had a busy day and the water being a bit choppy on their return, although it seemed languid enough to me. It was only the following day when I spoke with Dr Hans Kück from the University of Bremen that I was offered a more expansive account of the night before. He told me that Zach had not shown up at the agreed departure time in the harbour and that, after a short discussion, it emerged that Ange had been the last to see him. Heading into the locale where he had last been spotted, the group had split into mini-search parties to try and find him. It had been Dr Ballotelli that had pulled him, paralytic, out of a local cafe.

Ange was off with me for a few days after that night. One afternoon, I found her on deck looking desolate and I wondered if she had been crying. She fobbed it – and her atypical introspection – off as *mal de mer*, a consequence of the swell having picked up, making the Atlantic increasingly unpredictable as we charted our course back to Europe. It was unusual for her to be in such a mood but, when it did happen, I knew to leave her well alone.

Chapter 3

26 August 2017

It was only several weeks later, when we had returned to our regular and often split lives in Stockholm and Amsterdam, that Ange opened up to me about that afternoon cum night in Point-a-Pitre. We had been attending a work colleague of mine's wedding in Gothenburg. He had elected for a humanist ceremony in the Universeum, a purpose-built rainforest experience in the heart of the city designed to encourage an interest in, and conservation of, the world's biodiversity. What had been a bijou and touching ceremony, some readings – an excerpt from *Captain Corelli's Mandolin*, another from Pullman's *The Amber Spyglass*, some words by Plato – was followed by a selection of reflective jazz, Thelonius Monk and Duke Ellington if I recall, before a charabanc transported us across town for a wedding breakfast at Chateau Beirut, a cosy Lebanese restaurant, which had been commandeered for the occasion.

Ange and I rarely get tipsy but I am afraid we both succumbed to the free alcohol that was available to us throughout the celebrations. Ange had actually started the day in fine spirits, buoyed by a journalistic find that she refused to share with me. She said she had a little more research to do before going public with it and didn't want to 'break the spell,' as she put it. As I gorged on the exquisite falafel, shawarma, moussaka and kebbe, Ange was distracted and picked at her food, sipping gin and tonics on top of the champagne we had already enjoyed. I took a pull on my beer and asked: 'What's wrong? Are you not eating?'

'I am just not hungry.'

'Surely you are not still thinking about work? Why don't you have a day off and unwind?' I probed, hearing the hypocrisy of the words as I uttered them.

'No, I am not thinking about work. Well, I suppose I was in that I was ruminating over how to make the most of my discovery. How the NOW movement might be able to best leverage it to build momentum for their cause.'

After a contemplative pause, I probably came across more belligerently than I intended when I said: 'Oh, Angelina, do you really want to introduce more discord into the world? You know for every NOW supporter, there will be a detractor. For every internationalist, an anti-globalist. Just like for every communist there is a fascist, every Republican there is a Democrat, every left of centre advocate there is a right of centre adversary? Do you really want to give people one more reason to be at each other's throats, for there to be more schism, more hostility and distrust in the world, war even? Can't you see how dangerous all this is?'

She came straight back at me: 'But I believe that NOW's proposition is so compelling that the vast majority of people will accept it with open arms. It is neither a left-wing nor right-wing ideology, it is just plain common sense. Yes, of course there will be detractors, there always are, that is human nature. But they will simply be overwhelmed. After all, countries will remain the same, there will be no enforced changes to their political and economic systems or their religious beliefs. The new world order would just be about increasing the emphasis on countries working more closely together to steer the ship which is Planet Earth. That is all; more international cooperation to fight climate change, poverty and war. Who in their right mind would not want this?'

Whereas Ange believed that there wasn't much wrong with the world, it was just poorly organised, I had my doubts.

'You are just too Panglossian. If only it were so easy,' I mused before persisting: 'It is naive to assume that this will not lead to new conflict. Humanity is just too contrarian. Sometimes, I think our destiny is to wipe ourselves out entirely. And, do you know, I can't help but wonder if this might actually be the best thing for the world. Certainly if we don't sort ourselves out in the next couple of decades or so we will bring about our own ruin – not mass slaughter or genocide but omnicide, human extinction brought about by human action. You do know that 99% of all species that ever existed are now extinct? It does happen. Think of the Chicxulub Asteroid that crashed to earth and wiped out three quarters of animal and plant species, including the dinosaurs. There have been several biotic extinctions in our past and, right now, we are showing all the signs of careering towards the next. A clear indicator of this is the recent speeding up of the loss of living organisms. If we don't change direction immediately – and there is no sign whatsoever that we will - then it is now just a matter of time before we make ourselves extinct. The only question for me, is what is the biggest existential threat? Ecological collapse? Overpopulation? Catastrophic climate change? A pandemic? AI? A nuclear winter? We are in what Christians term the great tribulation or end times. I don't see the NOW movement stopping this. For me, the chances are they will accelerate it.'

'Ah, I see, I get it now. That's rather a bleak outlook isn't it?' Ange countered. 'So that would explain your reluctance to even consider having children, you assume their life or their children's lives will be cut short by Armageddon?' she said, tilting the whole discussion. Saying words and introducing subjects that can only be aired after drink.

I knew that Ange's biological clock was ticking and it was true that I had been fudging the issue of late. In my earlier years I had assumed that I would almost certainly have children, perhaps in my mid- to late-thirties but, as I approached that age, doubts had begun to creep in; it seemed there was more and more compelling reasons not to procreate. On one level, eugenically speaking, I thought it important that people like me and Ange produce offspring. I mean, I don't want to sound elitist but surely the world needs more people with logical, discriminating, caring, liberal and, dare I say, scholarly minds? However, I knew the planet was already overcrowded and, more to the point, as I have said, I believed – and still do – that the human race is now just rearranging deckchairs on The Titanic. We are thundering – at a speed way quicker than people realise - towards the iceberg of ecological catastrophe.

Laying down my knife and fork, I continued: 'Planet Earth can no longer sustain us. Demand for raw materials and food, overpopulation combined with poor management, pollution and climate change, has set us on an irreversible path towards extinction. Forgive me for not wanting my children to bear witness to their world going up in flames around them!'

Ange let my words settle, taking a moment to swirl her balon glass before savouring a large mouthful of G and T.

'Surely you can see that a world government is the only chance we have of solving these problems?'

A pause.

'And you say you don't want children? Okay, so where do you think that leaves us as a couple?'

Silence.

'Am I to go childless because you have given up on the human race? Your morbid belief that we are in the end of days? Well, for the record, it is my view that the creation of life is one of the few truly positive contributions we can make during our time here - one job that if we can, we are obliged to do. It is the natural conclusion of a marriage – of being in love. Perhaps not our duty, but our gift to the world.'

'I hope my work will be my legacy,' I snapped, feeling cornered. 'My concern, as an environmentalist, is the extra pressure we put on the earth's resources – and all the associated repercussions - by having children. By 2050, the world population will be 10 billion and, never mind each individual's carbon footprint, the point when there are simply not enough materials to support us is imminent. Things are going to get difficult. If I am honest, I have been considering the possibility of a vasectomy.'

Ange put down her glass and stared incredulously at me, momentarily lost for words. Finally she said: 'You're joking right?'

'No, I am not. Whilst vasectomy used to be the preserve of older men who didn't want any more children, it is becoming increasingly popular in developed countries among younger men. A recent study concluded that easily the best thing we can do to reduce our carbon footprint is to have one less child – this is way more useful than going without a car or taking fewer long haul flights. It is common sense really when you factor in all those polluting actions that will no longer be taken by a child that is never born.'

'You say "have one less child" as if you've already fathered a clutch but you haven't; you've just dedicated your whole life to yourself,' Ange interrupted.

Ignoring her interjection, I continued: 'This is before you even start to consider the horror that they will witness as the climate crisis intensifies. Some of my colleagues are anti-natalists and believe we, as a species, should end all reproduction, quietly allowing the human race to become extinct and, in the process, doing the planet a huge favour. For them, extinction is the end goal that must be quickly attained before we take down any more of the natural world. I am not that far along the road; I hope we can survive. I fear we won't, but I hope we can. You might say that not having a child is selfish but I think it is the most selfless thing we can do. There are already too many children in the world; I don't want to put extra pressure on our planet.' After a short hiatus, I offered the olive branch of: 'I might not be totally averse to adopting a child.'

Ange didn't respond, so I went on: 'During the course of any life, there will undeniably be suffering and death. There *may* be happiness but this is far from guaranteed. By choosing not to have children, we don't put that pressure on a sentient being. We negate the possibility of a life of suffering and then death. And let's think of us for a moment - how much time and money would we have to dedicate to this project?' Wrong word, I thought to myself as it issued from my lips.

Ange rolled her eyes, shook her head and glared at me. 'I wouldn't worry, it would no doubt be my time that was eaten up if we were to dedicate ourselves to this "project" as you call it. Anti-natalists? What a waste of time! As if the majority of the world is going to buy into that hogwash. And, as for money, since when was that important to us?'

'Since it enables us to live comfortably in two European capitals, to travel at will, to not worry about where our next meal is coming from,' I said, finishing off the last of the falafel by hand.

'And you think having a child will leave us struggling to keep the wolf from the door? We are not living in a fucking war zone or abject poverty.' The volume of Ange's voice was steadily increasing.

'No, I don't think that, but I think we will have less money, less time, less freedom and one of us, almost certainly, would need to put our work on hold.'

'I think we can guess who that might be,' Ange voiced. 'Is your blessed work more important than a human life – one that we would create together? And might you have discussed having a vasectomy with your wife or were you just planning on forging ahead and doing it regardless? If everyone had the same attitude as you then our world *would* come to an end; you have spent too much time in your books, hypothesising and dreaming up doomsday scenarios.'

Her words hung in the air for a moment before I retorted: 'Well, you could always call your drunk English boyfriend; I am sure he'd be more than happy to help with child rearing duties……'

I still don't know what made me utter those words. It wasn't something I meant – in fact it was something I dreaded. They were heat of the argument words, when things quickly escalate and you are looking for something to strike back with. And, reflecting now, I suppose subconsciously it had been bubbling away with me; I had been wanting to get out into the open, the evening in Point-a-Pitre. Before Ange could frame a riposte to my clumsy phrasing, I followed up with: 'I know you kissed him that afternoon on Guadeloupe. You were seen. It is why you have been so moody ever since. Feeling regretful I like to think.'

The colour drained from Angelina's face and she was fleetingly silenced: a mix of bewilderment, anger and no doubt guilt.

'That's not….how? Who? That was nothing … if it is what I think you are referring to? Zach was feeling a little low and I tried to pick him up by reminding him of all of his endearing qualities and, yes, I gave him a peck on the cheek. Nothing more than that.'

But I had clearly touched a nerve and both of us knew that she was lying or at least being economical with the truth. 'I really fail to understand what you can see in him?'

'Well, he is not quite as ridiculously self-important as you. He has a spirit about him, he is a character.'

'Plenty of spirits about him as far as I can see,' I couldn't help myself from quipping.

'Yes, he has his flaws but don't we all? He is human and not just a brain on legs. He likes to have fun – is fun,' was Angelina's withering response.

Both our voices had now become raised and we were starting to attract glances. Perhaps fortuitously – or even intentionally - our argument was halted as the father of the bride stood up, clinking his spoon on a glass to initiate the wedding speeches.

As I have already said, I had my suspicions about Zach from the beginning. His very presence on the *Esperanza* seemed just a little too opportune. I knew that it was commonplace for government agencies to plant covert operatives in NGOs and this seemed to me like the only plausible explanation for his late call-up. The only thing that made me doubt this was that, frankly, I wasn't sure he was the right calibre of man for such a job. He just seemed a bit of a gadabout, insubstantial and untrustworthy. Still, perhaps that is what whoever had placed him on the mission was counting on?

So, once back on terra firma and working on this hunch, I had done a little research into Zach. The saying about most men living lives of quiet desperation seemed to have been written for him. I called up one or two of Ange's friends from her university days, I spoke with her parents, with her brother Apollo, with his friend Geir, even with Philippe from the *Esperanza*. Some were more forthcoming than others. And, of course, we all leave a heavy online footprint. I discovered that after Amsterdam and having just scraped a pass on his course, he'd returned to the UK and spent a couple of dissolute years in London. Living at several different addresses it looked like he'd landed a few temporary jobs as a photographer but not enough to keep him from having to work a number of bars, most of which he was fired from for drunkenness and absenteeism. He'd returned to his hometown of Bolton – to the sanctuary of his parents' home - in considerable debt and checked himself into the local branches of Alcoholics Anonymous and Narcotics

Anonymous.

There then seems to have been a period of recuperation during which he dropped off the map, I could find no trace of him anywhere. The next job I could see him doing was with *The Bury Times*, where he worked prior to employment at *The Bolton News*, a role he had clung on to until the Greenpeace expedition. Meanwhile, his parents had moved to Hebden Bridge and he had gone with them. Not the average resumé of someone working for Greenpeace and he certainly looked like the kind of man who could benefit from a side hustle.

Immediately after the speeches and without uttering another word, Ange was on her feet and out of the door. She knew few of the gathering and felt under little obligation to make her excuses. I, on the other hand, did need to say a few goodbyes before I could get away. The majority of the party was going on for further drinks and a nightclub but this was of no interest to me. I apologised for Angelina dashing out, explaining that she had been feeling unwell and then slipped away myself, saying that I had been working really hard of late and was feeling a little fatigued.

Chapter 4

27 December 2017

Shortly after the wedding in Gothenburg, Ange returned to Amsterdam. We had by no means put our differences to bed. A little time later, she made a trip to Copenhagen to follow up on her 'breaking story' and, shortly after that, and with no pre-warning for me, she travelled on to see her brother Apollo in Madrid. From there, she caught the Renfe train down to Malaga before declaring, somewhat to my concern that she felt her life imperilled and that she would be taking some time out in the foothills of the Sierra de Almijara.

Prior to fleeing south, Ange had insisted we both install VPN apps on our phones. This was driven by her increasing paranoia and, she said, would afford us a little privacy. We spoke awkwardly once or twice via Skype but I knew the only way to straighten things out between us was eye to eye.

I stumbled off the bus from Torre del Mar to Cómpeta feeling quite nauseous after a vertiginous climb. The sprawling village was certainly remote but seemed to have a healthy population of ex-pats; as much as 50% Ange reckoned. Her apartment was small and meagrely furnished but Spain was not the sort of place for spending much time indoors.

After a couple of days of polite iciness, things thawed a little when, eating al fresco in the village square, she confided in me about the story that she was on the verge of breaking – and why, in doing so, she thought it may endanger her life. Ange had uncovered the unlawful killing of a Swiss academic, Professor Christoph Benvido, who had been close to revealing super-efficient solar panels that would have changed how we fuel the world. She showed me a copy of the CIA files on her laptop documenting Benvido's assassination;

procured, she said, from a member of the Swiss government by her brother in Madrid. Precisely who had hired the fire-starting killer was somewhat nebulous, but she felt the story served as a perfect exemplar of how our world has been manipulated for decades by the collusion of hydrocarbon companies and corrupt, antediluvian politicians. She did not, as yet, have copies of Benvido's designs but intimated that she was a good way along the road to tracking them down.

The scientist's potentially world-changing breakthrough had got him killed and now Ange had convinced herself it was going to be the end of her too. It did not come as a surprise to me that he had been bumped off; my work had shown me first-hand how desperate some people are to maintain the status quo for their own ends. I wasn't totally persuaded – much to my later regret - that they would go after Ange. I couldn't help worrying afterwards if my trip had inadvertently led to her being discovered there.

Chapter 5

5 February 2018

Of course, the funeral represented a nadir for me. Besides the raw grief of losing my soul-mate and the tragic curtailing of a beautiful life in full blossom, the service and gathering brought home some uncomfortable truths. It reminded me how popular and loved Ange had been. I used to tell her that you do not need to hug trees, they will come to you. She had been fully integrated into the world, a result of her personality and her work and very much unlike myself who, like Ange said, sat removed and distant in my ivory tower theorising, doom-mongering, pontificating and debating. As much as I tried to be warm and vivacious, I knew I was fighting the genes I had been dealt. It actually left me questioning my own stance on voluntary childlessness. If two people are in love – and I believe or believed that to be the case even taking into account Ange's minor indiscretion – then the natural conclusion is surely to bring a child into the world? Maybe I had been wrong. Perhaps, one child would not have been such a bad thing? But this was academic now – forgive the pun – the issue that was alive was my primitive desire to avenge Ange's death playing against my cerebral concern that galvanising the NOW movement might unleash further and untold damage on humanity and the planet, accelerating our extinction.

A day or so after the funeral, while I was still in Amsterdam, I was surprised to receive a pre-scheduled and encrypted email from Ange in which she sent me the log-in details for her YouTube channel. Within the platform was a film of her denouncing the fossil fuel industry and offering an impassioned plea for people to support the NOW movement, recorded, presciently, in case she was killed. Also, there were copies of the classified files that I had already glanced that documented the contract killing of Benvido; both were scheduled to go live within days and I could see that links would be sent directly to an impressive list of international journalists and publications. The receiving of these account details somewhat negated my having whipped Ange's laptop from under the police's noses.

To be honest, the email rocked me. It had, quite literally, come from beyond the grave. I resolved to take a short sabbatical and took it upon myself to undertake a little research into Benvido and his discovery. It did not take long to appreciate how fastidious he was about his work and how he was acutely conscious of the political ramifications of his new solar panel widget. Many scientists or academics pursue their studies in a silo, blissfully unaware that their work might be raising red flags outside their immediate orbit but I did not think Benvido would be so naive, particularly given the threats made to his family. I took a leap of faith and assumed he would have passed copies of his blueprints to at least one trusted colleague. A little bit of assiduous detective work, after all research is what I am good at, revealed this to be true. After a couple of false starts, I came up trumps with a Professor Isobel Zihla, who was still lecturing in the US.

Zach's Journal Part Two

Chapter 1

12 February 2018

I have been in New York for almost a week, staying at Sylvenie's flat. Serendipitously, Apollo is here too, spending time with his lover in the Big Apple. They make a fine couple; the romantic in me likes to think it might be a trial run ahead of them living together.

Using a VPN and incognito searches on the internet – I am now paranoid about being watched – combined with a little creative thinking, it had been relatively straightforward to work my way through the three names of Benvido's closest work colleagues that Mad Lizzie had furnished me with. All were now retired. Two were still living in Switzerland, one of which I caught in a hotel lobby while he was attending a conference and the other I located at his flat in Bern. The third person was a little more elusive but I eventually found her offering assistance in a homeless shelter in Mannheim in Germany. Each convinced me that they were not the person who had contacted Angelina. Interestingly though – and it was my only lead – two of them offered the same name as to who I perhaps should be looking for. A former colleague, a certain Professor Izzy Zihla, was someone that Benvido had written a number of academic papers with and it seemed that she now resided in Cambridge, Massachusetts. I considered just calling her but I knew this may well imperil her and it also afforded her an easy opportunity to fob me off; it was a gamble but I needed to see the whites of her eyes when she was talking to me.

On a whim, I had called Apollo on a burner phone to ask him if he thought Sylvenie might put me up; I had a notion that it would be easier to lie low in a flat in Queens rather than a touristy hotel in Manhattan. To my delight, he said that Sylvenie and he had flown out of Barajas Airport to JFK the previous day and they would love to host me for a few days. I was gassed too that she had a PC that I could make use of.

In a half-assed attempt to bamboozle those that almost certainly had me under surveillance, I'd flown into Philadelphia with a pocketful of dollars and checked into a cheap hotel in the heart of the city. I'd watched Bourne; I knew how to drop off the grid. Utilising my superpower, I'd hung out in dive bars until the early hours before weaving my way back to a stool in the hotel bar for another hour or so. Convinced by now that if someone was following me they must be wilting, I retired to my room for an hour before re-emerging and quietly slipping out of a back-door at 4.45am. Aboard the five thirty bus to Boston, I finally got some disrupted shut-eye before pitching up at the South Station Bus Terminal in time for lunch. A ten minute subway ride brought me out in Cambridge, bang in between two of the world's leading universities, Harvard and the Massachusetts Institute of Technology.

Professor Zihla still guest lectured at MIT and if I had my days and timings right, she was due to wrap up a talk on Classical Mechanics in the Kresge Auditorium. I could see into the building and, as the lecture theatre doors were thrown open and the students flooded the lobby, I stared through the 30 foot high windows attempting to pick out someone fifty years their senior – not quite as straightforward as you'd think given the average height of an American teenager. Unable to descry her, I slipped into the block as a group of students exited and found her still at the front desk of the lecture theatre, patiently answering outstanding queries.

Professor Zihla took my intrusion in her stride.

'Professor, I am so sorry to pounce on you immediately after a lecture but I really need to talk to you about a former colleague of yours, Professor Christoph Benvido, who you worked with on the CERN project. Do you recall him?'

She raised a quizzical eyebrow before confirming: 'Yes, of course I remember him. We worked together for 20 years and collaborated on several notable projects. This is public knowledge. May I learn who is asking?'

'I am sorry, I should have introduced myself. I am a photographer and close friend of a journalist called Angelina Fontana, who was recently assassinated for, among other things, uncovering evidence of the unlawful killing of your former colleague. His house, just outside Geneva, was torched deliberately. Shortly before her own death, Angelina was contacted by someone claiming to be an associate of Benvido; they told her that he had been deliberately killed, that the Swiss government was investigating his death and that they would make contact again in order to pass to her his draughts for some revolutionary solar panels he had been working on. I am trying to track down that person and those plans.'

'Well, in which case, let me congratulate you; you have come to the right place. It was me. Although I had this very conversation with a man from Sweden just a couple of days ago. I think he said his name was Goldstein; he told me that he was the husband of Angelina and that he was also searching for Christoph's plans. Perhaps you know him?'

'Yes, I do…we are on the same team, kind of…or at least I think we are. He was….here…. in Boston?' I stammered, momentarily taken aback. Then, '…Sorry, you just said he was; please, go on.'

'Well, as an Ecological Professor, or whatever he said he was, he promised that Benvido's invention would go to the right people and that the solar panels could revolutionise how the world produces green energy. He said he was going to meet with NOW's Candy Kitcatt in a few days' time and that he would talk to her about how best to utilise the drawings. I like the principles on which the NOW movement is founded; I think it might be our last shot, and I thought if I can help them in some way, then all the better. He was very convincing and I handed the lot over to him. To be honest, it felt like quite a relief to pass them on to someone else; they have been an albatross around my neck for too long. Sorry.'

This stopped me in my tracks and, before I could frame a response, she said: 'Come on, let me buy you a coffee. I need a little pick-me-up and you smell like you could use one yourself, then I will tell you everything I know.' She was not wrong; every now and again I caught a waft of last night's booze seeping through my pores.

Seated in a nearby café, both of us armed with macchiatos, Professor Zihla, started to offload: 'I saw the bomb blast story, it briefly made it on to American news feeds, I think I saw it on CNN. Angelina's death came as a great shock to me and I can't help feeling more than a little responsible for it. As I said, it was me that called her to give her the lead. I wish I could have given her more information on the technicalities of his invention but he flew solo on it. Of course, I looked at his drafts when he gave them to me; some of them I could understand but there were scribbles and computations that I could not decipher. I told Angelina that he had left a wife who might be able to tell her a little more.'

'Forgive me for asking but why did you hold on to the plans for so long without sharing them with the world?'

Looking a little sheepish, Professor Zihla muttered: 'Frankly, I was scared. No sooner had Christoph passed me them than he was dead. I feared they might come for me next. I thought of my husband and children. I reasoned with myself that it was a long-shot that they would come looking for me but, ultimately, I decided it was better to keep my head down. And then I became involved in other work undertakings before retiring from CERN and relocating out here; there were personal things I had to deal with relating to my children and life just moved on and, to tell the truth, Christoph's designs slipped from my mind for a long time. However, once I had retired or semi-retired at least, I started to think more altruistically and expansively about the planet; bigger picture politics if you like. And when, in 2015, the UN issued its 17 Sustainable Development Goals and an urgent call to action in order that we reach them by 2030, I knew it was the right thing to do to release Christoph's plans, even if it only moved things along incrementally, even if it might endanger me and my family.'

'But now you no longer have his workings?'

'I am afraid you are right. Angelina's husband convinced me that they would go to the right people. I believed him, although I have neither heard nor seen anything yet.'

'So you trusted him implicitly?' I asked, my disappointment clear in the timbre of my voice.

'Yes, I really did. He seemed so earnest. But, of course, having spent a lifetime in academia and working with unpredictable IT systems, I know the importance of keeping back-up copies of everything. So, of course, I took some photos of his project, but unfortunately I am no photographer and they are a little blurry; I am afraid when you zoom in that some of the detail is lost. You can have copies but you might be disappointed. If only I'd had a professional photographer to hand!'

'Yes, thank you, I would love to grab a copy of your photos!'

The septuagenarian then surprised me by opening up her phone and sending me a batch of photos via Android AirDrop.

'They might be usable,' I said, glancing at them and knowing full well that they wouldn't be. 'Don't worry, I will liaise with Jochen – Professor Goldreich not Goldstein – about the originals but your electronic files are useful. I know you've heard this before but, trust me, they really will be put to very good use; I have something in mind. I don't want to say too much at this stage but soon you and the whole world will see them, assuming nobody gets to me first.'

'That all sounds good to me; but please, keep my name out of it,' were the professor's parting words.

Chapter 2

13 February 2018

Done.

My video editing skills were a little rusty and it had taken me longer than I thought it would but, nevertheless, it had been a productive morning sat at Sylvenie's PC in her flat in Rosedale, Queens and I was just a little pleased with the finished product.

Jochen seemed to have stopped taking my calls; I wondered if he had changed his phone. I even tried his office via the switchboard at the Stockholm Environment Institute but was told he was taking some leave. I'd wanted to discuss Benvido's sketches that he had and to take photos of them but his behaviour was beginning to concern me. I devised a work-round solution but more of that later.

I dragged the cursor far left across the progress bar to the start of a file that was actually several short films spliced together into one and pressed play. My craggy visage, freshly shaved and hair combed, filled the screen as I began narrating.

'My life is over, I know that, but I implore you to give up 30 minutes of yours to watch this. It may well change how you see and live life. I have come to learn that we – and I mean the world when I say we - have a narrowing choice. We can continue how we currently live and sleep-walk our way into extinction or we can wake up and choose to prolong our time on Planet Earth. I hope the following footage will give you an insight into how the world *actually* operates, the behind the scenes éminence grise who really run the show. Trust me, I have learnt first-hand that the men in grey do not like those that shake the cage.

'I am Zach Boocock and I am a photographer. Several weeks ago, I received a message from an old and dear friend; an investigative journalist called Angelina Fontana, who told me how she thought her life was in imminent danger – a consequence of information she had unearthed for a news story that she had been working on. Less than twenty four hours later she was dead – blown to pieces in an explosion in a Spanish cafe. When I started to investigate her murder I found out that she had uncovered incriminating evidence relating to the killing of a CERN scientist, a certain Professor Benvido, who had discerned a way of harnessing solar power in such an efficient manner that it would offer cheap and universal energy - and which would blow the fossil fuel industry out of the water! His invention should have put the planet on a totally different trajectory some fifteen years ago. Angelina will tell you the full tale shortly.

'Sensing that she was being followed, my friend was so fearful for her life that she took refuge in a remote village in the hills near Malaga and started to schedule emails that would only be delivered to me in the event of her death. If she lived, she cancelled the programmed email. If she died, she knew that several days later, the email would come through to me. In it, she encrypted log-in information to a YouTube account, where I discovered two unpublished videos: footage of confidential Swiss government files investigating the hit on Professor Benvido, which included copies of CIA papers documenting his assassination; and a film recorded by Angelina, detailing her truth bomb news story on Benvido's discovery, which led to his - and her own - premature demise. Following that, you will see footage of two Americans admitting that both the professor and Angelina were the victims of professional hits as well as images showing the workings and illustrations of a prototype of Benvido's invention. I hope these can be interpreted and developed by scientists.

'What I should also come clean about is that I am in the employ of the NSA, the National Security Agency, which is part of the US Department of Defence. I was first contacted by them more than a year ago when I was called in at the last minute to be an assistant photographer on a Greenpeace expedition to the West Indies. Hours after taking the call, I was visited by an American agent posing as a delivery woman. She invited herself into my house and told me that they had deliberately engineered a car crash, debilitating the environmental campaigner's first choice photographer, my friend Geir. I don't know whether they somehow bullied him into calling me or whether he was innocently doing me a favour but I was on-board Greenpeace's ship, the *Esperanza*, because the Yanks wanted me there as a "sleeper". A monkey that wins the trust of others and feeds back juicy titbits to the organ grinder. All I had to do was report to them about conversations and happenings on the trip – although I am pretty sure the vessel was bugged anyway - and any subsequent dealings I might have with Greenpeace members. In return, I was on their books and would receive an ongoing stipend from them for the rest of my days and the "safety" of my friends and family would be guaranteed. How had I been recommended to them? Through a so-called friend, a certain Joseph Squibb, who I knew to be former police but, it turns out, was someone still on the books of the Secret Intelligence Service or MI6 as it is better known, having spent a brief tenure with them earlier in his career. Thanks for that pal.

'Within hours of receiving the scheduled email from Angelina, I had been contacted by the Americans again. As someone who could expose the hit on the Swiss professor, Angelina had been very much on their radar as a threat to national security. Whilst they could not yet decode the encrypted message, they strongly suspected that I now had access to the Swiss government files investigating Benvido's murder – they didn't, as yet, know I also had film footage of Angelina's damning commentary. Of course, once they decoded her email, I guessed they would not be quite so accommodating with me.

'How did they know I had received an email from Angelina, you may ask? Believe me, if the NSA wants to get into a mobile phone or PC or to track someone, they can and they will. The Agency intercepts and stores the communications of over a billion people. Many times, I have walked past the "golf balls" just outside Harrogate, otherwise known as RAF Menwith Hill, where we are all spied on from.

'Two factors enable this. Powers acceded after the 9/11 terror attack and the fact that much of the world's communications pass through the US or GCHQ, which is run by its close ally the UK – a benefit known to these countries' agencies as "home field advantage". And secondly, the proliferation of the use of digital technology has opened a window into our private lives. Our online data is hackable and metadata within our mobile phones means we all carry a tracking device with us. On top of that, the NSA can listen in on your phone calls, check your internet searches, read all your email messages and document downloads, spy on you through your desktop camera, listen to you through Google Home and Amazon Echo and track every penny you earn and spend. Yes, just as you suspected, we are living in an Orwellian world.

'For good measure, the US also surreptitiously taps into other countries' internet traffic through what is known as "boomerang routing" where messages pass through the US before returning to their country of origin. The NSA claims that this is necessary as part of its fight against terror. In order to find the needle in the haystack, it claims to need access to the complete haystack. Google, Microsoft, Yahoo and the like receive endless data requests from US intelligence agencies. These companies, along with the likes of

Facebook, Apple and AOL, all petition the Senate, demanding reforms to the amount of information they are compelled to hand over but, in the end, nothing much changes. Although online encryption of our information can slow things down, intelligence agencies decode it in the end - there is always access through a "back door". A back door which has been purposely created to allow NSA entry.

'Anyway, getting to the point, they wanted me to hand over the file sent by Angelina on a memory stick and arranged a meeting in Venice. In return, my ongoing compensation would be considerably increased, on top of which I would receive a one-off payment allowing me to purchase a home.

'Whilst they were correct in assuming I was a tractable and hopeless alcoholic who has spent most of his life half-cut, what they had forgotten about me was that I am a professional photographer and videographer. And, when I am sober – and sometimes even when I am drunk – I know right from wrong. I recorded our exchange in Harry's Bar using a tiny lens in a spy camera secreted in a pair of sunglasses and the voice recording facility on my phone. I've knitted everything together for you to watch in a moment. You will note how the Americans admit to the killing of both Benvido and Angelina. Sadly, but not surprisingly, Benvido's wife has also died in the last week or so. Just three more senseless deaths in the war against environmentalists. Nothing too surprising I suppose, currently three or four activists die every week, so a few more are easily hidden. Watch this space, I know I am destined to go the same way. Here's Angelina.'

The film flickered momentarily and then she was on screen and, even though I had now watched her recording several times, involuntarily my mouth went dry, my heart danced a little jig and my mind raced. She was sporting a faint tan from the Andalusian sun and perhaps a touch of make-up; I found it difficult to tell. Her hair tied back, a dab of eye liner and mascara;

she'd definitely made an effort for the camera. Behind her was what I presumed to be her rental flat, sparsely furnished and streaked by white shafts of late afternoon Mediterranean light that illumined the hovering dust. She looked a little world-weary, who wouldn't under the circumstances, but her usual verve and vigour quickly came through as she relayed her impassioned message. She was, I think, reading from an autocue.

'I hope no-one ever watches this film because, if they do, it means I am dead; assassinated at the bidding of a fossil fuel firm or several, or one of their professional bodies or perhaps by a national security agency. Just who is culpable isn't entirely relevant. The point is that I - and others - have been killed by the hydrocarbon industry. A sector that has always put profits before people. They wanted to silence me but this short film, recorded in January 2018, exposes them for what they are: greedy murderers who will stop at *nothing* to preserve their own wealth and the old world order, which has served them so well.

'I am about to show you how a handful of companies have radically transformed our planet and its weather systems, killing and displacing millions of people, polluting the environment, destroying economies, wiping out animal and plant species, depleting resources and annihilating pristine ecosystems. They have done this with an evangelical ruthlessness which has seen them bribe politicians and attempt to ridicule, silence and, yes, murder those who stand in their way. This has gone on for long enough; now it has to stop. Our ravished earth is weeping as we exploit and vandalise it. Now is the time for us to take control of our own fate.

'My name is Angelina Fontana and I am a freelance journalist. I am recording this film as I hide away in an isolated Spanish village, scared for my life. I do not work for a specific newspaper or news channel so I am not shackled by any political alignment; I can choose my own stories and say what

I want, predicated on incontrovertible evidence of course.

'Firstly, an admission: throughout my life I have been an avid environmental campaigner. If I am honest, I've always been slightly at a loss as to why everyone else isn't too. Why wouldn't you want to save this beautiful place where we all live? If your house is on fire with you and your children in it, do you just quietly sit in your armchair as the flames lick your feet or do you try and suppress the blaze?

'In this short film, I hope to show you how the oil industry will stop at nothing – and I mean nada - to further their own ends. We - and they - know their bloodied hand holds a smoking gun. The UN tells us that 7 million people die prematurely each year as a result of air pollution. We can see it with our own eyes in the miasmic grey skies blanketing most cities, most notably in India, China and Pakistan, where the air quality is four times worse than the World Health Organisation's maximum limit. Let us also factor in another 5 million deaths per annum from climate change and from polluted water, not to mention the tens of thousands that still die annually in the extraction of oil, the earth's black blood. For too long, corporate greed - an obsession with share prices and dividends - has supplanted a respect for humankind. The boards and leadership teams of the big hitters have, knowingly, negatively impacted every life on the planet. They should be tried for crimes against humanity and their companies made to pay reparations to all those suffering from the effects of global warming.

'Now we stand on the very edge of environmental ruin, brought about by the unremitting use of fossil fuels. Something the energy companies have systematically disputed for decades through policies of denial, obfuscation and political lobbying. They have intentionally delayed and blocked attempts at introducing renewable energy sources, including, as I shall prove, resorting to murder. Exxon Mobil, once the world's largest company, still doesn't see renewables as part of our or their future; it thinks our world can be saved through carbon capture alone! It is time for the insanity to stop and for the voices of ordinary people to be heard. We cannot let fuel companies run – or should I say ruin - our world.'

Angelina's image was then replaced by emotive footage of climate change carnage – swathes of what looked like Australia ablaze, aerial shots of a flooded Bangladeshi delta, storms battering a Caribbean island, glaciers melting, slabs of ice breaking off polar landscapes, huge chimney towers spewing out clouds of smoke, mud landslides, parched landscapes of cracked soil, rivers bursting their banks, burning oil wells and flooded cityscapes. All this dystopia as Angelina continued her excoriating narrative.

'Climate change is not something that might threaten us in the future; it's happening right now. On our watch. Some of the larger events we're beginning to see coverage of, especially in first world countries – I am thinking of Europe's soaring summer temperatures and flash floods, the melting of the ice-caps, Californian wildfires and Australian bushfires – but in poorer areas there is much that goes unreported and is already causing disruption, chaos and death. As we all know, it is the poor that always suffer first. There is the desertification of Central America, the disappearance of islands in the Pacific, the flooding of Asian deltas and turmoil in African climate cycles with intensified heat, increasing numbers of droughts and less frequent but more intense rainfall. Africa, with its growing population, is set to be the hardest-hit continent, even though it has contributed the least to our problems.

'The richest 10% of countries are responsible for almost half of the all the carbon dioxide that has ever been produced. Meanwhile, the poorest 50% have contributed less than 10% of greenhouse gas emissions. Global warming is a problem created by the West. Believe it or not, even now, only one tenth of people in our world have taken a flight and 80% do not own a car. Compare that with North America, where the average citizen consumes ten times more than someone from China and 30 times more than an average person on the Indian subcontinent. When we look at annual per capita emissions of carbon dioxide, the US, Canada and Australia are among the worst offenders. China is just above the average, but India is, so far, significantly below. In Europe, historically, Germany and the UK have a lot to answer for. If all world citizens were to live as UK nationals, we would need three earths. The UK represents less than 1% of the world population yet accounts for a twentieth of all historical discharge of carbon dioxide pollutants. But I am not on your screens to apportion blame to individual nation-states. I am here to expose the oil and gas industry for what it is.

'The recent Paris Agreement's central aim was to strengthen the international response to the threat of climate change. The target is to ensure that global temperatures this century are kept well below a 2° Celsius rise from pre-industrial levels. Let me tell you that we are absolutely *not* on a trajectory to achieve this. Moreover, the Agreement seeks to pursue the goal of limiting the temperature increase even further, to a maximum of 1.5°C. There can be no more delay and prevarication; this has to happen. We have one chance and it is now.

'While a degree or two of temperature rise does not sound like a lot and the human skin can probably bear it, for the planet, this would be calamitous. The UN has reported on the massive difference between average global warming at 1.5°C as opposed to 2°C; with the latter causing a vortex of more extreme weather, sea level rises, glacial retreat, food security threats, droughts and heatwaves, ocean acidification, ecosystem disruption and extinction as well as social upheaval to hundreds of millions of people. If you need an example of how just 1°C can make a dramatic difference, think of the agricultural heartland of the US around Nebraska. Six thousand years ago, when the world was 1°C warmer, this region was desert. During the Great Depression of the 1930s, due to a climate fluctuation, it was again transformed into a dust bowl which led to widespread famine and the mass migration of two and a half million Americans.

'If a 1.5°C increase is bad for the planet, a 2°C rise would be truly drastic. The former would see a loss of 70 to 90% of coral, while the latter would mean 99% disappearing. At 1.5°C, 8% of plants, 6% of insect species and 4% of vertebrates would lose more than half their habitats. At 2°C, these figures more than double. At 2°C, ecosystems covering up to a fifth of Earth's land mass can be expected to undergo transformation to another type, such as savannah to desert, whereas at 1.5°C, there would be less than two thirds of that impact.

A variance of just half a degree would be the difference between life and death for so many people. Despite the Paris Agreement, there is still a 90% chance – so a virtual certainty - that temperatures will rise more than the aimed for 2°C and a one in three chance that global temperatures will rise by at least 3°C. A rise of over 2°C and we will see millions of people starving in India, Africa and Central America. There will be failed states as civil administration collapses. History has taught us that hungry people tend to move and there will be hordes of refugees seeking food in pastures new. Africans into Europe and people from Central America fleeing to Mexico and the US. As we know, this forced migration is already happening. All the evidence points towards it getting worse. The end of the Amazon Rainforest will be as certain as that of the melting of the ice caps. This in itself will set off a cascade effect - another chain of catastrophic events as more CO^2 is released into the atmosphere - leading to an almost certain rise in temperature of more than 3°C.

'Above 3°C and most of Florida will be underwater, as will Bangladesh; cities like Bangkok, Mumbai and Shanghai will be swamped. Miami and most of Manhattan would disappear and Eastern England and Central London would be flooded. You could say farewell too to the Netherlands. This is now runaway climate change. Ice at both poles would melt and there would be a sea rise of one metre every 20 years, stabling off eventually at a 70m growth in sea level. At this rate of rise, a thawing of permafrost is triggered – two-thirds of Russia stands on this – and a "methane bomb" would be released as we career towards an inevitable 4°C rise. And so it goes on. Our situation is truly precarious.

'Why have we left things so late? Let us not forget that Paris was preceded by decades of climate change and science denial by the "merchants of doubt" – large oil, gas and coal companies who purposely obstructed public policy. We all know they are guilty as charged. Likewise, the politicians that smoothed their path. I ask again, why isn't somebody being prosecuted? These are crimes against humanity.

'Energy companies are far and away the biggest contributors to our climate crisis. Globally, just twenty oil, gas and coal corporations are responsible for one third of all greenhouse gas emissions in the modern era. They have contributed to the release of 35% of all energy-related carbon dioxide and methane worldwide. Let's name names. Four companies alone - BP, Shell, Chevron and Exxon - account for 10% of the world's carbon emissions since 1965. While these companies buy favour at the very highest levels, it is even easier for state-owned fossil fuel enterprises to act with impunity. The leading polluter is Saudi Arabia's Aramco. But let's not forget Gazprom, owned by the Russian government, the National Iranian Oil Company, Coal India and others. We have failed seven and a half billion people in allowing a couple of dozen companies and petro-states to build their fortunes at the expense of

Planet Earth.

The truth is that they – and we - have known about climate change for a very long time, since at least the middle of the last century. Back then, scientists were already warning how the burning of fossil fuels would heat up the atmosphere, making uncannily accurate forecasts that are now coming to fruition. In the 1970s a chemist called Frank Sherwood Roland summed matters up when he said: "What's the use of having developed a science well enough to make predictions if, in the end, all we're willing to do is stand around and wait for them to come true?" This was after he had been accused of working for the KGB because he had the temerity, correctly as it goes, to suggest that CFCs would destroy the ozone layer.

'For decades, the big polluters have denied climate change in the ruthless pursuit of lucre. They have lobbied politicians and the media and attempted to cast doubt on scientific theory. At the same time, most people have buried their head in the sand, buying up cheap flights and gas-guzzling SUVs. Mass cognitive dissonance. The fossil fuel industry has been our pusher and we its helpless addicts.

'Ever since the 1950s there has been a concerted effort to cast doubt on whether there even is a climate crisis and, if there is, whether humans are to blame. This clouding of the waters has gone on for years, influencing public opinion and delaying legislation, resulting in the deaths of millions each year from air pollution.

'In recent decades, energy firms have benefited from a similar strategy of scepticism that the tobacco industry employed, a scheme known as "Project Whitecoat" that sought to pit scientists against scientists. While all the evidence suggested that smoking caused lung cancer, the project saw tobacco companies recruit, train and pay so called "research specialists" who would question the evidence of experts. Over the years, Project Whitecoat, promulgated widely by a headline-hungry and right-wing press, has encouraged people across the globe to doubt facts and experts and has helped engineer a cynicism towards science. Concurrently, the tobacco industry abnegated its responsibility by promoting the concept that smoking was all down to individual choice.

'The hydrocarbon industry has employed very similar methods to Project Whitecoat, even rolling out some of the same so called "experts" to sow doubt about climate change. This was after researchers within energy firms had already reported on the havoc that climate change would doubtlessly wreak on the world. Now we all agree that smoking is bad for you and only an idiot would refuse to accept climate change but the deniers had done their job, squeezing out several more decades of billion dollar profits for big business.

'More recently, social media campaigns and a huge amount of money spent on Google ads have helped spread further distrust of science. Sensationalist misinformation spreads ten times faster than actual information on the internet. Across the planet, the orchestrated policy of deception, denial, doubt and delay on climate action has become the greatest PR campaign in human history. All for a few dollars more. Beyond the tobacco industry and the climate crisis, think of the misinformation that still circulates around vaccinations, GM crops and diseases. Modern propaganda is all about spreading falsehoods and questioning veracity. Facts and statistics have become completely malleable. We are in what has become known as the post-truth era; an anti-intelligentsia, anti-science world where it is the norm to doubt experts. Many have been subject to online abuse and trolling. This attitude has been propagated by those working on behalf of the fossil fuel companies and from elements within the media. The current catchphrase is "truth isn't truth".

'Another strategy from the petroleum industry has been to fund political lobbyists, also known as think tanks. They have petitioned politicians, ensuring that they work for them and not for the good of the general public. Of course, those in the business of energy have paid politicians to champion their cause for a long time. Almost a hundred years ago, back in the 1920s, Winston Churchill took £5,000 from two oil companies, Royal Dutch Shell and Burmah Anglo-Persian Oil Company, which was later to become BP, in return for him representing them in their application to the British government for a merger. A precedent was set.

'The US provides us with countless examples of think tanks and businesses coming together to aggressively lobby politicians and the media in order to further their own ends. Over the last few decades, it would not be too far-fetched to say that the multi-billionaire Koch brothers, whose fortune – surprise, surprise - is built on the energy business, changed the face of American politics by fighting "climate change alarmism" and funding right-wing enterprises, including the Republican Party itself. The Global Climate Coalition, formed in 1989, comprised major players from oil and coal, from utilities and from the steel, car and rail sectors. The Information Council for the Environment or ICE, was made up of US electrical companies. Both attempted to position global warming as conjectural theory not fact and employed top PR specialists to sow doubt which, in turn, fed a controversy-hungry press. PR practitioners know that truth does not always win out, it is more about how you present an argument, how frequently and how widely you get your message out there. These days, our equivalent is bots relentlessly flooding the internet with misinformation.

'And why wouldn't the hydrocarbons industry spend dollars on this? Studies show that the oil industry gets a 5,800% return on the money it invests in campaign contributions and lobbying in the US Congress – so for every dollar they spend they get $59 back! I have a very, very thick file full of data showing how much, over many years, fossil fuel companies have bought off politicians and governments around the world in order to pursue their own agendas.

'One of numerous examples would be Exxon Mobil who, from 2003-2007, gave £5.6m to 91 institutions to downplay climate change. Nearly all of these were right-wing think tanks that were strongly against regulation of any kind. With a little help from their friends in the press, they managed to equate climate change with the left and would argue against it on ideological grounds; over the years, many Americans have been brainwashed to believe that environmental concerns mean socialism and socialism means anti-American.

'Despite the formidable wealth of these dirty energy firms, each year the US government – or more accurately the US taxpayer – continues to provide $27 billion in subsidies for the production and consumption of fossil fuels. Meanwhile, whilst these companies enjoy their free handouts, many Americans struggle to get by - over 44 million live in poverty, with 10% of the population having no health cover. There is also bounteous evidence that energy companies promoted and funded protests and marches denying that climate change was happening at all! Of course, oil companies achieved their ultimate goal when Trump pulled out of the Paris Climate Agreement.

'There is no doubt in my mind that these spurious and ridiculous arguments have cost the planet 40 years. So far, staggeringly, no US or European energy company has set targets to reduce the carbon intensity of the energy it supplies. On the contrary, profits soar as oil and gas production continues to grow and is projected to increase further in the coming decades.

'And, as I have already pointed out, it is not just American citizens that suffer; communities around the world are massively impacted by climate change, oil spills and water contamination from drilling, fracking and mining. Governments must put an end to these corrosive subsidies, not just for fossil fuels but for industrial fishing and industrial agriculture too. The pendulum must swing and they must start properly taxing the big energy companies to help pay for the damage they have caused and to ensure that research into green energy is intensified. Duties that would be rendered much more stringently and easily by a global authority.

'Even though ninety seven per cent of scientists agree that we are responsible for the steady warming of the earth's climate, unbelievably - or perhaps not so given what I have just said - over 100 members of the US Congress know better and have expressed cynicism about humans being to blame and the need to reduce our emissions! All but one, of course, are Republicans. I will bet they are Republicans of a particular religious persuasion too. Some of the oil-heads in the Bible Belt defy reason – they are quite happy to believe that 3,000 years ago Noah's ark saved the animals from intemperate weather caused by God but are unconvinced about extreme weather - happening right in front of us - being caused by scientifically proven global warming! The Republican Party has regularly purged its own ranks of candidates who believe in climate change. It is a shame out of a population of 325 million, the US cannot find 500 or so virtuous politicians to represent them.

'Right now, globally, there are in the region of 1,500 oil and gas firms listed on stock exchanges and, combined, they represent $4.65 trillion worth of wealth. Exxon Mobil alone is worth $425 billion. A study showed that in the first half of 2012, between them, the five biggest oil companies earnt $62.2 billion; that is $341 million per day!

'Yet they invest next to nothing of their profits in green energy. What is scary is that fossil fuel companies, knowing their time is finite, have actually started to increase their level of plastic production. It is set to double by 2040! You would think that they would have learned a lesson but it seems not. Let's take an individual case – the humble story of the plastic spoon. Surely we have truly lost the plot when drilling for oil, shipping it to a refinery, turning it into plastic, shaping it accordingly, delivering it to a store, before someone then buys it and brings it home is deemed to be less effort than what it would take to just wash our stainless steel spoon after use?

'It is against this corporate antagonism to humanity's future welfare, the achievement in Paris – despite coming dangerously late in the day - should be weighed and celebrated. Really, you would think that if some of the stats I've quoted became public knowledge, it would appal most right-minded citizens. The sad truth is that this data is already out there and it has either gone unreported or quietly ignored as everyone focuses on their own everyday struggles. I think consciously or subconsciously we have all known that our usage of fossil fuels is going to catch up with us; well, now it has!

'Not only has the fossil fuel industry knowingly polluted the planet, they have also strived to block any attempts to move to greener technologies. Everything I've talked about is well documented but today I would like to share with you a story that has most definitely not been reported on. It is the sad tale of Professor Christoph Benvido, an eminent Professor of Physics with a long and distinguished career at CERN.

'But first – and bear with me, this is relevant – a little about how we might fuel our world going forward. Our future – that of the planet and everything on it – now depends on green, sustainable energy. We need to wake up and understand that renewable energy is the future and that we must accelerate our transition to it. This is the biggest problem for our generation – and possibly the largest issue to ever face humankind - how do we power our world without destroying it? It is not that answers or partial solutions do not exist – they do; it is more that we need to stop treating them as crank projects and start to intensify our research and investment in them. We need to urgently employ our very best minds to develop them further and to ensure that they are implemented at speed. Our very existence depends on it.'

Angelina disappeared from our screens again, this time to be replaced by film clips of oceanic wind farms, fields of solar panels, chimneys issuing clean geothermal energy and gushing cascades of water running down the face of a huge dam. Her voice continued over the images.

'Since Paris, some countries have performed better than others. Germany is the world leader in renewable technologies. China has invested more than a third of a trillion dollars in green energy. In the transition to a low carbon economy, China is a surprising frontrunner. Yes, we know all about their city smogs but these are diminishing as it focuses on reducing pollution. It has started to grow its delivery of wind fuel, more so than the US has ever done. Wind power currently accounts for 4% of worldwide energy and a third of this is generated by the Chinese. It also leads the world in generating hydro-electric power.

'India is on track to better its ambitious 2022 target for solar energy; Costa Rica is set to be a zero carbon country by 2021 and a significant shift towards regenerative energy is being seen in many other nations. Despite Trump pulling out of the agreement, 40% of the US population still live in states subscribing to the Paris goals. Since 2015, the selling off of investments in coal, oil and gas has almost doubled to over $6 trillion. Between 2009 and 2015, the US, thanks to Barack Obama, invested $150 billion in green energy. There is still hope.

'Back in the 1930s, America's greatest inventor, Thomas Edison, said: "I'd put my money on the sun and solar energy. What a source of power! I hope we don't have to wait until oil and coal run out before we tackle that!" I am afraid to say if the fossil fuel conglomerates have their way, it is looking increasingly like we will. But by then, it will be too late. We can have a short future with hydrocarbons or we can have a future; we cannot have both. Every year the world uses 35 billion barrels of oil. If we continue at the current rate of usage we will run out of oil and gas in 50 years and coal in about a century. Then what? Aside from the planet being utterly wrecked, how will we power what is left of our world?

'Energy from sun, water and wind sources currently provides about 15% of our requirements. If we consider the sun, it radiates 173 quadrillion watts of solar energy 24-7, which is 10,000 times more than our current needs. If you stop and think about it, our world is already predominantly solar powered. It gives life to us all, without it our planet would be a dark, ice-coated ball of rock, spinning in the void. Yet we are only just beginning to harness its power to provide energy - about 2% of the world's electricity comes from it. For years, scientists have grappled with how to make more use of it. Rather than let it destroy us, we need to ensure it saves us. To power the world, we need to exploit the solar energy from just 1% of the Sahara – this would mean a grid that spans 100,000 square kilometres. Given deserts are miles from anywhere, we then have the problems of efficient storage and transportation. This is where we need to spend our research money. For starters, we would need a series of grids placed across the globe. And this is where Professor Christoph Benvido comes into the story. His discovery could have saved us 20 *critical* years and millions of lives; we could be living in a totally different world.

'Benvido's work at CERN in Geneva was his lifetime obsession, but through a side project he was involved with, he inadvertently developed a technology capable of revolutionising the effectiveness of solar panels. While his invention was integral in the quest to create a perfect vacuum in the Hadron Collider, it was only when he retired in the early noughties that he had time to adapt and develop the mechanism so that it could be used in solar power. His work would have taken solar panel efficiency from somewhere between 10 to 15% to 50% or more. I know all this through speaking with his scientific colleagues and his wife.'

'His brainchild really should have changed our world. It would have decimated the fossil fuel industry. Imagine how things would have been turned on their heads: suddenly, the countries where the sun shines most, which, as we know, are predominantly the poorer nations, would be holding all the cards in terms of cheap, clean and perpetually renewable energy. In a nutshell, the ruthless oil companies could not permit this upheaval and they assassinated Benvido before he could take his invention to market. They burnt down his house, wiping out his work, killing him and seriously injuring – physically and mentally - his wife. Whilst the fire was blamed on faulty wiring, I have copies of CIA files which prove otherwise and you will see them later in this recording. Although they identify the assassin who "lit the match," they do not reveal who provided the matchbox. Of course, it's a shadowy, undocumented trail which leads from company executive to lobbyist to politician to intelligence services such as the CIA or Russia's Foreign Intelligence Service to private contractors to a further subsidiary to local mobster. His death may or may not have been authorised from the very top, although we all know that the fish rots from the head down. Whether his murder was sanctioned by an oil company, a trade association, a politician, a country or an inter-governmental agency like OPEC, we will almost certainly never know. Why would somebody want Benvido dead and the panels not on the market? Simple; too many people – be they individuals or companies or countries even - had too much to lose. Trust me, killing an academic would not have weighed on their conscience; killing an investigative journalist like me, even less so.

'But pause for a moment if you will and think of the countless lives that could have been saved by Benvido's mega-efficient solar panels. And the hundreds of millions, if not billions, of lives that could have been improved. The myriad animal species and natural habitats that could have been preserved.'

Staggering stats about flora and fauna extinctions then flashed on the screen in a ticker tape procession.

'And so, while solar power research was set back decades, it does still continue and, now that we are in a race against time, we need to bring all our great scientific and inventor minds together to focus on this and on developing the efficacy of bio fuels, wind power, hydro-electricity and geo-thermal energy. Given that it is not always sunny and the wind is not always blowing, we also need to further improve our capability for green energy storage.

'And while I have my reservations over nuclear energy – the Chernobyl disaster in 1986 reminded us all of the danger of nuclear power as the radioactive equivalent of 400 Hiroshima bombs was unleashed and, more recently, the Fukushima calamity in Japan reawakened our fears – I do know much work goes on in this field and that scientists are moving beyond nuclear fission and its inherent dangers and looking at power from nuclear fusion, which will address fears about accidents and radioactive waste. I am no scientist so I reserve judgement on nuclear but, what I do know is that *if* this is to be our pathway to carbon-free emissions, then we need investment and all the world's experts in the same room and working in unison, not tomorrow but right now.

'There is hope out there but we need to come together as a world to quicken our transition to using renewable energy. And to fight the fossil fuel companies - and the corrupt politicians and media that they have in their pockets - who continue to stand in our way. They have infiltrated our governments and built themselves an elaborate form of self-regulation. As I have explained, they are big business and, as such, put their own interests first and have, over the years, spent mega-bucks ridiculing green thinking and the eco-movement whilst doing all they can to maintain the current situation which sees us hurtling headlong into oblivion.

'So, with my death, and that of Benvido, we can add murder to the list of crimes that the fossil fuel industry is culpable of; and I know there have been many others. Their misanthropy is one more reason why we need oversight by an altruistic world governing body, an organisation that puts the interests of the planet first, not the balance sheet of energy companies. Believe me, there is a way that we can make things right. Instead of countries and companies working in isolation and against one another, we must unite to find solutions. We can no longer be victims of the "divide and conquer" mentality of those in power. A new one world government would better coordinate the disparate strands of research and would oversee the effective and efficient deployment of new technologies. In the same way that we need green technology experts in the same room, we also need to come together across the planet to steer and provide governance for new concepts such as artificial intelligence, robotics, virtual realities, biological and chemical warfare, cloning and all the other threats and opportunities that face us. We are being confronted by more and more compelling needs for international standards and cooperation. Please, I beg of you, support the next NOW march happening in your local city. Do it before protests turn violent and we start to see eco-groups planting bombs.'

Cue footage of NOW marches in several cities across the world.

'By all means vote for your local NOW representative if there is one but we simply do not have time to wait for the usual political processes and machinations to play out. Get out there and change the world for the better!

Governments will only listen when they see the strength of feeling. As I hope I have impressed upon you; the very survival of the human race is at stake. The philosophers say that the meaning of life is to plant trees under which you do not expect to sit – we, as a generation, now need to act on this in order to secure our future. Thank you for listening to me.'

There then followed a carousel of slowly revolving photographs depicting pages of confidential CIA files, documenting the killing of Benvido and including a confession of arson by a hitman from Sarajevo.

A slight juddering of the screen revealed the limitations of my editing skills and then we were looking at moving images again – namely the two American agents sat in Harry's Bar uttering their incriminating words. Recorded in 4k, I was rather pleased with how the film had come out. And then it was back to me and, as far as I was concerned, the pièce de résistance.

'I leave the world – for I know my days are now numbered - with a parting gift. Angelina had been promised a copy of Benvido's drawings and notes for a prototype of his new solar panels but, as a result of her premature demise, these never materialised. When I met the scientist's widow in Copenhagen she gave me the names of a few close colleagues and collaborators who she thought he may have passed his plans to. I tracked them down one by one and finally struck gold. To follow, you will find images of his blueprints, detailing the technicalities of the invention. I pray that they will be enough for scientists and inventors to make something of.'

There then followed a series of crystal-clear images of Benvido's sketches. As the whole piece drew to a close, surely, I thought to myself, there must be enough material here for a few people to stop and ask what is actually going on in the world?

Now I faced a straightforward conundrum – how to get the film to the right people before the wrong people got to me? Easier said than done considering I had already stood Candy Kitcatt up once and I knew the Americans were very much on my trail.

Chapter 3

14 February 2018

I

I chose to send the film that I had spliced together to Candy in Denmark via FedEx. I did not want to run the risk of anything sent electronically being intercepted or giving away my location. If it was to go 'missing in the post', then I still had copies of the original files and, hopefully, no-one knew of my whereabouts, I reasoned to myself. I had by now started to worry slightly less about being tailed and opted to take the easy option of using a local but still relatively out-of-the-way FedEx depot. It was on 147th Street, out near JFK, and it was only once I had exited the building and was back on the desolate street of anonymous business units that I started to get the vibe that I was being tracked. Lengthening my stride as I headed back to Rosedale, I started to curse myself for choosing such an unpeopled spot; someone had emerged from a car park and was certainly following me, about 40 yards behind and at precisely the same pace as mine. Whether it was pure chance was up for debate but it seemed unlikely. Where are the subway stations and buses when you need them in life? I considered running but opted to bluff it out, finding a bench in Brookville Park and calling Sylvenie to ask her to come and pick me up. My pursuer walked straight past me without a glance – male, a similar age to me, perhaps a year or two older but taller and of an athletic build. Thankfully, Sylvenie had been out in her beat-up Chevy Monte Carlo, shopping in the vicinity, and was with me within a few minutes.

The incident made me realise two things: my deposit at the FedEx depot would almost certainly be sequestered and that those hunting me were close at hand. It was time to move on. However, before I could do so, I had the small matter of a voodoo ceremony to attend.

II
15 February

It had been Apollo rather than Sylvenie who had talked me into joining them at the gathering in the basement of a bakery in Brooklyn in what is known as 'Little Haiti' in Flatbush. I often try and live by the axiom of trying everything in life except, of course, incest and Morris dancing and had agreed to attend. Apollo had promised me an amazing spectacle and convinced me that Angelina would be with us at the gathering, although Sylvenie was less comital on this issue. While the ritual did not provide me with any Angelina solace, he was not wrong in terms of the delivering of a spectacle.

It was easier to find a nail bar than a lounge bar in Flatbush but we had stumbled across a place called The Zombie House, which suited our needs. I think it was what is known as a tiki bar and before we had chance to find a table, a half-dressed and gregarious hostess danced over to us and around us before declaring herself as the talking menu. It was all a bit overwhelming for me but we ordered a round of cocktails revolving around Caribbean rum, which the joint seemed to specialise in.

Elevating our voices above the chilled Caribbean beats, we could just about make ourselves heard. 'Will I be allowed in? Am I going to stand out? Like an imposter, like an undercover cop?' I fretted.

Sylvenie placated me: 'You will be absolutely fine. The beautiful thing about vodou is it does not discriminate. It is enough that you are there. Tonight's ceremony will take place in what you would call a temple but what we call a peristyle and will be attended by anyone and everyone; no one is judged. There will be men, women and trans in the audience and from all backgrounds – everyone from doctors and lawyers to thieves, dealers and prostitutes; no-one is excluded. Freedom is the very soul of my religion. Many of those attending might be Christians during the day – it is not at all unusual to attend Church in the morning and to be a vodouist by night.

'The lwas – or spirits – are themselves either male or female and they do not discriminate when choosing who to enter or ride. Whoever they choose becomes known as a *chwal* or horse; it is a great honour for us mortals to be ridden by the divine, they only enter those that they love. There are many lwas, responsible for many aspects of our lives such as morality, reproduction, love, wealth and death. Each has to be elaborately prepared for, and each has their own unique, favourite demands of offerings from worshippers. My brother ,who has moved back to Port-au-Prince, is queer and he likes to wear make-up – while he could get away with that in New York, in Haiti it is acceptable in a peristyle but not on the streets. Tonight's rituals will be presided over by a *houngan* – a male priest – but it could easily have been a mambo, like me. I am told that he likes to dress up as Baron Samedi, a lwa of the dead, which is a little unusual. A priest's job, certainly back in Haiti, is something between a doctor, a spiritual worker and a social worker. At heart, vodou is a healing-based religion. Remember that in Haiti there might only be one doctor for 10,000 people. As you will see tonight, practitioners dance their way to ecstasy – it is the polar opposite of Eastern religions that think their way to nirvana.

'I hope you will enjoy your evening but shall we take a precaution to ensure that no lwa rides you? That can sometimes trouble neophytes. Would you permit me to rub some of this wax into your hair? It is a sensible precaution to keep the lwas away.'

I'd not expected to have my Barnet dishevelled by a gluey unguent but I knew that cats and dogs were surprisingly drawn to me and I wondered if it might be the same for spirits? All things considered, I thought it worth the inconvenience. Apollo did not follow suit.

We accessed the peristyle down some metal fire escape steps at the side of a non-descript store. Certainly not the sort of place you might just stumble across. The fire-door gave on to a small and square basement with a cement floor, dimly lit by hundreds of candles and sporting painted walls with elaborate depictions of skulls, snakes, crosses and trees. The room was hot and noisy, crowded with folks of all ages. Besides Apollo and myself, I spotted only one other white face. I discerned a small altar replete with colourful flags, candles, statuettes, a bottle of champagne, several rum bottles, various food offerings including a large cake and what looked like boiled eggs, flowers, brushes, perfume, figurines and a skull with three lit candles coming out of it at unlikely angles. No risk assessment or health and safety forms here I thought to myself. Sylve had suggested I bring some food offerings that Angelina might like so I pulled out a bunch of beetroot from a brown paper bag that I had been clinging to for the last two and a half hours and squeezed them on to the busy altar.

Sylvenie said: 'Now, follow me, just do as I do and you will be fine,' before bowing dramatically in front of a line of conga drums. Then somebody walked past me and poured a bottle of beer on my head. I was about to kick off but Sylve put her index finger to her lips and shouted: 'Don't worry, it is to help protect you.'

The houngan was instantly recognisable in a striking black and red top hat, a yellow frilly shirt, a white powder mask with blacked out eyes, nose and cheek bones and carrying a gnarled staff adorned with shells. He stood in the middle of the circle and it looked like things were about to get underway. Two thirds of the audience were dressed in white. Of these, perhaps half wore an incongruous hybrid style of traditional garb and streetwear; many had their

NY baseball caps at jaunty angles. Several were drinking beer and quite a few were smoking cigarillos. One or two had headphones on.

The houngan had a number of helpers, two of which were putting the final touches to the drawing of symbols on the floor with what looked like flour; their scrawls resembling flowers and leaves. Then the djembe drums began and, to my horror, a thrashing chicken was suddenly whipped from a hessian sack and a man with a three foot machete decapitated it. My stomach turned. Some of the dead bird's blood was spread on the floor by the mural, while the rest of it was mixed into a communal bowl of corn or something which was being passed around the room.

A small fire was lit in the middle of the circle. The houngan took a long pull from a rum bottle he was brandishing and spat it on the fire, all the time waving the headless chicken above his head, which was in his other hand. I noticed that many women had bowls of fruit on their heads and were circling in an anti-clockwise direction. They tilted and swayed in unison and then broke out into song, some of the audience started chanting whilst others danced. The whole scene was exhilarating but utterly disorientating.

Suddenly Sylvenie was thrown to the floor, as if an invisible wrestler had picked her up and hurled her there; someone screamed. Almost as quickly, she was on her feet again and was circling the priest backwards at great speed, her eyes bulging. I decided it might not be prudent to take her exactly at her word and to mimic *all* that she did. The priest also seemed possessed and was now stood in the flickering fire staring wildly. Then Sylvenie was back on the deck, face down in a star shape, her body seized by powerful convulsions. Her crashing to the ground had been softened this time by a coterie of helpers who haplessly tried to guess her next wild prostration. It was insanely intense.

Meanwhile, the sticky beer had somehow reacted with the beeswax in my hair to form a thick chewing gum paste. On top of this there was an intense smell of musky incense, the heat was stifling and the drums relentless and discordant. When a second squawking chicken was pulled out of the sack, I wondered what I was doing there and knew I was going to throw up.

I found the single loo through pure instinct, just in time to spew up my Zombie cocktails to the now dulled backdrop of pulsating ceremonial drums. Several minutes later, having recomposed myself, I opened the door to find a confused throng swaying about immediately in front of me. I noticed the drums had stopped and several police officers were pushing back against a dozen members of the congregation while a bible-clutching group of religious types were shouting off warnings about sinning and doing the devil's work. On talking to Apollo later, it turned out that purely by chance an evangelical God squad had arrived to disrupt the ceremony just moments before a police raid had been scheduled. The two groups had merged with those already in the basement and a chaotic ruckus had ensued. I took in the tableau in a flash before swiftly closing the toilet door and, using the rusted sink as a footrest, prised myself through a tiny window and out into the gutter. I had a strong premonition that the authorities were there for me.

Speaking with Apollo afterwards, he told me that nobody had been hurt but the disruption had brought a premature end to proceedings just as they were getting going. He also said that it had displeased the lwas and that Sylvenie was not herself at all; he thought she was still possessed by one. When it finally left her, he surmised, she would not remember what had happened for the past few days.

Meanwhile, I had problems of my own, finding myself on the streets again. I knew I had to lie low; these were a critical few days ahead of World Unification Day. Luckily going under the radar was something I was rather adept at; much of my life had been lived in a kind of low key obscurity. I still had a wad of notes and I found it easy enough to disappear into a nether world as a West Bronx barfly. The absence of bookies initially kerbed my fun but I soon found some slippery chancers who were happy to take 'off-track' bets for me. I never needed much of an excuse to sit in a dive bar all day and watch sport.

Jochen's Journal Part Two

Chapter 1

11 February 2018

As soon as I knew about them, I was keen to get my hands on the actual plans for the solar panels. I did not want to risk them being sent in the post so the only option had been for me to take a flight to Boston.

Having spoken with Professor Zihla face to face, explained who I was, and convinced her that I was not a spook or working for the oil and gas industry, she seemed more than happy to hand over the sketches that Benvido had given her as security in case the worst happened. In many ways, that had been relatively straightforward – the more taxing problem for me was what to do with them.

I was sat on the CIA files detailing the arson attack on the Benvido property, Ange's pre-recorded message cum promo for NOW and the Professor's actual blueprints, showing how to build his new, ultra-efficient solar panels. My index finger hovered, literally, between the send and delete buttons. I truly did not know which way to go. Send the files to Candy Kitcatt and, to a degree at least, avenge Ange's death by letting the world know why she was murdered and by whom. Might this set the wheels in motion towards a better world? Or, alternatively, expunge everything, thus disabling the auto-send to journalists and saving humanity from becoming further polarised by NOW? In my mind, I could already see the anti-NOW militias forming. If I had the opportunity to reduce conflict in the world, then surely it was my duty to do just that?

The question conflated in my mind with a recent paper I had submitted on how our natural world is shutting down as it prepares to go into hibernation while we destroy ourselves and the planet. My article had expounded how we are currently threatening a million species with extinction. The point I was intent on making was that we are not just living on Planet Earth, but that we are part of it. If we continue along the same path, soon we will not be content with having destroyed numerous animal species, we will wipe ourselves out too. One of the things that spending a lot of time analysing marine ecosystems has taught me is that all creatures and plants, however small, matter and have a role to play. If we do not preserve each and every life in the ocean then, long term, we do not preserve ourselves. It seems we are hell-bent on self-abuse, causing our own slow suicide; the ocean is dying and what happens to nature, happens to us for we are part of it.

On land too, our world is in great distress. Many mammal, bird, insect and plant species are disappearing. So many are in danger – everything from bees to gorillas. Wildlife populations have fallen by two thirds in the last 50 years. Since 1900, we have lost 90% of the big fish in our oceans. Each year, we kill as many as 100 million sharks. It is estimated that 150-200 species are becoming extinct every 24 hours. This is a rate of destruction that has never been seen before. It is unsustainable. If we continue to degrade soil like we are currently doing, we have about 50 years left or, put another way, just 50 harvests to reap. Yet for some reason, most people do not seem to care. As you can imagine, it can be very depressing for a man in my line of work. It is almost as if what can't be witnessed first-hand, can't be happening. But now, I think our indifference is beginning to impact the West; perhaps the First World will start to pay attention soon?

Or was there a compromise? I knew our world desperately needed to clean its act up. One option was for me to delete everything except for Benvido's designs, which I could send to a scientific journal. No-one need necessarily know about the professor's murder. Having just the drawings published should, in theory, push us towards a greener world without risking the catastrophe that an incentivised NOW movement might unwittingly cause. Besides, I did not entirely trust Candy and wondered whether, once she had her hands on the super-boosted solar panel drawings, she might hold the world to ransom? As a trained academic, my instinct was for the middle ground and balance and this course of action seemed like the way forward. It might just buy humanity a few more decades, maybe longer? I certainly knew of people who would love to get their hands on the outlines. My hunch was that The American Chemical Society's Photonics Journal might be the place to publish but I would seek guidance on the matter. After that, I was convinced that it would be relatively straightforward to find commercial partners and to get the product into mass production.

Chapter 2

22 February 2018

I lunched with Candy at *Carmine's* near Times Square. I was a little surprised that she knew I was in New York and even more shocked to secure such a highly coveted invite to meet with her. She said she had a surprise for me. I have to say the whole experience was somewhat unsettling. She seemed like someone from another world - the future perhaps – certainly unlike anyone in my sheltered and prosaic, academic orbit. And, boy, could she talk. I can barely remember half of it.

Once we'd been shown to our table and had ordered our family-sized platters of Southern Italian fare, we settled into conversation; Candy's security hovering none too discreetly at the bar, sipping on their sparkling waters.

'My dear Professor Goldreich, what a delight it is to meet you again,' she opened in her raspy Danish brogue. 'How have you been since the funeral? I hope things have not been too unbearable for you. Mourning is such a drain on our energy levels. Quite unpredictable too as to when it can overpower you. Life conjures up so many unexpected reminders of our loved ones – words, smells, sounds, music, food, opinions, places. Grieving is a rainbow of colours, many dark but there is brightness too. I am sure you are coping in your way. Most of us internalise our grief. I've lost family including both my birth parents, not to mention several dear friends along the way. They say that you never get over losing someone but that it is possible, eventually, to get used to it. But the death of people your own age, or younger, feels viscerally wrong. Angelina was such a darling too, a real sweetie. With such a mind! You must be so proud of her? Anyway, I won't go on. I often think about death though – I guess it is part of my life living as a trans woman, which, as I am sure you can imagine, has its moments. Anything from funny looks when I visit the women's loo to vicious online abuse and death threats. I suppose, on the flip side, I get lots of love too. Being a popstar no doubt helps. People can be more forgiving if they like your music. I always think of Freddie Mercury back in the day. So many macho Queen fans had to come to terms with the gradual unveiling of their idol's true sexuality.'

Sensing I might not get a word in and keen to steer the conversation in other directions, I managed to interrupt her breathless monologue: 'You must be encouraged by the traction that NOW is gathering?'

'I am. I really am. Did you see our simultaneous student demos last week when 195 boys and girls, each of them carrying a different national flag, presented themselves outside the UN buildings in New York, Geneva, Vienna and Nairobi? It was, I thought, a beautifully choreographed moment, a wonderfully symbolic gesture; those young people just stood there accusingly, facing the offices in complete silence before they were forcibly removed. Hats off to our ingenious campaign team for that one.

'And soon it will be World Unification Day; I couldn't be more excited! My vision is being realised. I always saw the decisive demo as being in New York, the "crossroads of the world," a protest that winds its way to the United Nations' headquarters and the World Federalist Movement's offices opposite. It seems right that we should transition to a new world in what is still, just, the most powerful nation on earth in our "old" world. It also seems right that the flagship march, which will for many be motivated by our climate crisis and a hatred of fossil fuel companies, should take place in a country where so many politicians are still in their thrall; there will be much rich symbolism at the end of the old world order and the beginning of a new one!

'People are finally expanding their thinking. Love of self and love of country are extending to a love of others and of the world. I am confident of disruptive strikes and a humungous turnout across the planet. Once the people have expressed themselves, the politicians will fall in line very quickly. I have said this many times but we *are* in paradise, it is just that, up to now, selfishness, greed, petty political differences, a lack of vision and poor management have got in the way of what could and should be the realisation of our very own Eden. We will look back on the last few hundred years as a time of necessary restless floundering and violent foment before world unification.'

Jumping in as she caught her breath, I asked: 'By the way, did you call by my hotel the other evening?'

'No?' Candy replied, looking slightly befuddled.

'Not to worry, it's probably nothing. Tell me, have you always been a world federalist?' I asked.

'Yes, and no,' was Candy's enigmatic response. 'I've always strived for a better world – one that is predicated on egalitarianism. A system that delivers for us all, not just the elite. I have always been, and remain, unconvinced by blinkered individualism, regionalism and nationalism, where all the focus is on outdoing the "opposition" – be that the neighbour, town, state, region or country next door. Too many people lose in life through this structuring of society. I've always fought for a more collaborative approach, where we embrace one another and work together for the greater good of all rather than for individual entrepreneurs focused on their own pursuit of wealth. I believe in "we" not "I". Mutual aid and succour, I believe, are innate human characteristics, however much capitalism tries to deny and suppress them. Quite simply, there should be no billionaires in the world. That, to me, feels instinctively wrong. I would much rather see the steady progression of society than the stellar rise of a few individuals.'

'What have you made of the recent rise in populism?' I asked, beginning to feel like an interviewer.

'Ah, yes, "the people against the elites," as it is sometimes crudely depicted, has been instructive hasn't it? It has shown us that people can still influence political parties or side-step them entirely. Both left-wing and right-wing populism paint a picture of those running the country—the politicians, judiciary, media, banks, business owners—as being pro-immigrants, pro-international business, and pro-foreign countries, all at the expense of the indigenous people. While there is clearly much to worry about with populism, it is undeniably a force where those with little say in society get to challenge the dominant forces. We need to re-educate and re-direct this distrust of the present system and harness it in our favour. People need to be roused into agitating for a global assembly, which has long-term vision and seeks to balance the best interests of individuals with the planet; a system that identifies, addresses and solves our problems in a coordinated and sustainable way. I would argue that we need to take back control of the word "populism" and harness it in our favour, as we make the argument for a world that would be run to benefit the global population not just the super-rich. I mean, across the planet, really, how many people would choose to live the life they live? If we are honest, how many, if they could, would choose to rewind their lives and live it all again? Not many, I would say. We can and must do better than this.'

A brief pause and then: 'Going back to your earlier question about whether I've always been a world federalist, I would say that, over the years, my philosophy has remained much the same, but I have gone from local to global in my approach. When I was younger, I was an anarcho-syndicalist; very much influenced by the writings of Proudhon, Kropotkin and Bakunin. They took me to my happy place as I watched my dad fall apart after my mother had run off with another woman. More recently, I have great respect for Noam Chomsky.

Of course, Christiania, where I was brought up, is a living example of how an anarchist community can work. I have to be clear though, the political system that I believed in was the very antithesis of Communist states like China and Russia – it was, and still is, my view that power corrupts. I believed in a grassroots democracy or decentralised Communism, free from hierarchies and bureaucratic central government and based on the voluntary collaboration of self-governing communities and workers' collectives. If roles and responsibilities were required at all in these co-ops, they would be rotated amongst its constituent members. After all, this is how we lived for millennia. It was only with the rise of towns and cities that institutions of control and authority came into existence. Call it naïve but, at essence, it was a belief that no human being should exploit another. The nearest we have ever come to a modern day society running itself like this was during the Spanish Civil War. In *Homage to Catalonia*, George Orwell described tens of thousands of people living alongside each other without class division and masters. There was collectivised running of factories, farms, hospitals and schools. Of course, it didn't last long as Franco's fascists won out in the end.'

'But now you want a one world government? Surely that is the ultimate globalisation of everything? An absolute hierarchy?' I asked, genuinely confused.

'Many "anti-globalisation" protestors object to the very term that is used to describe them. What they are protesting against – me too – is multi-nationals and blue chip financial firms currying favour amongst politicians, mistreating their workers, polluting the environment and homogenising every high street, reducing us to a McWorld monoculture. What many activists are actually calling for is trans-national cooperation in areas such as human rights, fair trade, justice and sustainability. While my political vision has matured and continues to evolve, I still hold true to these values. I certainly see myself as being aligned to and promulgating the left-leaning workers' associations which were founded last century on the principle of international solidarity. My dream would be for us to move through three stages. Firstly, a world government would show us how we can prosper by working together, which in turn would lead to more countries adopting Socialism and this would be the pre-cursor to us becoming free to ultimately, one day, reach the perfect state of Anarchism.'

Candy was confirming my worries about NOW: 'I can see you might have detractors,' I opined. 'People's natural instinct will be to fight being dictated to by a remote world super-state. I know you are a pacifist movement but you must anticipate resistance?'

'Strong government, democracy, opportunity and education for all, the eradication of hunger and poverty and the promotion of positive health outcomes, social justice, equality, freedom, a decent standard of living – prosperity even - and peace. Who doesn't want these things? A global cosmocracy would be much better equipped to deliver these aspirations than individual countries with maverick and transitory leaders. When it is explained to them clearly, I think people will see the overwhelming case for strong international government.

'After all, a one world federation would not be looking to micro-manage every detail of local and regional policy; it couldn't possibly do that even if it wanted to. The clue is in the word *world* – it would seek to deal with macro-issues that impact nations. Individual countries would still have the right to self-determination: to choose their own political systems, leaders, religions and laws. But, a world government would take care of global concerns. For instance, what could be more important than the safety of the planet on which we live? As we know, the threats facing us are serious and universal, be they from climate change, pandemics, terrorism or cyber-crime. Imagine AI in the wrong hands? Someone reminded me just the other day of the ever-growing network of cables that stretch across our oceans in "no-man's land" which will need protecting. As we become an increasingly symbiotic world, geopolitical tensions have consequences for us all.

'Just think how, with a single global authority, we would actually be able to plan ahead. Consider, for instance, the world population. Yes, right now it continues to grow but, by the end of the century, predictions suggest it will be in decline. This is already the case in South Korea and Japan and many Eastern European countries. Birth rates are set to plummet and by the end of the century almost all countries will see serious population decline. By then, most nations will be competing for migrants as they try to keep their economies vibrant enough to pay for the care of increased numbers of the elderly, while at the same time, a handful of countries will be struggling with burgeoning population growth. The re-distribution of labour will be integral as to whether humanity prospers or withers. A world government would, of course, be uniquely placed to manage this situation and to facilitate the organised migration of people – for those that wanted to move of course.

'And imagine, if you will, that we were to organise things propitiously so that we started working in a coordinated fashion across borders. We could live in a world where everyone works but we all work less hours, freeing up more time for family, friends and leisure. Something that I think, for most, would be a turn for the better. In 1930, the economist John Maynard Keynes imagined a future in which technological innovation, efficiency gains and long-term capital growth might usher in what he called a "golden age of leisure" – he predicted that by 2030 we would be working no more than 15 hours a week. I always recall reading the book *Paths to Paradise* by Andre Gorz in which he laid out a practical roadmap to liberate ourselves from the shackles of work. These utopias are, in theory at least, now within our reach.

'Think too of a world where there would be universal education. What progress civilisation would make when all – not just a small percentage – of minds were fully developed and utilised!'

A world of forced migration, labour camps and stifling, homogenised education, I thought to myself but I did not interrupt.

'One of the worries for self-centred first world inhabitants is that by sharing resources and power, somehow this will be deleterious to their own life. I don't believe this to be true at all. And anyway, let's just say I am totally wrong and we have to take a slight dip in our living standards, is that such a price to pay in order to allow others to live? Does every member of the family really need their own car? Do we really need three flat screen televisions in our homes, whilst many villages across the world share a single TV set? If you and I are stranded on a desert island, do we pool resources and physical and mental toil? Do we work together or do we try and go it alone and think to hell with our cohabitee? Of course, we collaborate, sharing our skills and resources in order that we might survive.

'Given all the world's problems, don't you think that nations will increasingly have to come together anyway? Already there is evidence of this as we gradually improve the life chances of people around the world.'

On this point, I saw some common ground: 'I am not sure "gradually" is quite the right word. We so often overlook the progress that humankind makes. Even though our population continues to grow – and it has doubled since 1970 – indicators suggest things are getting better for most people. For one, we are living longer. Since the turn of the century, our healthy life expectancy has improved by an average of five years in almost every country – Syria being the exception. In Rwanda, children born this century can expect to live 22 years longer than the generation before them.

'Much uplifting work detailing how the world is a better place than we think has been done by my compatriot, Hans Rosling. In terms of health, education, access to energy, clean water and sanitation, and a host of other criteria, we do move forward as a species. He argues that we are psychologically geared towards thinking that everything is getting worse – experts refer to it as our negativity bias - but actually the evidence tells a different story. Essentially, we are programmed to catastrophise and pay more attention to scary things. As he rightly points out, newspapers play on this and revel in reporting disasters, crises and calamities; it is very unusual for them to feature positive news as it just doesn't grab our attention.

'But there is plenty to celebrate. Over the past generation or two, extreme poverty is down 80% and, believe it or not, deaths due to war are down by 95%. In 1950, global average life expectancy at birth was 46 years of age. In 2015, it was over 71. This is largely due to the gap between rich and poor countries diminishing. During the nineteenth century, every third child in the world died before the age of five. The young are acutely vulnerable to disease but child mortality rates have fallen significantly – by more than 90% in developed countries and by 80% in the least developed countries - all thanks to vaccines and improvements in hygiene, nutrition, healthcare and clean water access. These days, we are less likely to get killed at work or by a car accident or in a plane crash. Europeans can thank the EU for improving much legislation in these areas.

'Across the world, individual life experiences are improving. In recent decades, child labour rates have reduced, so too income inequality and gender inequality, per-capita income is up as are education rates. Despite all the headlines, the chance of being a victim of violent crime has dramatically reduced over the centuries, particularly in Europe. Capital punishment, once a worldwide norm, will likely disappear entirely in the next 10 years.'

'Yes, I read Gosling's book too,' said Candy. 'Whilst we can thank the UN for much of this work, just imagine where we might be if it had been operating unencumbered and at full tilt?' and, ruminating further: 'It seems self-evident to me that our lives could be so much better with just a little careful planning and forethought. If our current world was a ship, then one person would live in extreme opulence, a couple might live reasonably well, then the bulk of the crew would toil tirelessly for next to no wages and a sizeable group would be left in a corner to starve or die of treatable diseases. But we wouldn't accept that, would we? Were we to set sail, we would compute how long we would be at sea and how many of us there were; we would share the workload and ration our supplies. Likewise, we can do this for the world. Granted, it will take a little more planning and organisation but it is not beyond our wit and wisdom. It just needs a universal will – and cooperation on a global scale – to make it happen. We either find a way or continue to watch millions die of poverty, war, disease and hunger. Who does not want world peace, human rights, enough food and good health outcomes for all? Well, it *is* achievable, it *is* now within our grasp.'

'And if - or, should I say, when - a NOW administration is realised, how do you think it will look?' I asked.

'This is a good question. How will we fashion the assembly? As you can imagine, I've given this a good deal of thought. The easiest way will be to revisit the UN's Charter and to refresh and turbo-charge this in order to seriously empower it. We could utilise much of its existing infrastructure and political apparatus and no doubt make use of its offices throughout the world: in New York but also in Geneva, Vienna, The Hague where the International Court of Justice resides, Nairobi, Addis Ababa, Beirut and Bangkok. I would envisage a slimming down of its 37 agencies. There would need to be something analogous to the UN's General Assembly, which is where each of its 193 countries currently has a seat. We would need to re-assess, if not scrap, how the Security Council works; for too long, its five permanent members – Russia, the US, China, France and the UK – have been able to veto vital interventions. Not a single country from Africa is represented. That has to change.

'A NOW government could be shaped along similar lines to the UN Secretariat. Doubtless, there would be merit in setting up departments that oversee key areas such as international trade, conflict management, the battle against drugs and crime, maritime law, counter-terrorism, safety and security, appeals and dispute tribunals, the exploration of outer space and the like. There could be a mirroring or perhaps expansion of the Economic and Social Council, which strives to develop a sustainable world through circular economies while promoting cooperation between nations on financial, social and cultural issues. Such a body would seek to ensure there is employment, health and wellbeing and higher standards of living for all, whilst safeguarding human rights and fundamental freedoms, irrespective of sex, race, language, religion or creed. There would also need to be a reinvigorated entity serving the same purpose as the International Court of Justice, which currently settles legal disputes between states as well as giving legal advice to UN agencies. And, to start with at least, a serious bulking up of its military capabilities. If we are serious about bringing an end to war and conflict, then we need to ensure that going up against the UN would be like a Nursery child trying to take on the heavyweight champion of the world. Do you know what I would do? I would centralise world energy and give the NOW assembly the power to cut off supply to any aggressive nation! Don't you think that is a cool idea? Anyway, the current structure will doubtlessly need some rethinking. Despite its good intentions, the United Nations has been tying itself up in knots for decades; its efforts regularly paralysed by just a few intransigent countries. Whilst ensuring we retain the democratic process, an improved mechanism for making prompt and impactful decisions needs to be put in place in order that urgent actions are not blocked.

'However, if it is felt that the UN belongs to the old world, then there are, of course, other options. International governance could come through strengthening trading blocs that already exist; those such as the African Union, the South-East Asian Nations, the League of Arab States, the EU, the Organisation of American States and the Union of South American Nations. By using them as building blocks and bringing them closer together, you start to have a nascent new world government.

'Another possibility would be to unite the growing number of democratic nations and to hope that, in time, other countries see the benefits of joining such a pact. A bit like what has happened in Western Europe. Also, thinking a bit more radically, some globalists have mooted the possibility of running the planet through the creation of a world constitution, which would give direct voice to the people as they vote on how to resolve major global issues. It's a thought.

'Let's also remember all the other international infrastructure that is already in place and could be made use of. Besides the UN, we can consider reshaping and bulking up the likes of the World Trade Organisation, NATO, the International Monetary Fund, the World Bank, Interpol and the International Criminal Court. Or we could build from the G20 countries – so the likes of China, India, Mexico, Russia and the US. These countries must account for more than two thirds of the global population and certainly incorporate the most popular religions of Christianity, Islam, Judaism and Buddhism. Think too of all the humanitarian and altruistic NGOs – the Red Cross, Médecins Sans Frontières, Oxfam and the like - that could all be drafted into a new world congress.

'I see it as my job to get us to the destination; I am not overly concerned as to the logistics of how it might work when we get there. Your wife told me that the Dutch have a saying that a person who is outside their front door has the hardest part of their journey behind them. I believe we are outside our door. We know from history that if the people of the world protest and march in large enough numbers, politicians will find a solution quick enough.'

'And yourself? Are you comfortable with being a leader, given what you said earlier about the sharing of responsibilities and power corrupting?' I questioned, trying to trip her up.

'My role as NOW's principal is ephemeral. It is a necessary evil if it gets us to where we want to go. Much like NOW itself, it is merely a vehicle.'

'So, where do you see the world going?' I queried. 'Do you really believe there will be a paradigm shift to international collaboration and a people-first world?'

'Yes, I do. Without doubt. In fact, I think it is probably going to come about quicker than I first imagined. Across the world, momentum builds. People have had enough of being lied to, of seeing profits put before humanity and our beautiful planet; of so much being sacrificed in order that a select few can live opulently. As Bob Dylan once said: 'Is your money that good?'

'The rise of NOW has been, and still is, exponential. We have been receiving amazing feedback from all around the globe about how many people intend to march with us on World Unification Day. If the predictions are right, it will be a pivotal day in history, although I've always hated that word his-story, let me say our story.

'Never have we lived in such exciting times. Not just politically but scientifically and technologically. As you will be aware, there are all sorts of wonderful predictions for the coming decades – everything from space tourism to self-healing concrete to solar powered super highways that recharge driverless automatic electric cars to intelligent robotics taking over repetitive tasks. We stand on the precipice of so many developments – everything from energy being provided by renewables to embryo-editing that allows for the removing of genetic disease.

'Humankind develops at a staggering pace. We adapt our world to our needs and, at the same time, adapt ourselves to the environment we live in. Androgyny is the future. I mean this has nothing to do with the NOW movement or world federalism, this is just between me and you and is my opinion on where we are going as a species. Soon we will be able to be whoever the fuck we want to be and fuck whoever we want to without a need for badges such as hetro, homo, bi, transitioning and all that complicated nomenclature. We will just be. Even terms such as non-binary, epicene or genderqueer will become redundant. How liberating will that be? It is clearly happening before our very eyes, I am just amazed how few people have picked up on it.

'People's yin and yang are becoming increasingly balanced. Surely you have noticed younger people becoming more gender fluid, not only in their minds but in their looks and physicality? A manifestation of this can be found in the strange world that is the fashion industry where models and clothes are becoming increasingly genderless – skinny boys and girls with gaunt physiques and high cheekbones are all the rage. As are transgender models, something that I can personally vouch for. I was recently asked to parade up and down the catwalk in Milan. Of course, they wanted me to model the latest asexual suits but I only agreed to do it on the proviso that I could wear a collection of vibrant and, dare I say, risqué but always tasteful and elegant dresses. What we choose to wear or not wear defines us. I can't imagine living life with a mind so beaten down that you wear a grey suit or jeans and a checked shirt, day after day. I look forward to the time, not too far around the corner, when we can print out our self-designed clothes, mapped to our own bodies.

'Going back to my androgyny theory and, as I say, this is between you and me, but I believe it is connected to the lower male sperm count which is being caused by ever-increasing levels of plastic in the environment. It's known as "Spermageddon" of course. By 2045, more than half of couples will need help conceiving. Male and female are gradually merging into the same sex. Of course, this isn't an entirely new thing. Historical and literary tracts reveal hermaphrodites, or androgynes as they are now known, were present in many ancient cultures. Greek mythology told the tale of the first humans to have four arms and four legs and one head with two faces and, fearing their power, Zeus split them into two separate parts. From thereon, so the story goes, men and women have sought their other half in order to become one again. Epicenes have often be used to symbolise unity and wholeness – remember the line from Orpheus, "Zeus is male, immortal Zeus is female". And let's not forget that many ancient religions view their deity as genderless. Some countries already recognise a third gender – what is known as the hijra community in the Indian sub-continent.

'Too many people, for too long, have defined gender by genitals. Now, a heightened understanding of our physiology has allowed us to understand that we are not just defined by what is tucked away in our underwear but that we are all shaped by a complex network of hormones, chromosomes, neural signals and environmental factors. I certainly suffered from gender dysphoria as a child; trust me, I *knew* I had not been assigned the right genitals at birth. Advancements in scientific understanding, diagnosis and record keeping have taught us that there are significant numbers of people who are born intersex, some clearly misgendered at birth. Acceptance of this is becoming more commonplace.

'I know it is not quite the same, but think of the increased prevalence of iconic cross-dressers over the last century; for me, proto-types of an androgynous future: Marlene Dietrich, Coco Chanel, David Bowie, Twiggy, Prince, Annie Lennox, Boy George, Eddie Izzard, Harry Styles ….. you get my drift. It is not only gender, races too are merging as we blend into one being, a human. In no time at all, our skin colour and other traits and genes will have become so blended that most of us will resemble present day Brazilians. Across society there is a gradual diminution of stereotypes, fewer extremities of toxic macho-behaviour or overt femininity. Globally, we continue to see an increased inter-sexing of male and female – I have heard it referred to pejoratively as the "fanitisation" of men, coupled with women increasingly taking on what have traditionally been seen as "male characteristics" such as being assertive and ambitious. Think of the concept of the "new man" where males show more gentleness, compassion, sensitivity and empathy. The young no longer relate to the Marlboro man of yesteryear. In the workplace there are, quite rightly, vanishingly few divisions between "men's jobs" and "women's work". Our language changes too to reflect these changes – staffing rather than manning, Chairperson not Chairman, spokesperson instead of spokesman.'

'And what of procreation if we are to become human rather than man or woman?' I queried, although I suspected Candy would have an answer.

'Technological and medical innovations will take us there,' was her instant come-back, as if she had been waiting for me to ask the question. 'Within our lifetimes most babies won't be born as a result of sexual congress. Designer babies are already possible thanks to what is known as CRISPR research, which allows labs to genetically modify embryos – it can be to take out inherent disease or to add in characteristics such as strength and beauty. Same sex couples will be able to have their own genetically edited offspring and we edge closer to children being born from a single parent. Stem-cell research offers the possibility for children to be born from our own cells - so a female could potentially produce sperm from her cells and a male could produce eggs from theirs. In theory, doctors could take a woman's egg and sperm cells from her skin, create embryos from them and insert one of these into her womb for childbirth. Do you remember Dolly the Sheep? Humans are next, trust me, cloned babies are right around the corner. By the end of the century we will be watching our babies grow in incubators. This would give a whole new dimension to the term "in breeding", don't you think? And then there is the whole area of trans men having babies – you know, when a person assigned with female genitalia at birth is part way through transitioning to a man but still has her reproductive organs in working order and becomes pregnant. It happens. As you can imagine the newspapers love it. And don't even get me started on babies born in the metaverse - our immersive future - they will be an option for some within decades. Children that you can give back or can have live as perpetual toddlers if you like!

'Longer term, we are set to become a planet of androgynous cyborgs. Remember, we are always evolving. First we were simple anemones in the sea, then we lived in trees, in caves and so on. Next we will be cyborgs. It may just save us as our bodies become diseased through the ingestion of microplastics. Consider a walk down any street and how many people are staring at their phones, effectively tuned into another network? Our brains are already in the process of integrating with our devices. How long before we climb into them and merge with them? Prosthetics, electronic and bionic body parts, sometimes controlled by our smartphone, are becoming more and more common. Increasingly we will look upon our bodies as being fallible to disease and breakages; mortal, limited and imperfect carriers for our own computers –

our brain. To me, it is inevitable that we will join with machines. It will probably be a case of either merging with artificial intelligence or, as machines replicate and better-design themselves, being overtaken by them. Soon the speed of AI will be accelerated further through quantum computers, which all the big tech companies are racing to build. This integration has been labelled the moment of technological singularity. There is genuine hope that AI will lead us to a better world, bringing huge benefits to our health, our safety, the environment, clean energy and so much more.'

'Sounds dystopian to me, a future nightmare,' I couldn't help differing.

Completely ignoring me, Candy continued: 'As I said, these are exciting times. Right now we are the artist's blank canvas on which anything can be drawn. Our empathy, ethics, understanding, caring and compassion are the traits that will differentiate us from robots. These will still be required in many fields - medicine for one - as we move forward. Advances in AI and drugs will strengthen and shape our bodies in unimaginable ways in a process known as transhumanism. Some argue that we would become god or at least demigods but don't quote me on that! Our capabilities will be so developed that we will have become post-humans. Living in perpetual bliss, you might argue that we will have finally reached heaven! Creativity will be needed too. If, having had our brains scanned, our minds are transferred to a computer then we need them to be as beautiful as possible! This opens up the potential of living forever and having the capability to download yourself to a robot anywhere on the planet for a little stroll around every now and again!'

'Mmm, that's quite a future that you prophesise, even if only half of it comes true,' I mused, my head spinning. 'Some of it is quite worrying. A life driven by technology? And what of faith in this brave new world?'

'Religions – or, as far as I am concerned, superstitions – will no doubt continue to exist for some time yet, although I imagine they will eventually wither on the vine as people realise the only things worth worshipping are science, what we see in front of our eyes and the planet itself. For now, these, along with death, are the only absolute truths we have. But that is another discussion entirely and I have no particular axe to grind on that subject. Each to their own and NOW would certainly allow for multiple belief systems, indeed it would go out of its way to protect the religious, ethnic and cultural rights of every world citizen.'

'If you don't mind me asking, do you personally face this future alone or with a partner?'

'Professor Goldreich, are you making a pass at me?' Candy teased and, sensing my fluster, continued: 'Well, right now, as you ask, there is no one special, although I have lots of friends and, of course, each one of them is special. That will be one of the appealing things about the future; it will be much more commonplace and acceptable to be partner-less. After the moment of singularity, we will not only be amazingly intelligent but we will be able to experience pleasure way beyond our current ambit. Sexual liberation and transhumanism are inextricably linked. Cyborg sex is the future. The ultimate erogenous zone is the mind and, essentially, we will be looking at the conceptual transformation of the sexual partner into a masturbation device. Virtual reality and brain wave headsets will allow us to live out our wildest sexual fantasies without the risk of violence or pregnancy or STDs or, depending on your thing, arrest! At the moment, we are a tactile species, so sight and sound will not be enough for us. Lightweight haptic exoskeleton suits, or wearable robots as some people call them, will allow us to feel and touch and thus fully immerse ourselves in our virtual worlds – these uniforms add flexibility and strength to our bodies, conjuring up the possibility of boundless energy and all kinds of positions. Wonderful news for the disabled, the old, the unfit, the obese, those suffering with a lack of oestrogen or erectile disorders, don't you think? In time, all our senses will be improved and updated by technology. Pleasure and orgasms are the result of chemicals firing in the brain and very shortly scientists will be able to replicate those feelings by shooting signals from an implanted chip or a brainwave headset giving us the potential to turn on and off endless orgasms! Believe me, this is not as far away or as fantastical as it sounds!'

To be fair, as deranged as she sounded, I could have listened to Candy's fascinating predictions for longer but, as I laid down my cutlery, utterly defeated by my eggplant Parmigiana, she flipped the conversation by asking me, 'But I have talked too much. What about you, Professor Goldreich? Tell me about *your* life. What are you doing in New York?'

'To be absolutely honest – and I don't say it often – but I am actually enjoying a few days away from the office. I've been very busy of late, submitting a couple of research papers, along with the usual teaching and plugging away at my book. Ange's death had originally made me double-down on my work.'

'Tell me something about what it is that you do. What have you been focused on?'

'There are so many crimes against our planet, it's often difficult to know where to begin. When I return to work, I will continue my investigations into the US's "Pacific Proving Grounds" policy. I am sure you are familiar with this. It took place during the Cold War when, during the middle of the last century, they exploded over one hundred nuclear "tests" in the Marshall Islands in Micronesia. Sixty seven of these atomic explosions took place on the atolls of Enewetak and Bikini.'

'As in Bikini Bottom in the cartoon series SpongeBob SquarePants?' Candy exclaimed.

'Actually, yes, there are lots of subliminal references in the programme which I don't think many people pick up on – but that's another story. One of the bombs exploded on Bikini Atoll was named "Bravo" and was the equivalent of 1,000 Hiroshima bombs. Many of the islands and islanders are still radioactive to this day and there has been untold ill-health and cancers in the region. In order that the experiments could take place, hundreds of people were exiled from their homes and have still not been able to return, whilst some islands were vaporised completely! Just for good measure, they threw in some biological weapon tests too. The radiation left by these explosions won't dissipate for thousands of years.

'During the tests, enormous craters were carved into the landscape and one of these was used as a dumping ground for nuclear waste. The Runit Dome on Enewetak, where radiation levels are *still* as high as at Chernobyl and Fukushima, is known as "The Tomb" by locals. The bomb-created basin, right next to the ocean, was filled with radioactive material, some of which was imported nuclearised soil from the US, and then capped with a concrete lid. Consideration was given to lining the crater with concrete but it was decided this would be too expensive. Of course, this was in a time before our climate crisis and rising sea levels. Right now, the dome is in imminent danger of flooding as the groundwater creeps up each year. Now we await the next catastrophe to hit our seas. I thought the whole story served as something of a metaphor for how our very existence is balanced on a knife-edge. And, by the way, right next door in French Polynesia, the French were doing exactly the same.......'

Candy cut across me, glancing at her fitness band and butting in with: 'I am sorry Professor, but it is later than I realised. I have a surprise for you for dessert but it entails us leaving our seats right now.'

More than a little intrigued, I allowed her to guide me to the bar where the screens of the two large suspended televisions suddenly started flickering and the volume seemingly rose of its own accord. We needn't have left our seats as the whole restaurant had no choice but to turn and watch. Try as they might, it seemed like the staff could not change the channel or turn the monitors off either. To my utter amazement, it was Zach's face that filled the screen as he said: 'My life is over, I know that, but I implore you to give up 30 minutes of yours ……'

Some half an hour later, having watched Zach, Ange, some film footage from a Venice bar and photos of Benvido's plans, the audio muted and the screen returned to a basketball game. One or two people had walked out but everyone else had sat transfixed throughout the utterly surreal interlude. The only other time I could recall a whole bar being so captivated by a TV screen was during the unfolding of the 9/11 tragedy. Candy Kitcatt was electrified; it had been a wonderful promotion for NOW.

'Oh my god! It worked – such a powerful message; your wife speaks so well and we actually managed a blanket takeover of the popular channels of communication. That should bolster World Unification Day numbers even more. Just one question Professor,' she said, her tone now slightly threatening, 'Benvido's drawings?'

'I have them – or at least I thought I had them,' I said, wholly nonplussed.

'I think if you look in your safe, you will find you don't actually have them. Zach liberated them and handed them over to us,' said Candy, her face now a menacing rictus. 'But, tell me, what were you thinking of doing with them?'

'My plan was to release them to the scientific world.'

She glanced at her security before looking at me questioningly.

'Truly, it was,' I pleaded.

Zach's Journal Part Three

Chapter 1

26 February 2018

Welcome to CBS This Morning on what looks like being an extraordinary day.

New York, the Eastern Seaboard – indeed most of the world - is at a standstill as we prepare for what is being termed World Unification Day: 24 hours of international strike action and protest marches. Schools and universities are closed, banks are shut, hospitals are fully stretched, almost all department stores and restaurants are shuttered and the transport system is operating a skeleton service. The global downing of tools has effectively turned what is, for many, the first working day of the week into a public holiday Many people are using the day to join synchronised demonstrations around the world in support of the New One World movement.

A significant crowd looks to be building in central Manhattan as NOW continues to gain international traction. The pressure group, which originated in Copenhagen and has recently seen dramatic growth in popularity across Europe, will be demanding a new paradigm shift to a world government which would oversee the political and economic stewardship of the planet. On top of the mass industrial action, it is thought that over 100, largely concurrent, demonstrations will take place across six continents, with the New York protest culminating at an assembly point outside the gates of the United Nations' offices on East 42nd Street.

Midtown's Bryant Park is already full and huge swathes of people are assembling on Fifth Avenue, which has been shut down to traffic for the day. CBS's Lucy Bentley joins us live from Times Square where people have been arriving since early this morning, joining many that have camped overnight.

Christina, thank you. As you can hear, we are standing right in front of an already noisy gathering of hundreds if not thousands of protestors. They are being overseen by a large, visible police presence – you can see and hear helicopters circling high above Manhattan's skyscrapers - although rally organisers have insisted that today will be a peaceful protest. Right now, there is almost a carnival feel and you can sense the energy building ahead of the march which is due to begin at midday and ultimately head to the UN headquarters. The event will end with a rally and celebration in Central Park when charismatic leader Candy Kitcatt will address a worldwide audience as she simulcasts to co-ordinated protests.

The NOW movement predicts that one million people will march through the streets of New York, which would make this the largest political protest to ever take place in the city. It's too early to say whether this prediction will be met but it certainly looks as if tens of thousands will be gathering across town.

With me now is Aneta Dimitrova, a NOW activist and one of today's organisers. Aneta, what is all this about and what are you hoping to achieve?

I think people are finally seeing beyond domestic politics. Our current system of national governments is broken. We now live in a global community with problems that need transnational solutions. There are so many urgent issues that can only be fixed when countries work together in a United States of the World. Only then can we fight climate change and pollution and all our other problems. People across the world have now come to realise this, even if the politicians are still playing catch up. Finally, we have something to unite our broad church. Whilst some governments will inevitably meet the strikes and demonstrations with repression – I think we can guess which - I honestly believe momentum is on our side. I think we have reached a critical mass which will enable us to make the transition to a new world order. We stand on the verge of a cosmocracy. Either that or we continue to sleep-walk into extinction.

Well, it's certainly going to be a busy day right here in New York but what about the rest of the US and the world? Are you anticipating interest across the continents?

As a publicity stunt we started offering world citizen passports and international identity cards, but people have taken it seriously and demand has gone through the roof - we are struggling to keep up! When Candy speaks to the world later today and politicians begin to understand the groundswell of public support for a new world government, I think it will make them realise that things need to change quickly and dramatically.

Thank you Aneta. And, lastly, do you anticipate this being a peaceful march? We know that counter-demonstrations are expected across Manhattan.

Yes, we are a pacifist movement. Nothing permanent has ever been built on violence. We seek to change hearts and minds through logic and learning not through violence and intimidation. You can't pick up anything with a closed fist. There will probably be some small pockets of counter-protesters - a few groups of people who we still need to convince but I think they will be utterly overwhelmed by the numbers on today's demo. Nobody's domestic political system is in danger, it is just that each country will need to cede a little power to the greater good. We all need to tune into a global consciousness. In a way, nothing changes but everything does.

Thanks again Aneta. Ordinarily, standing where I am, I would be mowed down by heavy traffic but, as you can see, today I am in the middle of a sea of banners – If not NOW, When? Right Here Right NOW, Come Together, Ready for Better, NOW for Tomorro, World Super State NOW, It's NOW or Never, People Before Profit, Our Time is NOW, My Nationality is Humankind, NOW Now, We Are the 99% and there's a banner that has the A in USA crossed out and replaced with a W for World; another one simply proclaims We Not I. Let me see if I can just grab a few words with some of the demonstrators, many of whom have been here since first light. Morning sir, can I ask you why you've joined the protest today?

Sure. This is a massively important day; I am here to be part of history. I travelled in from West Copake yesterday and couldn't find any hotel accommodation so I bought a tent and camped overnight. Climate change is wreaking havoc on us all and we need to come together to fix it. It's that simple. We've all had enough of watching our world flooding or burning or melting and witnessing the suffering that follows. It's time to stop being passive spectators. We can suffer in silence no more. We need to be active participants in the fight to save our planet. They stole the world from the people, now we are stealing it back! Let's bring all the best brains into the same room and have them work together rather than against one another. Enough is enough. The clock is ticking.

And you, madam, thank you for putting your megaphone down for a moment. Why are you here?

Today is where it all begins. I am celebrating the start of the transition to a new and better world – where we work with nature rather than against it. Just look at how many beautiful people are here. People of all races, all creeds, all sexual orientations, of all religions and none. For years, millions of voices have been silenced –environmental campaigners, anti-fascists, peaceniks, pro-women marchers – well, today is our day. This is our Woodstock. Today is a parade not a protest. This is celebration day; it's party-time! Woo! Let's go!

Thank you. And with that, for now, I hand back to the studio.

Thank you Lucy. The noise and excitement certainly seem to be building. They say that passion is a contagious emotion and that looks to be the case in Times Square right now. Don't go away, we will be returning throughout the day.

The size and impact of today's demonstrations have been bolstered after the recent release of a YouTube video in which a journalist, who was subsequently assassinated, denounced intelligence services and fossil fuel companies for murdering a CERN scientist who, she claimed, was on the cusp of changing how we power the world through his invention of super-efficient solar panels. The film, recorded just days before the journalist's murder, flooded screens across the globe two days ago. Commentators believe its release will significantly swell today's numbers.

NOW leader Candy Kitcatt's speech will be broadcast live to numerous worldwide rallies, including in Dhaka, where it will be 1.00am in the morning, Karachi, New Delhi, Mumbai, Moscow, Istanbul, Cairo, Berlin, Paris, London, Rio, Sao Paolo and Buenos Aires.

Earlier, largely peaceful demonstrations took place in Auckland, Sydney and Tokyo; although in Shanghai, Beijing and Hong Kong there were scenes of sporadic violence after marchers defied a ban on protesting. There have also been unconfirmed reports of unrest in Pyongyang in North Korea.

The effects of today's protests have impacted so many aspects of our daily lives, not least the financial markets. Tabs Goldman, our Business Analyst, joins us now to talk about how the world's stock markets have been reacting.....

'Sir, can I ask again, are you okay? Are you sure I cannot fix you some breakfast?'

I lifted my head from the bar or, it seemed to me at least, I pushed the bar away from my head and focused on the fretful waitress. I had been up all night, after all I was in the city that never sleeps, so why not?

'Oh okay, I'll have another double rum with a splash of soda water.'

'And nothing to eat with that?'

'No, most definitely not. Anyone who needs to eat breakfast is clearly not drinking enough.'

Re-running the last week or so over in my mind, I once again congratulated myself on how I had hunted down Jochen in New York. Immediately after the funeral and drinks soiree at *Discordia*, I had visited Ange's flat in Amsterdam, using the key that Jasmine had slipped me. As was to be expected, there was nothing there of relevance but I did, quite by chance, happen to notice a pen from the illustrious Waldorf Astoria. I'd taken a punt and assumed it would be where Jochen would be holed up in the Big Apple. Knowing how his mind worked, if one or both of them had stayed there before and liked it – and the chances are they would have, given its reputation – he would use it again. I made a quick call and asked to be put through to his room. When I was connected and heard his lofty tones, I knew

I'd struck gold.

'A little later, I had reception call his room during a quiet moment in the evening to proffer him an invite to meet Candy Kitcatt in the lobby bar. Scanning the block of lifts to ascertain which level he came from, I then sidestepped his unmistakable gait and hung out on his floor until he returned to his bedroom, puzzled as to why Candy had stood him up. His room number suitably identified, it was then a case of coming back early the following morning and waiting for him to take breakfast. When he did, I audaciously tapped on his door while the cleaner was in there and took my chances by asking for a moment alone in my room. After just a few tries, I decoded his safe—Ange's date of birth, what else?—and replaced Benvido's prototype sketches with a red carnation, the flower symbolising revolution. As I had suspected, Professor Zihla's photos of them had been altogether inadequate, but now I had the originals, which I passed to Candy shortly afterwards when I briefly met with her in Central Park to discuss the airing of the film.

I also replayed in my mind, the FedEx double-bluff. Whilst I had been reasonably certain I'd shaken off those tracking me, I knew better than to trust my instincts. Just minutes after I had left Sylvenie's flat with my package bound for Denmark, Apollo also exited the apartment, roller-blading his way to the FedEx depot at Cross Island Plaza in Rosedale to post the actual memory stick to Candy. A faint smile traced my lips as I thought of the interceptors ripping apart my package at the 147th Street depot only to find an empty memory stick and a red carnation.

And, within days, my reel was out there. I knew that NOW would simulcast on social media but I was surprised when my mobile phone and iPad came to life with the same footage, not to mention the TV channel in the bar where I was sitting and which had been showing an English Premier

League game; Angelina was across all platforms whether you liked it or not. The film was even projected onto outdoor screens and prominent buildings across the globe. When it ended, the football match I had been watching had finished and the proprietor punched the channel to a music station. Nick Cave's 'Into My Arms' was playing. I took it as an affirmation from Angelina, a moment that left silent tears rolling down my cheeks. I'd not cried since I was a child. Slumped, with several days of growth and donning a rasta tam, no-one in the bar had recognised me.

It had been a nice stunt by the NOW hacktivists, I thought to myself as I switched my attention back to the screen above the bar and wondered how the day might unfold.

Printed in Great Britain
by Amazon